I0769707

SECOND EDITION

Library of Congress Control Number: 2025921909

ISBN: 979-8-9918157-2-7

Cover Art: Younness Elh

RABBIT-TRAPPED

NATIVE LEGENDS BOOK ONE

By

Jacquelyn Holmes

Titles by Jacquelyn Holmes

Rabbit-Trapped
The Thrown-Away Son
Twisted Hearts

Author's Note

I don't pretend to be the best representative of the Creek Nation. I'm part Creek myself, but did not grow up in the Creek culture, or any Native American culture, for that matter. Part of writing this book was trying to learn about my ancestors. Many of the fables mentioned here are real Creek myths, that have been adapted respectfully to the purposes of the story. There is a lot of information I had to improvise, because there is little information available concerning how the Creeks lived before Europeans came to the Americas. A lot of the information after their arrival is biased and conflicting because it is from the perspective of the invaders, not the Creeks themselves. However, they were cultured, spiritual and bold, just like my fictional Creek Woman. I have tried my best to represent these great people well.

Prologue

Creek Woman

My story began long before all of this happened. Sometimes when I close my eyes, I'm transported back to those times and places. I smell the cooking fires of my people. I can still see the great swamps and forests before they were defiled by the oncoming horde of white men.

While I was yet a girl, I was marked by a wise woman for an unnatural life. She told my mother that I would take too many steps for one life, that my steps would go beyond what any of them would see. My tribe began to believe that I was immortal, that I could not die. This was the main reason I was chosen to be given over to Big Man-Eater. They believed he could not kill me.

They were wrong.

I have been called many things since then, but not my true name. My true name burned away with the rest of my past, all those years ago.

Elliot, age 12

Elliot was alone. He wasn't supposed to be, but he had wandered away from the family. Well, his mother and brother. Father was dead. Elliot remembered his corpse as if it were smiling at him.

"You're stuck here alone, little one," it seemed to say to Elliot. His brother cried and he couldn't understand why. Didn't he see that smile? Didn't he hear the corpse's awful voice?

Elliot was throwing pebbles into the water. Would they hit the little fish that swam there? Would the fish die if the pebbles hit them?

Elliot was starting to notice that he was different from other people. He noticed that other people didn't like the things that he liked. He noticed that they were repulsed, rather than attracted...

What was that? Beneath the surface of the water, Elliot thought he saw something. He threw another pebble, listening to the tiny *glug* as it dropped into the cold water.

Then there it was.

A face.

But no, how could anyone be in the water? Elliot had been there a while, no one could hold their breath that long. The surface of the lake was undisturbed, like the frosting on a birthday cake.

The face smiled at him. It smiled like his father's corpse. It surged forward, out of the water.

✦ ✦ ✦

"Elliot! God, wake up!"

Elliot's eyes snapped open. Mother was shaking him and tears were in her eyes. His brother's face looked white next to her.

"What?" he asked, realizing he was wet. Why was he wet?

"We found you in the water!" Gerald whispered. His hands shook as they drew back from Elliot.

Mother pressed him to her in a clumsy embrace. Her skin felt clammy next to his. Elliot pushed her away.

"What do you mean you found me in the water? I wasn't in the water!" Elliot's voice was insistent, but he knew it must be true. How else could he have gotten so wet? He felt his face grow hot and clenched his fists. "You did it!" Elliot yelled at his little brother. Gerald's shoulders tensed. "You threw me in the water! This is all your fault!"

"Elliot!" Mother said. "What's gotten into you?" She petted Gerald's hair, as if to console him. He wasn't the one who was wet and filthy!

Elliot stood and ran away. He fled into the woods, seeking out the darkest place he could find. He was angry and didn't understand why. He didn't understand why he felt as if someone were laughing at him.

Chapter One- Five Years Later

Creek Woman

The first thing you should know about me is that Rabbit and I are not friends. We are unlucky companions because he will simply not die. Believe me, I've tried to kill him.

Rabbit is a trickster who has plagued my people, the Creek all down the line of our history. And in my own life, he has caused great hardships with his practical jokes. It's true that at times, his tricks have benefitted people. His nature is not to be cruel, but he doesn't consider the consequences of his actions either. His nature is to play games, no matter the price.

One of my earliest memories is of a great burning. I can still smell the smoke, hear the cries of the old who could not outrun it. I can remember the great heat under my heels, threatening to consume my flesh.

There is an old story among my people, a legend now, about Rabbit and Alligator. Rabbit asked Alligator if he had ever met the Devil. Alligator said that he had not. Rabbit asked if Alligator was afraid to meet him. Alligator said that he was not afraid. So Rabbit told Alligator, "That's funny. I just saw the Devil, and he said you were afraid of him."

"I'm not afraid of the Devil," answered Alligator. "Please let him know that the next time you see him."

The conversation continued, Rabbit goading Alligator into meeting the Devil. He told Alligator that on the next day, he should climb to the top of the grassy hill and wait. Rabbit would bring the Devil and Alligator could prove that he was not afraid. And Rabbit told him also, "If you see smoke, do not be afraid. That is just the Devil passing by."

"I understand. I am not afraid. Bring him and I will meet him."

The next day, Alligator trundled up to the top of the hill and waited to meet the Devil. Rabbit, however, went to the edge of the field and started a fire. He fanned it so that it grew and it swept down towards Alligator. Alligator waited, believing it was only the Devil passing by. Finally, he ran back to the water, his feet and belly burned from the fire from waiting so long.

Rabbit just laughed and laughed and kicked his heels. He loved a good trick.

I sat in a tall tree at the edge of the field that day. I saw Alligator waiting, saw Rabbit's trick. I saw the fire sweep towards my village, and I ran across the hot, burning field so that I could warn them.

I was too late. By the time I emerged from the field, the thatch roofs of our homes were already alight. I called to any who could hear, "Flee! Leave the village!" Many were already running. Many could not run fast enough. We lost our homes that day. We lost many elders and a few children too. It was a terrible day.

Still, Rabbit laughed and laughed. He did not seem to understand the suffering his joke had caused.

And because I emerged from the fire, the others looked at me differently. How had I survived? Was I truly immortal? And if I was, was this a good omen or bad? Had I offended the trickster and caused the fire myself?

My mother and father shielded me from many because I was a full-blooded clan member. I had rights. I belonged. But things changed for me that day. Many of my clan grew wary of me. I began to worry that I would be unable to make a good match for my future. I could not have known the way life would make so many choices for me.

Neveah

Rapunzel, Rapunzel, let down your hair.

Snip, snip.

Neveah frowned. Having a grown man climbing your hair seemed like a terrible
way to meet people.

Snip, snip.

The hairdresser made quick, economical movements with her hands. Fluffing
Neveah's hair this way and that, assessing how it lay against her scalp.
Neveah wondered if this hairdresser went to other people's houses to
give private haircuts. Or was it just Neveah who was indulged like this?
Surely it was an unusual request? Neveah's mother insisted though.

For the last three years, Neveah had rarely left her family's estate. She was a bit like Rapunzel herself. Maybe that was why her mother insisted she cut her hair short? She didn't want to discover people using Neveah's hair like a back door. Neveah grinned at the thought. She doubted her mother was that paranoid about "suitors."

Her father on the other hand, well, that didn't bear thinking.

Her father was the one paranoid about her safety. Neveah's mother was just the enforcer. It had to do with her father's business dealings, but he went to great lengths to keep that information out of Neveah's path.

Sigh.

Snip, snip.

"What do you think, Mrs. Winters?" The hairdresser asked Neveah's mother. She was looking at Neveah in the mirror's reflection though. Neveah appreciated this subtle nicety. The hairdresser was also interested in her opinion, it seemed. Neveah looked at the reflection of herself smiling timidly in the mirror. The hairdresser nodded her head slightly in acknowledgement.

"It will do. Thank you, Anita," Neveah's mother, Jillian Winters, said in a cool, professional tone, inherently dismissive. Anita packed her things away. Neveah stood as soon as the plastic apron was removed from her, and she followed her mother out of the room as expected. At the door, she turned back and said, "I like my haircut so much. Thank you."

Out in the hallway, Neveah's mother waited impatiently.

"You're too casual with the help, Neveah." It was an often enough refrain between the two of them. Not much else needed to be said as all the lectures had been heard and repeated. Neveah had few small rebellions in her life, but this was one of them.

"I know, Mother," Neveah said, averting her eyes. She knew what she would see there: hardness, disapproval.

"Go to your room. No diving practice tonight. It's supposed to rain, so I don't want you roaming around on that horse tonight either."

"Yes, Mother."

An hour later, Neveah sat on her horse, Sunbeam. She had escaped from her tower room (actually, upstairs bedroom) in a daring escape. She had pocketed a few biscuits and a carrot from the kitchen, with the help of one of her secret alliances (the chef, Harry). She had army crawled through the den, so Mother wouldn't be able to see her from her post in the living room. Neveah had carefully opened the back door and ducked under the windows until she was on the other side of the house. The groundskeeper kindly ignored her goings-on. The stable master had Sunbeam saddled and ready for her, bless him! She wordlessly handed him the biscuits and gave Sunbeam the carrot.

Freedom! No hair climbing involved!

She was far enough away from the house now that she wasn't worried about her mother glimpsing her with a casual glance out a window. Neveah gave Sunbeam her head and let the reins go. She pulled out her digital camera and leaned back as far as she could in the saddle. The light filtered down to her through treetops and she snapped a few pictures. A bird was perched on a lower branch and Neveah captured its image mid-song.

These were the moments that she lived for. Pleasantly quiet and away from the pressures of life at home, she felt like her true self. The only drawback to these little escapades was that she was still alone, like Rapunzel.

Elliot

Elliot gently pushed aside a low tree branch and watched. He'd been following the dark-haired girl on her solitary horse rides for some time now. He saw the camera she clutched in her hands and wondered if he was lurking in the backgrounds, unseen, in any of her precious photos.

Elliot slipped his hand into his pocket and felt his phone. Since watching her so enraptured with photographing nature, he'd begun photographing what he loved. His phone was now filled with images of the animals he'd caught, the traps he'd laid for them. He began to understand her interest in photography. He found himself pouring over his own photography for hours.

There, she snapped a picture of a robin. A female, he surmised, as the bird was only a dull rust color instead of the brighter hues of a male. Elliot mentally filed away the image of the bird. He would try to catch one just like it tomorrow. He would keep its feathers. Maybe its feet, too. One day, maybe he would show these trophies to the girl.

Elliot felt a tightening in his chest. His vision began to darken. There was The Face, pressing in on him again. He blinked and shook his head, not wanting to let go of this moment.

Then blackness.

✦ ✦ ✦

Elliot looked around and saw leaves. It was early fall but the trees had shed more than they had kept. The leaves were stuck to him because of the dew. Despite the wetness, they looked as if they were on fire. Elliot reached to peel them away and reminded himself that they would not burn. They wouldn't even feel hot.

The forest also looked on fire. Elliot reminded himself that that was just because the sun was setting. If the forest were really on fire, there would be smoke. The animals would be restless or gone already. He would smell it in the air.

Lately the gaps were growing. He sometimes was afraid that he would get lost in them. At first the gaps in his memory, the blackouts frightened him. With time, the lost time stopped mattering. But now, he was gone for longer and longer periods of time.

And now he was beginning to dream in the gaps. He dreamed about the girl. This time, in the dream, he gave her a present. It was a tiny box wrapped in silver paper. She smiled at him, her eyes big with surprise. Her small hands unwrapped the paper. Her hands bled, more and more as she unwrapped the present, from a thousand tiny papercuts.

Elliot savored the memory of the dream.

17

Ash

Ash hated putting in insulation. Even with gloves, he felt itchy for hours after. He always imagined pieces of it under his clothes or in his hair. But it had to be done. Ash wasn't sure where his step-mother, Abigail, got the money to flip houses. The only thing she ever spoke to him about were ways to cut more corners and save more money. And then every time Abby sold a house, Gerald and Elliot got some new toy. And Ash? The only thing he got was more work. The last time, his step-brothers had gotten a car. Ash had gotten another house to fix up. He felt bitterness rise up in him like bile. Ash pushed the feeling away. *That won't help get this insulation in any quicker*, he thought. Besides, the truth was that he didn't want to know where Abby got the money, or how. Some things were better left alone.

Oddly, Ash was thankful to Abby for the work. With all of this forced labor, Ash now had the skills to work almost anywhere that construction was going on. He could support himself, maybe even save enough to go to college. It was hard to imagine having that much money to his name, but he knew that men supported families with construction work. Surely he could support himself.

Also, because of his work on her little house flipping projects, she had reluctantly bought him an old truck. She had grown tired of making trips to the hardware store, hauling lumber and other things she called "common work." That truck wasn't worth much, and

18

certainly wouldn't survive a long road trip, but it gave him a new level of freedom. As long as he didn't wander too far, he could put gas in it every week. It was hard to complain about that arrangement, especially as it helped him with his other business, the one that actually made him money.

Ash finished the insulation and washed his hands and face from the outside faucet. He hadn't put in a sink yet, so it would have to do. This house hadn't really been a smart buy; he'd had to tear it down to the studs. Abby hadn't been happy about that, but the housing inspector knew her well enough that she couldn't fudge all the details. It just had to be done. Ash wasn't afraid of hard work, or even long hours. It kept him in good shape and taught him valuable skills. He just wished she would pay him for it.

Loading tools in the back of the truck, Ash saw a familiar figure coming his way. He felt an instant guttural fear and forced it down. Elliot was drawing near. Ash had spent a lot of time and effort over the last few years ensuring that he was never alone with Elliot. He couldn't explain why exactly that he feared Elliot. They were the same age and roughly the same size. Elliot had never hurt him outside of the rough bullying that he engaged in with his brother, Gerald. However, there was a glint in Elliot's eyes that promised so much more, if only he ever had the chance. The part of Ash's mind that was still animal instinct always reacted strongly to his presence. He knew, in some intuitive way that Elliot was dangerous.

"Ashes, Ashes, we all fall down." Elliot sang it softly, with a smile on his face. He casually leaned against the truck and watched Ash pile tools in the back. "More work for the little mouse, eh?" Elliot chuckled to himself.

"You're in a good mood, Elliot," Ash said, as he wrapped an extension cord.

"Ah yes. I caught a squirrel today. Have you ever done that?" Elliot examined a thumbnail as he talked. "They squirm so. It's rather lovely."

Ash repressed a grimace. Elliot loved to catch and torment animals. Ash had rescued any number of squirrels, cats, birds, and mice from Elliot's little traps.

"I know I'm not supposed to talk about it. Mother gets rather cross with me when I do. But I say, why hide it? It's who I am. Isn't that what all the social justice is about these days? Speak your truth?" Elliot's face held a taunting grin.

"Somehow, I don't think that's what they are talking about," Ash answered drily. He walked to open the driver's door of the truck. Elliot was there in an instant.

"Aren't you going to offer your dear brother a ride home?" Elliot pressed Ash against the side of the truck. Ash felt the alarm bells in his mind ringing out, *Danger! Danger!*

"I didn't think you'd agree to ride in such a piece of crap truck as mine. *Dear brother*." Ash ground out the reply from between his teeth. Elliot grinned again. The menace was wiped from his face. He stepped away with a laugh.

"Never any fun and games for you, is there, Cinderfella?" Elliot said. Ash gave up trying to follow his cryptic answers long ago. He was just relieved to see Elliot turn and walk away.

Elliot

There it was again. A black cat. Elliot had noticed the cat a number of times, always hanging back just out of sight. It was as if the cat was stalking him.

Elliot laughed.

Thus far, he had encountered no predator more dangerous than himself in the woods. Let the cat follow him.

Just then, Elliot had seen the cat in a tree nearby. It carefully watched him through the cover of foliage, still as the tree itself. The Face rose up in his consciousness like it had out of the water that day, so long ago. Elliot had never heard its voice, had never spoken to it directly, but he did get feelings from it. The Face did not like the cat.

How peculiar. Elliot had never known The Face to dislike anyone or anything. Normally he sensed from it a sort of laughing curiosity. It loved to play tricks on others above all else. Elliot himself did not much care for the games but indulged The Face on occasion. He had learned that denying it just meant more gaps, as it seemed to take over him and do as it pleased anyway. Elliot often felt as if he were sharing headspace with a willful child.

He continued on in the woods, but kept track in his mind of the watching cat. Elliot would have to learn more about this, and why The Face in his mind disliked it so much.

Elliot remembered the first time he met his mentor. He had been studying a koi pond at some event Mother had dragged them to. They flitted through the water, sleek and shining. Little lily pads were scattered around, and the fish would hide beneath them, then dart forward to catch a mosquito with their wide mouths. If Elliot cut the fish open, would he find the mosquitos there? If he cut the fish open fast enough, would he see its little heart still beating?

A hand fell at his shoulder.

"Beautiful, aren't they?" He said. William. A large built man with red hair that was going white at the temples. He had hands like a butcher and a smile that stretched a bit too far over his face. Elliot was certain that if he cut him open, no matter how quick, there would be no beating heart inside.

"Yes. Lovely fish. I wonder if they are as beautiful on the inside?"

"Truly, they are. I love throwing a fish on the fire, listening to the skin crackle. I used to make myself dinner that way in the woods, as a boy. Have you ever done that?"

"I haven't. I've never burned anything." Elliot's mind flickered back to the last time he'd been alone in the woods. He had not been able to coax a fire out of the wood he'd gathered.

"I've always found flames beautiful. You might try it sometime," William said simply. He pulled a lighter out of his pocket. "This would do. If you set fire to something small, it's gone so fast, you miss the beauty of it. But be careful. Wouldn't want you to burn down your house or anything."

William handed the lighter to Elliot. It was heavy. A large ornate W was etched into the metal casing. Where had he bought such a thing?

"And also, son. If you don't mind me saying so, it might be wise to keep these talks about fire to yourself. Most people won't understand. Do you follow what I mean?"

Elliot thought of Mother then, and her disapproval. "Yes, sir."

"That's a good boy. Perhaps we will run into each other again in the woods."

"I'd like that, sir." He slid the lighter into his pocket.

William had walked away that night and, Elliot later learned, began an illicit affair with Mother. For some reason he sunk his claws into their family. The gaps were already beginning to cloud Elliot's views of what was important and what wasn't. Otherwise, he would have thrown that lighter into the koi pond.

William had meant what he said when he spoke of meeting in the woods. There was a strip of forest that lay between his property and theirs. Over the years, they met numerous times. Elliot began to notice that whatever force that brought on the gaps in his memories chose to lie dormant when William was around. And for that, he met him as often as he could.

William was not a nice man. He was, however, very competent. He taught Elliot many things about hunting and tracking, starting fires and slipping unnoticed in the shadows of trees. Elliot assumed that this was what his own father would have taught him had he lived.

Soon he came to a small clearing. It was deep enough in the forest that it was unlikely anyone would accidentally walk through. Elliot had met William here numerous times over the last couple of years. It was very important to William that their meetings remain a secret.

Particularly since William was cheating on his wife with Elliot's mother.

Elliot was not supposed to know about that part. His mother would be terrified if she knew he was aware of it. William would be angry. He should not, however, be surprised. It was William, after all, who had taught Elliot how to track people unnoticed.

Elliot had followed his mother on one of her more secretive outings. He couldn't say he was too surprised when she met William at a diner at the edge of town. Nor was he surprised when they went to a hotel room together. His mother always seemed to have an unexplainable amount of extra cash. She worked late a lot for someone who worked at a county courthouse that closed at 5 sharp. She came home in the wee hours of morning often enough that he had already guessed what she was up to.

William appeared at the edge of the clearing, carrying a small satchel. He opened it up to reveal several short lengths of ropes.

"What do you know about tying knots?" William asked, a hard grin on his face.

"Not as much as you do, apparently," Elliot answered. He reached out for a piece of rope. The two men sat next to each other companionably. William began to show him a knot, without preamble. It fell silent as Elliot tried to repeat what William had shown him.

"What is this one for?"

"This would be good for tying off a boat to a dock."

"Doesn't seem like something I would need to know. I don't care for boats."

"Always be prepared, I say." It was an often enough comment from William.

"Isn't that the Boy Scout motto? Were you a scout?"

William was silent a moment, untying his own knot and taking another length of rope out for another demonstration. "I was."

Elliot did not respond. He was able to mimic William's knot on the first try.

"Here's a good knot if you're ever climbing the bluffs." William continued showing him knot after knot. They fell into a working silence, William tying, Elliot retying.

"Do you have a daughter?" Elliot asked quietly. He knew the answer of course. A Winters daughter, hidden on their estate.

William's hands instantly stilled. "Why would you want to

know about something like that?"

"Do you teach her how to tie knots as well?" Elliot knew this would irk William. He refrained from smiling. William stared at Elliot for a long moment.

"I suppose there's a reason you're asking me this?" He fished a cigarette out of a pocket and lit it with his heavy engraved lighter. It was the only outward sign of his irritation. Elliot did smile then.

"You have a daughter. She is my age. Why have I never met her?" Elliot set the rope down in front of him. "Are you embarrassed of her? Or me?"

William took a long drag on the cigarette then ground it into the soil at their feet.

"I'm not embarrassed of anything." He began gathering the ropes and stuffing them back into his bag. He stood to leave and paused. "Never go near her."

Elliot leaned back against a tree with his hands behind his head. He smiled as he listened to William disappearing into the forest. "How very interesting!"

Ash

"Asher Price!"
Ash's head snapped up. He'd fallen asleep in class.
Again.

The teacher was glaring at him in a decidedly unforgiving sort of way.

"Thank you for finally joining us, Mr. Price," she said in a sarcastic tone. The teacher turned her back to him and continued with her lesson.

Ash felt his cheeks redden. He hadn't meant to fall asleep. However, Mrs. Nelson was unlikely to believe that since it happened so often. He generally liked her too, so it bothered him that he kept sleeping in her class.

A nudge at his back caught his attention. A note was stuffed into his waiting palm.

Dude! You are going to get detention if you keep sleeping in class!

Ash was well aware of this and didn't need the reminder. He turned around and glared meaningfully at his friend, Gilly, who had passed the note. Gill was holding back his laughter.

Some friend!

Ash rolled his eyes and deferred his attention to his teacher for the last 15 minutes of class. It was brutal, but he managed to take a few notes. Hopefully Gilly had gotten more and would share.

The bell rang and Mrs. Nelson said in a tone that brooked no argument, "Stay, Mr. Price."

Oh no.

Ash gathered his things and stood, but didn't leave. It seemed like it took a long time for everyone to leave the classroom while he lingered there awaiting his punishment.

"Yes, Mrs. Nelson?" He tried to be as polite-sounding as he knew to be.

"Have a seat."

Not a good sign.

"I'm a little concerned about you, Mr. Price," Mrs. Nelson said. Her tone and expression were serious, but there was a bit of softness in her eyes. It was going to be one of *those* talks. He'd had a few since his father died.

"I'm sorry I keep falling asleep in class. Really, I don't mean to," Ash said, trying to inject genuineness into his voice.

"I realize that you aren't doing it on purpose. However it does mean that you are falling behind. If you keep falling behind, you could fail. It would mean not graduating on time." She paused meaningfully. "I get the feeling you want to graduate on time."

"Yes, ma'am. I do." Ash looked away.

"Would you consider after school tutoring? It would help you catch up."

"I...I don't have money to pay someone for tutoring, ma'am. I'm sorry." He paused. "I will try harder."

Mrs. Nelson looked at her gradebook. Her expression told him what her mouth didn't want to say: It wouldn't be enough.

"You need to find someone to help you. Could you come to my classroom at lunchtime?"

Ash grimaced inwardly. He usually napped or caught up on homework during lunch.

28

"I could make it work, I'm sure."

✦ ✦ ✦

On the back edge of the property, there was a little metal gate, the kind anyone could buy at a hardware store. Ash walked through it now and looked around. He was definitely out of sight of the main house, she'd seen to that. By now Elliot and Gerald would be off to their own entertainments. Ash had some time to himself for now, and this was often where he spent it.

There were three rows of modest stones tucked neatly inside the fence. Ash had worked to keep them clean and the grass mowed. The fence, however, he had let the vines overtake. It was to give his family some privacy. In the spring, tulips bloomed happily on the graves. He always hoped Mother could see them from wherever she was now.

Ash settled down beside two of the stones and watched the sun go down.

"It won't be too much longer until I will have to leave you two. I hope you can understand. It's not that I don't love you, but I can't stay. If I don't leave, I'll always sleep in a shed and I'll always be looking over my shoulder for trouble. I want to do something with my life so that you'll be proud of me when I finally see you again."

Creature jumped down from a fencepost and sauntered over. She sat in front of Ash as if she had something to say. Her tail gave a quick swish and she turned and walked away. At the gate, she stopped and looked at Ash expectantly.

"I guess you're right, Creature," Ash said with a chuckle. "Mom and Dad wouldn't want me to sit around feeling sorry for myself." He stood and left the graveyard. His shed was settled right nearby, and he was inside in a moment.

As far as sheds went, Ash's wasn't bad. His stepmother couldn't literally leave him in a shed. Not while he was a minor in her custody. So she had doled out the cash to have their shed outfitted with a sink and toilet, a mini fridge and a stove. He had a bed and a desk. What else could her peasant stepson need?

Actually the arrangement suited him just fine. He didn't exactly relish the idea of sleeping near his step brothers. They were likely to get ideas about further tormenting him in his sleep. At any rate, sleeping, eating, and living in the shed meant that he had more time to himself and away from his ...whatever they were. He didn't consider them family. His family was sleeping in the little graveyard.

Ash carefully scouted around his shed to ensure he was alone. Elliot had a knack for sneaking up on people unexpectedly. The last thing Ash wanted was Elliot knowing his secrets.

Ash had taken up a few hobbies to fill his time. Unbeknownst to his stepmother, Ash had started making dollhouses. It wasn't that he had some secret desire to play with dolls. It was more that he was able to do it. And carpentry was a family tradition. Before his mother had fallen ill, his father had been a master carpenter. After she died, he couldn't seem to pull himself together well enough to hold down a regular job. He still had his business, but it dwindled dramatically. His heart just wasn't in it anymore. Love had made him a strong man while his wife was alive, but her death had destroyed him. They had had to sell more and more of their custom pieces, their family heirlooms. Even in the end though, he could still tell his son about his lifelong study of wood and how to turn it into something beautiful. The only things his father had left him, that no one else could take away from him, were his memories and his love and knowledge of carpentry.

Back in his shed, Ash checked on his sketches again. One by one, he carefully pried up the floorboards in his shed. Underneath were his cutting tools, boxes filled with wood glue and clamps, and extra pieces of balsa wood. He took great pains to put everything back underneath when he finished working for the night. He wanted to make sure that anyone suddenly peering in would see nothing except a normal 17-year-old boy's room.

Ash had sold four or five of the dollhouses now. He didn't advertise publicly, but found people by word-of-mouth. He had pocketed a little cash, quietly selling them to mothers and grandmothers of little girls who loved their dolls.

He carefully counted out his stash of money. It was a woefully small number. He remembered his plan, his goal: *I'll throw my stuff in the truck. I'll drive west. I'll find work. I'll survive.* It was his mantra of sorts. He fell asleep that night whispering to himself, "I'll survive. I'll survive."

Neveah

Neveah was supposed to be doing research for an English paper. She had read yet another Shakespeare piece and was supposed to be comparing it to something-or-other. That's what she was supposed to be doing.

What Neveah was actually doing was stalking local teenagers on social media. Her keen interest in photography naturally led her to Instagram. It started as a harmless pastime. She loved photography, she missed people. Here was an entire world of both, all at her fingertips. She didn't have a cell phone, of course. Her father felt that having a phone was taking on an unnecessary risk. She could be tracked. She could be hacked. She could have some semblance of a normal life. Obviously that was out of the question.

And then, she found the name of a girl she knew in elementary school, the last time she attended a public school.

And then she found that girl's friends, all students living in or around the nearby town.

People. And even better, teenagers. It was like after a lifetime of hunting unicorns, she found a unicorn night club. Teenagers, who were so absent from her life, were suddenly everywhere.

Of course, these people didn't know who she was. And she couldn't post pictures of herself. Her father would go completely mad if he found out. But she did post some of her photography. And people actually liked it! It was an unimaginable kind of magic in a world of private lessons and loneliness.

Neveah was addicted. Every spare moment of unsupervised computer time became a dive into the world of Instagram.

Neveah was supposed to be doing research, but the tutor had left early, so that *obviously* was not going to happen tonight. She was on a mission.

There had been some event at an art museum that was not too far from where she lived, the Regional Art Museum of Sebastian County. She learned from a previous internet binge that a notable photographer was going to have his work on display there. It was a one night event as part of a fundraiser. Surely there would be pictures? The museum's website only offered three, as a teaser and incentive to come and spend money. But Instagram rarely let her down in these matters.

"Neveah, are you studying now?" It was Mother, leaning into the den to check on her.

"Yes, Mother," Neveah answered. Her laptop was turned so that Jillian couldn't see the screen. She paused what she was doing, waiting for her mother to leave.

"Did your tutor leave early again?" Jillian's tone could have frozen the wine in the glass she was carrying.

"Yeah." Neveah's tone was flat. She wasn't very impressed with her current tutor, either. The woman seemed to practically run from their house at the slightest excuse. "Today she left because she said she had to get back to feed her neighbor's dog. Apparently, the dog is on a strict regimen, can't get its food late."

Neveah and her mother shared an eye roll. Jillian was already pulling out her phone when she turned and left. That will be the last of that tutor. Not that Neveah was especially heartbroken. This was her fourth tutor since starting her high school curriculum. She had stopped getting attached to them.

Neveah heard her mother's voice fading down the hallway. Neveah let go of a breath she hadn't realized she'd been holding. Back to her mission...

After a few minutes of getting the right tags she hit on some images. Most of them were of smiling couples or groups of friends. But there, shining in the background was the real imagery she had wanted to see.

This guy was certainly no Henri Cartier-Bresson, but he had talent. Of course, Neveah would consider herself lucky to be considered as talented as this photographer. He at least could get a showing at an art gallery. That was more than she could say for the hundreds of photos stored on SD cards in her desk drawer.

Click, click, click.

She had looked at about a hundred photos when suddenly a face leapt off the computer screen at her. She felt an instant stab of shock. Then immediately, denial. *It can't be!*

There on the screen was the face of her father.

With another woman.

Ash

School was a total loss the next day. Ash couldn't think about trigonometry or physics, not when he was too busy worrying about passing high school. What would he do if he failed? It was an unbearable thought, but the very one he couldn't shake.

"Earth to Ash." It was Gilly, waving a hand in front of Ash's face.

"Huh?" Ash answered dumbly. "What?"

"Are you going to eat your toast, space cadet?" Gilly asked, indicating the food untouched on his lunch tray.

"Whatever, dude. Take it."

"Did you just call me 'dude'?" Gilly laughed at him. He stuffed the toast into his mouth. "What planet are you on today?"

Ash shook his head and changed the subject. He wasn't ready to talk to Gilly about this. Gilly was a good guy, his friend, but he would not understand. Even worse, he might start asking questions that Ash just couldn't answer.

➹ ➹ ➹

Ash left when school was over and went straight to the little house. Hanging drywall wasn't his favorite job, but drywall meant the insulation was done, at least. He'd seen on a TV show that most professional crews used a pneumatic nail gun to nail up the heavy sheets of drywall. It meant infinitely less effort and time to finish the job. Ash had asked Abby for one, but she'd just laughed at him. So here he was, muscling in screws with a handheld drill, praying the battery would last longer than the work.

Drill, drill.

Another handful of screws. His hands were chalky from the drywall. He felt sweat on his neck and down his back.

Gilly had asked him to come over this weekend, to hang out and play video games. Normal teenage guy stuff, Ash assumed. He'd told him that he had too much homework. It was true, Ash did have homework. But he also had a house to finish. He was hoping to finish the drywall before the weekend, so that he could spend Saturday and Sunday painting and installing the bathroom tub and shower surround. Manual labor, endless manual labor. And when he eventually finished this house, Abby would just get another for him to work on.

Ash felt the frustration rising up in him. He squashed it down. He could play video games another time. He'd find time.

The drill slipped in his grip. His hand banged against the wall. A sudden flash of red appeared where his knuckles had grazed the head of the screw.

With a roar, he threw the drill across the room. It slammed against the studs of the opposite wall and thudded to the ground.

"Why do I have to do all of this work anyway!" He yelled, "It's not fair!"

"Dear brother," said a voice from behind him. "Haven't you heard the old saying? Life's not fair."

Ash went from hot with frustration to cold. He turned to see Elliot appear out of the unfinished kitchen. Why hadn't he heard him come in?

"What are you doing here, Elliot?" Ash asked, his voice flat. Ash hadn't meant for Elliot to see his outburst, and he was determined to not give him the satisfaction of seeing anymore.

"Can't I come just to chat with my lovely sibling?" Elliot's grin was back in place.

He paced the room, looking over the unfinished walls, and paused at the thrown drill on the floor. "The work getting on top of you these days?"

"Come off it, Elliot. I'm having a rough day," Ash said, retrieving the drill with intent to continue his work. Generally, Elliot left if he was ignored enough.

"If it's so bad, why do you stay?" Elliot asked. He sounded sincere, but Ash wasn't fooled.

"You know full well why I stay. I've got no place to go. And no money to get there, for that matter." Ash was irritated. He pocketed more screws and started lining up another sheet of drywall.

"So it's the money, eh?" Elliot said. He intentionally leaned against the wall, right in Ash's way. It forced Ash to stop what he was doing and face Elliot. "What if you had money? Would you leave then?"

Ash paused. It was dangerous to confide in Elliot, even in the best of times. However, it was no secret to anyone that he wanted to leave.

"Probably, yes." Then he nudged Elliot out of the way.

"Then here. You can have this." Elliot casually pulled a handful of money out of his pocket and handed it to Ash. He was shocked to realize that Elliot was holding hundred-dollar bills crumpled as if they were worth no more than old gum wrappers.

"Elliot. What are you doing?" Ash pulled his eyes from the money to look at his step-brother's face. "Why would you give this to me?"

Elliot shrugged, noncommittally. "What's it to me, anyway? Mother will give me more money. You know that." Then he looked at Ash sideways, a smile at the edge of his lips. "Besides, maybe I want to do something nice for my dear brother."

↗ ↗ ↗

Ash had never held so much money in his life. After Elliot had slipped away (there was no other way to describe Elliot's movements, he didn't just walk like a normal person) Ash had counted the money with shaking hands. Fifteen hundred dollars. It wasn't enough to live off of for long, Ash wasn't stupid. But it was enough to get him the hell out of here.

At his shed, he had thrown his few belongings in a duffel bag, and tore out of the place as if it were a house on fire. He slowed down long enough to say goodbye to his parents. He truly regretted leaving them, but it wasn't as if they could come along.

His old truck protested as he went flying out of the driveway and down the highway. *Free, I'm free.* It was all he could think. Once he crossed the county line, he'd decide where to stop for the night. Then he could figure out his next move. Ash had learned from previous attempts to run away that there were schools that would let him finish his high school diploma or GED in night school, while he worked during the day. It would be the opposite of what he did now, and he wasn't intimidated by the workload.

But how far could he get on fifteen hundred dollars? The farther away the better. He just had to be out of Abby's reach until he turned eighteen. Just a few months. Bouncing on the seat of his old truck, he felt like the very air was supercharged. He just had to survive for a few months and then no one could touch him. He could do it.

The county's end was up ahead. As he was driving, he realized he'd never been outside of the county, never made it past this little road marker up ahead. In all of the little adventures he'd gone on with his dad, they had never really left home. He wondered if they had left the county while his mother was still alive. Surely, they did.

Ash noticed a rabbit hunched on the side of the road. He slowed, in case it decided to bolt in front of the truck. Instead, it seemed content to perch underneath the sign marking the end of the county. Ash was distracted by the rabbit; he wasn't sure what happened next.

Wham!

Suddenly, Ash wasn't in his truck anymore. Looking around, he was on his backside in the grass. Looking up, his truck was parked next to the road. It looked as if he had pulled over, gotten out of the truck, and laid down in the grass.

What the...? Ash thought.

He stood and brushed the grass off of his pants. The rabbit was still there, a mere few feet away, eating clover and watching him. Ash stepped up to the truck, climbed inside. The keys were still in the ignition. In fact, the truck was still running. Ash never left the engine idling like that.

He put on his seatbelt and shifted into gear. The county line was a few feet in front of him. Checking his mirrors, no one was coming from either direction. He was alone. Well, except for the rabbit.

A moment later and Ash was sitting in the grass again.

"What the hell is going on?" Ash said, aloud this time. The rabbit's nose twitched, but otherwise he was met with silence.

A second time, Ash stood up from the grass and brushed himself off. He walked a little quicker back to his truck. It was in the same condition: keys in the ignition, engine running, parked on the side of the road.

"I've lost it. I've actually lost my mind," Ash said to himself, looking around again. Not a soul to be seen.

He reached in, turned off the truck and pocketed the keys.

It couldn't be. Ash was deeply shaken. Of course he'd heard the rumors that everyone else had. Children aren't great at keeping secrets, so he'd been confronted with the idea of being cursed in elementary school. But curses aren't real.

Slowly, Ash stepped forward, his hand outstretched. The end of the county was a few feet in front of him. A foot. Inches. Ash stopped, his hand lingering.

Ash pushed his hand forward, and *felt* the edge of the county. It was as if the county line was edged in a clear membrane, a bubble. His hand bounced back from it, physically rebuffed.

No. No, it can't be. Ash pleaded, internally. He felt sick. He felt lied to. He felt trapped.

Ash balled up his fist and punched the barrier.

This time, when Ash awoke in the grass, he wasn't shocked. He was disappointed.

"I'm trapped. I really am trapped." His voice sounded lost, even to himself.

A familiar figure appeared out of the trees nearby. A feline form, deepest black.

"Oh, Ash. I'm so sorry."

Chapter Two

Creek Woman

After the great fire, our clan rebuilt upriver. We had new homes and new fires and were happy for a time. It was not long however, until the hunters of our clan began to go missing. We learned soon after that the neighboring forest was home to one of the great Man-Eaters, a creature of spirit and hunger. They were mysterious and violent and all of the clan began to worry and pray to our Creator for a solution. Should we relocate again? Could we pacify the Man-Eater?

One of our elders decided to meet with Big Man-Eater. Others protested. No one wanted him to be eaten.

"I will go and try to come to an agreement with Big Man-Eater," he said. And then he left, in search of the beast.

He was gone for four days, and when he returned, he appeared despairing and conflicted. The people gathered around him to ask what happened.

"I have met the Man-Eater. His hunger is vast. He wanted to eat all of us," he said. The people quailed with terror. Some shouted, "How did you survive?"

The elder calmed everyone. "I only survived because the Man-Eater wants something from us. A trade."

There was a murmuring in the crowd. What could a Man-Eater possibly want from us?

"Big Man-Eater wants a woman. He has decided that he will take a wife from among us. In exchange, he will not eat us. If he is satisfied with this wife, he will protect us from others. He said we could choose from among us. But she needs to be young and fleet of foot. It is the only trade he will make to not eat us, because he is so very hungry."

There was a lot fear in the clan members, especially parents with daughters. No woman could please a Man-Eater and would surely be eaten! The elders met that night to discuss what our clan's options were. Should we just move again? But rebuilding again would be a great hardship on the clan, and this new home was rich and fertile. Was the price of one daughter worth this?

It was not long until they remembered the words the wise woman had spoken over me. A daughter who would live forever. Surely, this one daughter could survive the Man-Eater? And after the fire, few of them wanted me to remain in the village anyway. It seemed like a fair trade. One unlucky immortal girl in exchange for the village's protection.

It was decided. I would marry Big Man-Eater and the clan would be saved. I was honored by my village for my sacrifice. My mother sewed me a new dress and edged it with beads. My father gifted me a strong bow and arrows, so that I could hunt for myself. We did not know if Big Man-Eater would provide for me the way a normal man would.

The elder who had found Big Man-Eater before, led me through the forest. Big Man-Eater was waiting under a large sycamore tree. He was in the form of a large mountain lion. His head swung back and forth as he smelled all the creatures of the forest around us. He paced impatiently, and his paws left prints in the dust as large as a woven basket. I was filled with fear.

He knew we were coming, but did not settle from his pacing until we were upon him. The elder held a hand on my shoulder, and I could feel his nervous sweating. He was a proud man and tried his best to appear brave in the face of this beast. I knew though, if I could sense his fear, the Man-Eater would likewise sense it.

To my surprise, the Man-Eater spoke with a voice like any man's. "Is this the girl?" He asked without preamble.

"Yes. This is her," answered the elder.

"Is she fleet of foot?" asked Man-Eater, plainly looking me over.

"Yes. She is one of the fastest girls in the village." This was not necessarily true. I was no faster than any other girl. No slower either. Maybe they hoped that the Man-Eater would not know the difference.

"She will do." Big Man-Eater said simply. He turned to walk away. The elder looked at me and I could see the regret in his eyes. He did not want to give me away. I tried to smile, but failed. My knees were weak. My heart beat so quickly. I was not sure I could step forward on my own.

"I've changed my mind. I will take her back to the village. You cannot have her," the elder said proudly. He was shaking, but firm in his words. I felt a moment's relief, followed by fear. Would the elder be eaten now?

Instead, the Man-Eater simply turned and growled at him. It was low in his throat but so loud that the old sycamore tree rumbled with *it. The elder fled in fear. I should have fled also, but I found that I could not move. I was rooted there as if I were another sycamore. Big Man-Eater looked at me and simply said, "Come."*

I went with him.

Neveah

The face glowed on the computer screen, staring back at her.

There was no denying that it was her father. There was also no denying that this wasn't a work outing, or a woman he considered simply a friend. His arm was around her waist, holding her close.

Neveah flipped through a few more pictures. There, in the background of instagram photos, she followed her father and the strange woman around the museum. They held hands. He stroked her hair.

Neveah felt like she might not ever breathe again. She felt as if all the air had been sucked out of her, out of the room, maybe out of the whole earth.

Oh god, does Mom know?

Neveah slammed the laptop shut. She drew, forcibly, a large deep breath into her chest. It was as if she had swallowed a live wire instead of air. She couldn't sit still. She stood and practically ran from the room.

"Neveah! Where are you going?" Jillian called from a the quickly fading kitchen. Neveah didn't bother with an answer as she tore out the backdoor.

Neveah's shoes skidded on the concrete floor of the stables. Sunbeam whinnied, her head rearing up, when she saw Neveah coming. Neveah grabbed her bridle, but skipped the saddle. She just leapt onto her bareback and left.

A few minutes of galloping at full speed and girl and horse were both deep in the dark woods surrounding their lands. Neveah hoped there wasn't another living soul around for miles but suspected that wasn't the case. It was less than a mile to another house, if nothing else. For once, lonely Neveah wished she were really alone.

How could he do this to their family? Who was this woman who had torn her father away from her mother? Did her mother know of the affair? And even worse, was this the first time this had even happened? The questions circled her mind like horses on a carousel.

At least one question would get answered. Neveah knew how to find people online. She'd find out who this mystery woman was, and as much about her as possible.

And what about her father? Neveah always knew that he was keeping things from her, but she assumed it was the pressures of business, not something so nefarious as cheating on her mother. It begged the question: What else was he hiding? Neveah wasn't sure if she could find those answers on Instagram, but she would start investigating this mystery as well.

Neveah was lost in thought and didn't know where she was anymore. She guided Sunbeam in a circle, turning them around, hopefully in the direction of home. She tried to squash down the feelings about her father, tried instead, to focus on the more present issue of getting out of the ever-darkening forest.

Rustle, rustle.

Neveah's head jerked towards the noise. What could it be? At first there was nothing. It must have been a raccoon or something.

Then the underbrush parted and a man was there.

"Who goes there?" Neveah asked, pitching her voice so that it could be heard clearly. It was what people said in movies, so it seemed appropriate.

The man was younger than she originally assumed. He smiled at her, auburn hair dim in the low light. His smile didn't touch his eyes. It unsettled Neveah instinctively.

"Are you lost?" While he said it in a congenial tone of voice, Neveah couldn't shake her instinct of fear.

"I can't be far from home." Neveah felt Sunbeam shift her weight. Her horse seemed a little unsettled as well. "My family will be looking for me soon."

The young man's smile quirked up higher on one side. "I'm sure they are." He stepped forward, as if to pet the horse. Sunbeam shied away further. "I don't think your horse likes me very much."

"Do you know the way to the Winters estate?" Neveah asked, thinking her horse was generally a good judge of character.

"Winters estate? You must be their lovely daughter." His fingers brushed the hair of Sunbeam's mane delicately. "I've wanted to meet you, and here you are. A gift from the forest herself."

"I really need to be going." Neveah said. She began to wheel her horse around to leave.

"Well, it's that way," he called, pointing a course slightly to the left of her current direction. She fled into the night. Sunbeam seemed glad to escape and put on a burst of speed. The boy faded into the dark, gone from sight but not her mind.

Ash

Ash's eyes flew open. It couldn't be real. It had to have been a dream. It was the only explanation. Ash sat up in bed.

"Good morning," said the cat.

Oh no.

"I thought you might need to talk about what happened out there," the cat said.

Very practical, talking cats are.

Ash rubbed his hands against his eyes. "No, no, no."

The cat licked and rubbed at her tail, generally ignoring Ash's crisis of reality.

"This can't be real," Ash said. He gestured to the cat. "You're a cat. Cats don't talk."

"What makes you think I'm a cat at all?"

Ash didn't know what to say to that.

He got out of bed and washed his face. Maybe he'd wake up and this would be a dream.

He didn't.

"Okay. So you talk. That part's real. What happened yesterday? Was that real too?" Ash asked the cat.

"It was real. You can't leave the county." The cat did not stop cleaning herself to answer his questions. It was distracting.

"How is that possible?"

"I told you, you're cursed."

"Well, then, how is *that* possible? I didn't think curses were real. I'm not sure I believe it now," Ash asked, rummaging through his clothes for a clean shirt.

"Should we go back to the county line so you can be reminded? Curses are real. Just try to accept it."

Ash gave her a flat stare.

The cat sighed and sat up taller. "Okay, fine. It's a very old curse. And it's not just you that is cursed, it's your entire family."

"That's ridiculous!"

"Can you ever remember your father leaving?"

Ash was silent for a while, reviewing his memories. He couldn't recall a single time.

"How could I not know about this?" Ash asked. His voice sounded pained to his own ears. The cat stopped moving, making eye contact with him.

"I believe Nathan was waiting for you to get older to tell you." Her voice was soft.

"Did you know him?" Ash asked, noting that she had said his name.

"Oh yes. I've known all of your family line for a long time." The cat looked away.

"How can I end the curse? I have to get out of here, there must be a way." Ash asked.

The cat hopped down from Ash's counter and headed for the door. "I don't think you can, young Ash."

"What? Wait!" Ash walked quickly to the door, looking the direction she had disappeared to.

The cat was gone.

Neveah

That evening, Neveah found herself at home alone.

Well, as alone as she ever was. There was a cook and maid who lived in a wing of the house full-time. Her private tutor had left for the day. Her diving coach wasn't scheduled until Thursday.

I hate swimming, she thought to herself. Neveah went downstairs and out the back door. She could see the pond in the distance, and even further out, rows and rows of grapevines. Sometimes, sitting here, she felt a swell of emotion she couldn't fully define. It happened again this evening. A longing filled her and pulled her to her feet unwittingly. Rapunzel-itis, she called it.

A few errant steps away from the house and she realized she was not alone. "Oh Midnight!" Neveah exclaimed, scooping the stray cat up. She had befriended the black cat some time ago when she had wandered onto the patio looking for scraps. Soon she had wandered into Neveah's heart as well. Sometimes, Neveah thought "Midnight" might be her best friend. A sad thought indeed, she pondered.

Tonight Midnight did not want to be held long. She hopped down and swished her tail at Neveah. She obviously had an agenda of her own. Neveah was content to let her go her own way, but after a few steps Midnight turned to see if Neveah was following her.

"Pardon me," Neveah said, half-bowing to the cat and obligingly followed along. She flipped on her digital camera. Curiously, the cat did seem to want her to follow. Every few steps she would look back to check that Neveah was still following. If Neveah started to wander her own way, Midnight promptly meowed. Neveah snapped a few candid shots of the temperamental feline.

Together they skirted the pond and wandered past the grapevines. She looked upward and noted that the sun was setting. The buzz of summer insects had begun to die down, reminding her that true fall was right around the corner. She smelled grapes overripe and falling off the vine. She focused her camera lens in on their forms, finding beauty in their deaths. Looking back, she realized she'd wandered quite a ways from her home, but was not concerned. The beastly place was large enough that she wasn't likely to lose it. No one would be looking for her anyway. She trudged on after Midnight.

It wasn't long before she was in unfamiliar territory. What her father called the "estate proper" ended and the true fields began. She did not spend much time out in the fields because her father didn't want her "consorting with the workers." *As if they were monsters or something,* Neveah thought. Many of them rented the land from her family and used it for their own purposes. She had often wondered about the people who lived nearby. None of them ever visited her family.

Suddenly Midnight stopped. Neveah was so lost in her own thoughts that she almost tripped over her. Midnight gave her a knowing look before Neveah heard a voice nearby. It startled her at first, because she could see no one. Then she realized that it was coming from behind a nearby fencerow. Vines had overtaken the fence to the extent that she could not see the other side. She quietly walked toward the voice on the other side. The fence had to be at least six feet tall.

"... didn't tell me. In all that time, you could have said something. I can't believe I never even noticed! I guess I'm going to live in this dumb shed forever now."

What strange words! She wondered who was on the other side of the fence, but wasn't tall enough to see for herself. Looking down at the cat, she swore that Midnight was listening as well. The cat looked directly at her, then climbed the fence and hopped down on the other side. Neveah waited a few moments. Maybe Midnight would come back.

"I guess you're right, Creature," the voice said in a surprisingly lighthearted tone. "There's no point in getting mad at them now."

Huh. Do people really live in sheds?

Neveah, realizing her escort was gone, having deferred to another admirer, turned and headed back home.

"Having been abandoned by her trusty sidekick, Rapunzel returns to her castle tower," Neveah muttered to herself.

➶ ➶ ➶

As she closed the back door, she heard the clinking of glasses in the den. Neveah assumed it was her mother. She was shocked to find her father and a stranger sampling the wine instead.

"Daddy?" Better sense would have caused her to keep walking up to her room, but she was somewhat startled to see him there, and therefore didn't think. Lately she felt startled every time she saw him. It was the knowledge of his affair that so unbalanced her. This time was even worse. She was not used to strangers in the house.

"Neveah, darling. Come in." William gestured broadly for her to enter the room. The man next to him was younger, probably in his mid-twenties. He had red hair that was cut close to his scalp. His eyes glinted in the low light of the den. He smiled at her, slightly raising his glass in acknowledgement. "This is Conner. He's been working quite closely with me lately. We decided to take a break and get a drink."

There was a smile on his face, but she sensed an edge of danger directed at his colleague.

"Hello. I'm called Neveah," she said to Conner. "It's nice to meet you." Neveah was edging out of the room though. It wasn't actually nice to meet him. It was creepy.

"Going somewhere, little sister?" Conner asked. *Very creepy.* She gave a nervous chuckle, and looked to her father.

"Yes. She has homework. Don't you dear?" William answered firmly. His look to her was unquestionable, *you need to leave.* She didn't need any further encouragement.

Elliot

On a nearby property William had an old storehouse filled with huge bubbling vats of wine. Elliot liked to go there sometimes and catch mice. He also liked to eavesdrop on William's secret meetings that sometimes went on there. Elliot, of course, was not supposed to know about these.

Elliot had caught two mice. Could he manage to tie their tails together? He mulled the idea over in his mind. The Face occasionally flashed images to him, suggestions on how to play tricks on the mice. Elliot and The Face often carried on this way. Elliot would think about one thing, The Face would present an image with another idea. Eventually they would settle on something.

He had the two mice in a burlap sack, the end tied closed. They jumped around inside, trying to find a way out, making little *thump, thump* noises against the sack. Elliot pulled a length of kite string from his pocket and began peeling apart the three strands of the rope.

In the open space between the vats, Elliot heard the heavy footsteps he associated with William. William was a large man and even the softest-soled shoes seemed unable to hide his tremendous presence. Elliot paused what he was doing and peered around from behind the vat. Naturally, Elliot wasn't supposed to be lurking around the place. William would never know he was there.

William carried a notepad in one hand and seemed to be checking the gauges on the vats. Elliot was always surprised to find William doing legitimate work, instead of his usual business. William insisted that it was important to appear as the owner of a valid business to the outside world, which sometimes necessitated doing normal valid business. William owned a sprawling and productive vineyard, which was mostly run by other people. Still, he was a mistrustful man and often did checks of the business himself to ensure he wasn't being cheated.

Elliot settled in for a long and boring wait. If discovered, William would kick him out. William would likely not approve of Elliot's antics with the mice. He strongly encouraged Elliot to set aside his childish pranks on harmless creatures and turn to more productive activities. Elliot knew that The Face needed the little tricks though. He had not told William about The Face. Elliot hadn't told anyone about The Face.

Soon there were more footsteps, these quick and loudly tapping against the hard floor.

"What is it now?" William's voice sounded bored. Elliot considered taking a picture with his phone. Peering further around, he could see William's back and little else. Whoever else was there, William's body was blocking Elliot's view.

"You know damn well what it is!" The second man said. His voice was not the deep baritone of William's, but still that of an adult.

"No. I can't imagine you are here to ask anything else of me." William sounded dangerous. Elliot's interest piqued even more. He slid a little closer.

"I'll ask what I want of you. You've taken everything from me! My home, my family." The voice echoed around the building.

"That was a long time ago." William's voice was calm.

"It was only yesterday that you parade me in front of my own family like a stranger. And I've worked like a dog for you all these years. It's time. I want my family back." The second man's voice had grown softer, plaintive. Was he actually begging something from William? Elliot was surprised that anyone would attempt it.

"It's not going to happen."

"I'll find a way. Just you wait! I know what stands between me and my family, William Winters! I'll find a way!" The man said. Elliot heard his footsteps fading away as quickly as they had entered. Elliot held his breath in the silence that followed. What on earth had that been about?

"Elliot, I know you're back there. Come out, boy."

No point in hiding now. Elliot slipped out from behind the vat and stood next to William.

"Who was that fellow?" Elliot asked softly. He had begun separating the strands of the rope again.

"A problem that is likely to pop back up again."

"Should I take care of it?"

"No. Unfortunately I can't handle him the same way I have the others. For now, just let him be." William patted Elliot's shoulder and turned and walked away.

Once he was gone, Elliot returned for his bag of mice. They had gone still, but were alive. The Face was pressing closer, peering out through Elliot's eyes at the two mice. Carefully Elliot caught them by their tails and began tying them together with the string.

The Face was distracted by the mice, but Elliot's mind was reviewing what he had heard. William had done a lot of things, but taking a family from someone? That was an odd thing. No, he would need to learn more about this. William took people from their families, not the other way around. What would be the profit in that? Elliot wished he had caught a name in the argument.

By now the mice were running frantically, hindered by the string tying them together. They scurried in different directions each pulling the other off course. The Face was laughing with glee, all the merriment of a child surging out of him. Elliot found his laughter infectious. Elliot laughed too.

The mice were caught around the foot of a ladder now, running in haphazard circles around each other, winding the rope even tighter with each pass. They were caught, they could go no further. Elliot, still laughing, squatted down beside them. He could see their hearts beating through their little veins as they lay there, fatigued beyond their fear. He pulled out his knife and cut the hearts from their tired little bodies.

Neveah

Neveah looked down at the still blue water and took a deep breath. She had jumped from the high dive a hundred or more times, but there was always this short moment of trepidation. The water looked so perfectly still, for a moment, she was sure she would crash into it, rather than through the surface.

She jumped.

She straightened out her arms and legs to cut the air, then the water quickly. A gasp of air, then she was in the pool. The water was silky smooth and cool against her skin. The chill of early fall was turning the water colder and colder.

Her head broke the surface of the water, and her coach was waiting at the edge of the pool.

"You haven't been practicing, have you?" She was a petite woman in her middle thirties. Of all the people her family employed, Coach Yeats babied her the least.

"How can you tell?" Neveah asked, pulling herself from the water.

"You aren't pointing your toes like we talked about last week. That tiny bit of drag makes a difference."

Neveah frowned. Her father forbade her from competing formally. It seemed a colossal waste of time to worry about pointing toes when this was essentially a very complicated P.E. class. Coach Yeats seemed to know her thoughts.

"I could always just make you run laps or something." She raised her eyebrows.

"I'll practice this time," Neveah answered.

✦ ✦ ✦

"I had thought to schedule more diving lessons this week. In a few more weeks, it's going to be too cold," Jillian said to Neveah over dinner.

"I wish you wouldn't, Mother. I'm really loaded down with homework this week. I have a paper to write." The words poured out of Neveah. Hopefully that meant they were more believable. She'd finished the paper the night before. It was probably the angriest research paper ever written in the history of mankind, but it was done. Neveah had been convinced she was going to break the keys from typing so hard.

"I'm worried about you, dear." Jillian didn't show any outward emotion except for a subtle softening of her features. "Maybe your tutor is giving you too much work. Do you need a break?"

Is it because Mother is so harsh? Is that why he's found a new woman? Or is she harsh because she knows? Neveah's thoughts seemed to always turn back to these questions. "No, Mother. I'm okay. I promise." Neveah tried to smile.

Jillian clearly did not believe her, but let the matter drop anyway.

She excused herself from dinner and begged off to work on her "research paper." Laptop under her arm, she ran to her room and was logged on to Instagram within moments.

I'll find you. Whoever you are.

Neveah was lost for a while in the searching, more photos, more tags. Follow this person who had taken the picture of them in the first place. Look through their photos for tags. Check the photos by this other person who had been at the event. Surely someone knew her.

She was so lost in her investigation that she didn't hear her bedroom door open.

"Ah, here you are, little sister." It was Conner. His voice slippery smooth.

"What are you doing in here?" Neveah asked, instantly nervous. "This is my room."

He laughed. "Of course it is. What do you think I was looking for? The bathroom?" He stepped closer to her. The sun had set and the room was poorly lit by her nightstand lamp. He pulled a hand out of his front pocket, and it was clutching something.

Switch.

A knife!

Neveah screamed. And it didn't matter what she'd been doing or that she was mad at him. In that moment, her scream was, "DADDY!"

Conner blanched. "I won't really hurt you, Neveah." His hands reached out.

"Get away from me!" Neveah shouted, scrambling backwards.

In moments, there was a crashing sound. Then he was there, filling the room with his enormous presence. William tackled Conner to the ground. The knife flew across the room.

Jillian was in the door, yelling, "William! Be careful!"

Neveah had rushed to the far side of the room. Now she looked across the two forms struggling on the floor to meet her mother's terrified gaze. They held eye contact. Jillian held her arms out to Neveah, and that was all the invitation she needed to go to her.

Neveah and Jillian held onto each other and cowered in the hallway. Neveah wasn't sure when she had begun crying, but now the tears had wet the whole front of her mother's shirt.

"William let him go!" Jillian cried out.

"I just want my family back!" Conner was shouting, his cries wild. Then he was silent.

"Don't look, baby." Jillian whispered in her ear and guided her away. Other bodies rushed past them, men coming to her father's aid. Neveah didn't see any of them. She only knew the softness of her mother's voice as they withdrew from a moment of horror.

Elliot

Elliot saw Gerald playing video games in the front room and settled beside him on the floor. He pulled out his pocket knife and began cutting out individual threads of the carpet.

"Mom will kill you if she catches you doing that," Gerald said without looking away from the TV. Elliot thought of his father then, and smiled.

"Indeed, she might." He closed the knife and shoved it back in his pocket. He tried to follow what Gerald was doing on screen, but couldn't muster up enough interest.

"What?" Gerald said, making a face at Elliot.

"For such a delicate flower, you sure spend a lot of time pretending to kill things," Elliot said, indicating the video games.

"I'm not a 'delicate flower,' buttwad." Gerald went back to the game.

"You almost never go outside. You don't do anything except play these silly games. You're terrified of water. You can't even swim. What exactly would you call someone like that?" Elliot knew he was goading Gerald too much, but couldn't stop. Gerald's face and neck were turning red. He gripped his controller harder.

"You know what doesn't make any sense? Why *you* aren't afraid of the water," Gerald said, slamming his controller on the floor. He stormed out of the room.

"Why would I be afraid of water?" Elliot asked the empty air. "What a stupid thing to fear."

"Leave him alone, Elliot." Abigail was setting her things down on the kitchen table. She must have heard the end of their conversation. Elliot shrugged.

"It is a stupid thing to fear, though," Elliot said again. He watched his mother put away her things with her usual strained expression. He supposed she was an attractive woman. Men, like William, certainly seemed to think so. Elliot mostly just found her tired-looking.

He sighed. He often did not understand others. It did not trouble him much. He walked into the kitchen.

"What have you been up to today, Mother? Killed anyone?" Elliot asked, smiling at his joke. Abigail blanched, her face tightening and her hands jerking away.

"Watch your mouth!" She said in an angry whisper, leaning around him to see if Gerald had heard.

"It was just a joke, Mother. Relax." Elliot smiled as she frowned at him and left the room.

The Face pushed forward, suddenly interested. He sensed that Elliot had played a little trick on his mother, but did not understand the joke. Elliot left the house, taking a run through the forest to clear his mind. While he ran, he replayed what happened in his mind. Elliot and The Face often shared information and memories this way.

🕊 🕊 🕊

Gerald played with the ferret in their living room floor. Mother told him for the billionth time not to let it get loose in the house. He shrugged his acknowledgement and continued to hold it in his lap. The ferret's eyes darted around the room, widening with apparent fear. Elliot could smell the little beast from where he sat across the room.

"Father will be mad when he comes home." It was a statement of fact, not an argument. Elliot's mother's eyes shaded over. She knew he was right. "I hope he kills that thing."

"What! Why would you want that?" Gerald said, finally looking away from his new pet. His eyes were wide.

"I wanted a mouse," Elliot answered. He toyed with a pocket knife, opening and closing it over and over again. "And I hate ferrets. They stink. The whole house will smell like it if we keep the stupid thing."

"That's enough, Elliot," Mother said.

Elliot snapped the pocket knife closed and shoved it in his pocket. He stood and walked to his room, leaving them alone with the ferret. He felt the anger rising up in him. It was happening more and more often. He did not understand it, and that only made him more angry.

Inside the room he shared with his brother, he kicked his bedpost hard. There was an immediate answering pain in his foot. The pain did not deter him. It soothed him. Elliot closed his eyes and thought about how the pain felt. Did it have this effect on others? He didn't think so.

Elliot took out a box from under his bed. It was filled with his favorite things, secret things. At first, he had collected things any child might: bird feathers, a turtle shell, moltings from cicadas. Then he had found a squirrel stuck in their fence. It had tried to squeeze between two fence posts and gotten caught. Now Elliot had its tail among his precious belongings.

No, others were not like this. Better to keep this a secret.

Gerald had secrets, too. Didn't he? Gerald had boring secrets. Elliot had gone to some pains to discover what he whispered to his friends on the playground. He liked a girl. What a stupid thing to care about. Elliot hadn't yet met a female that was worth much attention. They twittered and whispered to each other at school. At twelve, they were starting to notice each other, the boys and the girls. Elliot had noticed, then quickly dismissed. Girls, in his estimation, were useless creatures.

There was a door slam. Father was home. Elliot lingered at the doorway, waiting to hear what would happen. The usual greetings could be heard, then silence.

Father had seen the ferret.

Then Gerald was crying, sobbing like a baby. Mother was pleading to him, "Please, please! He's a little boy! Little boys have pets all the time! I'll take care of it! Please!"

Elliot crept down the hall, hoping to see the altercation but not involve himself. Father was stalking across the room, Mother hauling on his arm. A pointless maneuver, Elliot knew. Father plucked the ferret out of Gerald's chubby baby arms and in one quick motion broke its neck.

The room went silent. The ferret's body plonked to the ground. Father left the house as quickly as he had come. Gerald was white-faced. Mother looked up and noticed him standing in the hallway.

"I told you he would kill it."

That was the last time Elliot saw his father alive.

Elliot awoke later that night to police lights shining through their bedroom window. Gerald was still asleep and he left him there. He had cried for hours over that stupid ferret. Elliot wasn't about to start that up again.

Mother was standing in the doorway in her robe. There were two policemen talking to her. They all were talking in quiet voices and the policemen looked stone-faced. Mother's face was tight, her eyes distant. Did she even hear them? She seemed to be thinking about something else. Elliot avoided their gaze and turned to the kitchen instead. Probably telling her that Father was falling down drunk and got into another fight or something. Mother's coat and shoes were by the back door.

Odd. She was always so fastidious about her housekeeping. It was unlike her to throw things on the floor. Elliot looked again with new eyes, reaching out to touch the items. The mud on Mother's shoes were fresh, her jacket still warm. She had to have just taken them off.

Elliot looked back at where she stood with the policemen. He spotted the t-shirt she had been wearing under her robe. It would be no unusual thing to anyone but family. Mother was partial to silk nightgowns for sleeping. Elliot padded quietly back down the hallway to his parent's bedroom. There, in the far corner, the gun cabinet door stood ajar.

It couldn't be.

The policemen left. Their vehicle lights faded away. The front door closed. Mother walked back to her room. Elliot was sitting at the foot of her bed, waiting.

"You killed him, didn't you?"

Mother's face drained of blood. Her tongue seemed to stick in her mouth. She swallowed and answered, "What are you talking about?"

"Do the police suspect you?" Elliot asked, not moving from his place.

"Of course they don't-"

"I won't tell anyone, Mother." Elliot watched her process his words, the slow blinking of her eyes and clenching of her hands against her robe. They stared at each other for a long moment. Elliot could just hear Gerald's soft snores across the hallway, and knew that she was hearing them as well.

"You won't?"

"No. I won't." Elliot stood and left the room. He did not touch her as he passed her. He went to his room and stretched out on his bed. No more Father. What would they do now? Elliot looked at his brother sleeping in the bed next to his.

"We should've got the mouse."

❧ ❧ ❧

It had only been a few moments of running, when his path strayed close to the fields behind William's house. His eyes caught the figure of a lone person walking there. He crouched down and hid to watch.

The girl.

He'd seen her a few times. He'd met her once. She was William's daughter.

She was beautiful. His body reacted to her appearance, filling him with a heat he was unaccustomed to. This feeling, new to him, came on suddenly and strong. It frustrated him. He wanted to touch the girl. He wanted to take her with him into the forest. His sudden need for her angered him. She was beautiful and he hated her for it.

She wandered further away, out of his sight. For a moment, he considered following her. What could he do, if only he caught her?

But no. William would surely kill him. He stuffed the mental image of her walking through the field into a deep part of his mind. He would take out that image again later, when he could do something about it.

He ran on.

Neveah

Neveah had much to think about these days. She had been guarded so closely her entire life that she had little experience with deciphering the character of others. People were either good or bad, right? These revelations about her father had blurred the lines considerably though. He was always loving and kind to Neveah, she assumed that her father was good. But doesn't everyone think that about their parents?

Neveah wandered the fields outside her home, her camera dangling from her hand. She had thought to escape into her photography, but it wasn't working. She couldn't seem to shut out the whirl of worries in her mind. Not to mention the frequent flashbacks to her father fighting with Conner in her room. Her heart skipped a beat, thinking of the knife in his hand. And lately she was tired, probably from the sudden resurgence of night terrors. She hadn't experienced those since she was a child.

No birds on the pond today. No life at all, it seemed. As if Neveah's dark thoughts were chasing away all the little woodland creatures. Surely this wasn't how it worked for Rapunzel. At least in Disney movies, the little animals seemed to love the princesses. Feeling deflated, Neveah was reminded that this was real life, not a game of play-pretend.

A rustling sound came from Neveah's right. She instinctively tensed, remembering her encounter with the strange boy in the woods. With a start she realized she was back at the same vine-covered fence Midnight had led her to a few days ago.

She stepped closer.

What if it's that same guy from the woods?

Meow!

Midnight appeared at the top of a fence post. She continued to meow. The rustling stopped.

"What are you doing, Creature? Is someone there?" A voice said from the other side.

Oh no! He's coming! Hide! Neveah frantically cast around for a place to hide.

More rustling, a creaking of hinges.

"Oh." A male face appeared. There was a gate she hadn't noticed before. "Hello."

"Hey," Neveah laughed nervously. She looked around. "I was just...uh...I was..." She remembered the camera in her hand. "Taking some pictures!"

The stranger came further out from behind the gate. He was a young man, about her age. He was tall, with dark hair and...

70

...oh my god he is so hot! Neveah blushed.

"I'm Ash." He held his hand out to her politely. She gingerly took it in her hand. His hand was rougher than hers; she could feel calluses. She noted the muscles of his arm and was unusually aware of the grass stains on her jeans.

"I'm called Neveah." She tried to smile. "It's nice to meet you."

A moment of silence. *Say something, dummy!* But for the life of her, she couldn't think of a thing to say.

Midnight was perched nearby, cleaning a paw and totally ignoring Neveah's personal humiliation.

"Umm...do you live here?" Neveah asked. It was all she could think of. A real Rapunzel would have thought of something more interesting to say than that!

"Not exactly. You can come look for yourself, if you want," Ash said, running a hand through his hair.

Curiosity overtook her embarrassment and she went inside the gate. It was decidedly not a residence. It was a graveyard.

"Oh." It was all she said.

"A little morbid, I suppose. But it's where my parents are buried, so I try to keep the place cleaned up." He shrugged, stepping back from the gate to give her more room.

Neveah looked around. There were several graves in the small fenced area. Maybe twelve or so. They were all neat as one of her mother's suits. Fall flowers were blooming on some of them. For a graveyard, it was...

"Beautiful," Neveah whispered. Her fingers itched to take pictures. "Can I?" She asked Ash, indicating her camera. He nodded easily.

For a few moments, Neveah was lost in her photography. She took pictures of the headstones, especially the older ones. They were weathered and mossy and held a sort of gothic beauty that spoke to her. She took close ups of the flowers, caught a bee sampling from their blooms. The newest headstone was only a few years old and glistened in the fading sun like a rock fresh from a river.

It wasn't until she started taking a few pictures of Midnight that she realized that Ash was still there. Watching her. Waiting politely for her to finish.

"Sorry," she said to him suddenly. "I guess I got sort of caught up in what I was doing." Her voice came out as a nervous chuckle. Neveah started to turn off the camera.

"Wait!" Ash said, his hand reaching out and then pausing. He seemed momentarily embarrassed. "I...uh...can I see them?"

Neveah paused. No one had ever asked her that before. Of course, no one had ever been around *to* ask.

"I guess so. If you want." She turned so that they could both see the small screen on the camera. She flipped through the pictures.

"I like that one," he said, pointing to a picture she had taken of one of the older headstones. He was standing close to her, and she found that it was hard to focus. This took her attention though.

"Really?" Neveah exclaimed. "You like it?!"

He laughed and looked at her eyes. "Yeah, I do." Neveah laughed too.

"I'm sorry. I don't usually get to show these to anyone. In person, anyway."

"Why not?" Ash asked. "Are you too shy or something?"

"Oh. Um. Well, there's usually no one around." The laugh was fading from her voice. "I'm homeschooled." This was generally enough explanation for the few people she had encountered in the past.

"Oh. Is that cool? Being homeschooled, I mean?" Ash asked. He seemed genuinely interested, not making fun of her.

"It's...well, I don't know. It has its perks, I guess. I kind of miss being around people though." Neveah shrugged. Ash nodded his understanding.

"Well, I'm not an expert. But I think these are cool." He smiled at her. It was a sort of lopsided smile that made her knees feel wobbly.

"Thanks." Neveah floundered again for something to say. She thought back to their conversation. "Wait, didn't you say your parents are buried here?" Neveah felt a wave of horror overcome her. She'd been casually taking pictures of his parents' graves? Was that an offensive thing to do? Should she apologize?

"I'm really sorry!" Neveah blurted out, panic evident on her face.

"No, it's okay!" Ash said, his hands raised in front of him, as if he were calming a horse. "Really."

"Oh my gosh! I can't believe I just glossed right over that when you told me! I'm such an idiot!" Neveah's hands went to her face. *Please let the earth just swallow me up where I stand!*

Ash gently placed his hands on her shoulders, and Neveah froze. "Really, it's okay. It happened some time ago, and I'm not offended or anything." He smiled at her. "In fact, they rarely get visitors, so this was kind of nice."

Neveah looked at the headstones again. The name Nathan Price was carved into the newest one. *Loving father, husband and friend.*

"I'm sorry, Ash's parents." She whispered the words, but Ash heard. He paused, blinking his big blue eyes at her.

"I don't think anyone has ever spoken to them before. Other than me."

✦ ✦ ✦

Neveah couldn't stop smiling. *He liked my pictures,* she thought for the thousandth time. *He smiled at me*. She sighed, the thousandth sigh since leaving the graveyard. Neveah opened the back door and headed for the den.

Jillian was at the country club again. William was off "on business," which could mean any number of things. Neveah shoved away the instant thought that he was actually meeting his ...whatever she was. Mistress? Girlfriend? Neveah felt nauseous at the thought.

With a start, she realized that this was the first time she had been alone at home since Conner had attacked her. Her body tensed at the memory. She could see in her mind's eye the glint of the knife in his hand. She closed her eyes and took a deep breath. After the whole incident was over, William had assured her that he could never hurt her again. Neveah assumed he had been arrested.

It was odd though. She hadn't seen any police. Only her father's personal security team.

Neveah settled into her favorite chair, a big overstuffed thing that swallowed her. *Ash was so hot!* Neveah smiled to herself and rubbed her cheeks with her hands. Looking around for the TV remote, she turned to the side table. A newspaper was laying there, she picked it up to look underneath. Neveah absently noted the date at the top, today's newspaper.

She dropped the newspaper back on the table. Her hands trembled. There was the headliner, shouting out an unspoken accusation about her father.

It read: *Local man found dead along river bank*. Underneath was the unmistakable photo of Conner.

Chapter Three

Creek Woman

No one was more shocked than I to see what was waiting for me. I followed the great mountain lion through the forest and finally we came to a shore that I did not recognize. He faced me and turned smoothly into a man. He was golden-skinned and strong and as beautiful as any man of my people there had ever been. He reached his hand out to me. I was shocked and confused and still frightened. I took his hand carefully.

He led me forward to show me that there was a house waiting for me. It was made of wattle and daub, with a new roof, as fine a home as any in the village. I had no idea that Big Man-Eater lived in a home like any other person. I was shocked again.

"This will be your new home from now on," he said, gently leading me forward. "I have made it for you. You are my wife now. I will live with you here always."

It was such a simple declaration, but it was filled with meaning for my future. Would I be allowed to visit the village of my clan? What would be expected of me as his wife? Could I ever expect to feel safe, much less loved, by such a creature as him? My mind whirled with the implications, and so we walked quietly to our new home together.

In the coming days and years I was surprised by much of my life as Big Man-Eater's wife. While truly he was a wild beast, and he did actually love to eat men, he was kind to me. He would sometimes slip off in the night and the next morning I would know that his belly was full and he was satiated. I would silently grieve for those he had killed. It was a gruesome reality to an otherwise happy life.

I had a nice warm home, and there was always food cooking over the fire. Big Man-Eater provided fresh meat for me. He transformed into a wild boar and dug a garden for me. He transformed into a great eagle and collected seed for me to plant. He was magnificent and resourceful. It became easy to love him, with all of his care and thoughtful gifts.

And I learned the reason he had wanted a wife fleet of foot. Big Man-Eater spent so much of his time as a large cat, that like cats of all sizes, he loved to play. Big Man-Eater would chase me playfully through the woods and across the shores. Laughter filled trees. It did not matter how fast I ran, he always caught me. He would pounce and capture me in fallen leaves or a carpet of pine needles, and we would make love in the forest.

The only shadow on my life, aside from his appetites, was the village of my clan. I was allowed to visit, but learned soon that it was not wise to do so. While Man-Eater took no qualm with my visits, the people there did. I was treated as strange and dangerous. The people seemed to think that a woman who could satisfy a beast like Big Man-Eater was unnatural. They distrusted me deeply. My visits always left me with a bad taste in my mouth, and so with time, I visited less and less.

I had been wife to Big Man-Eater for some years, I forget how many. I had not visited my people in some time. I was only just beginning to notice that I did not age as others. My brothers and sisters had grown old and died, while my hair was still dark and my arms were still strong. I believed that it was some magic of Big Man-Eater's. He had taught me many things, and yet there was still much about him that I did not understand. And these differences between myself and my clan eventually became disturbing to me. To them also. It was unsettling to see my nephews and nieces grow old, while I did not change. So you see, I had lost touch with much of my family when one day a visitor came calling.

An old woman came trudging through the forest. She held a cane in one hand and had a scarf wrapped around her head and shoulders. She seemed to walk with difficulty, but was deliberately walking towards our home. Big Man-Eater was with me that day and asked if I knew her. I told him that I did not, but had not visited the village in many summers. Who would I know of them now?

She came closer and was wheezing with the effort. Big Man-Eater met her and asked her who she was. A relation of mine, she claimed. It seemed plausible enough. I had many relations in the village and would not likely recognize any of them. Big Man-Eater let her inside. We fed her, entertained her. She told us news of the clans. She thanked Big Man-Eater for his protection of the village. And after a while, my husband went to sleep on a rug in front of the fire, as he often did.

"Does he snore when he's sound asleep?" The old woman asked. "My husband used to do that. I still miss it sometimes, if you can believe it!"

"I believe it! Yes, he does snore when he's sleeping soundly. Sometimes he wakes me in the night. Though if he were not here, I would *miss him greatly," I answered. An odd conversation, but she seemed harmless enough. Eventually she tired as well and I made her a pallet to sleep on.*

In the night, she rose and took a knife from my kitchen. She took the knife and she killed Big Man-Eater. She cut off his head.

When his cries woke me, I came running to him. But it was too late. I looked at the old woman in horror, to realize much too late, that it was not an old woman. It was Rabbit. Rabbit had killed my husband.

Ash

The cat talks. Ash was thinking yet again. *The cat talks. I'm cursed, somehow. I can never leave this awful place. And I just stole a set of walkie-talkies like a third grader.*

It had been an eventful couple of days.

Ash checked over his shoulder. No one was following him. No one was calling out for him to stop. He had successfully stolen. Again.

Ash walked away from a discount store and entered a hardware store set in the same shopping center. He needed tack nails for his newest dollhouse. Browsing through the long aisle of nails and screws, Ash mentally reviewed again what he had learned: *A cat told me I can't leave the county. I tried it, it didn't work. Definitely can't leave the county. What now?*

Frustration ran over like water in a sink with the faucet left on too long. *I can never leave.* In a moment the anger flooded him. He felt it down into his fingertips. He grabbed a box of nails and threw it on the floor. The box tore open and the nails went skittering across the worn tiles.

A store stocker walked around the corner and took in the scene in an instant.

"I've had a very bad day!" Ash yelled at him, kicking the pile of nails. "But I'll definitely pay for these! Now please bring me a damn broom!"

The stocker turned and actually ran away from Ash. *Nicely played, you idiot*, Ash scolded himself.

In a few moments, a different store employee came. He was just in time to see Ash throw part of the box overhead a second time and slam it into the floor. He had a broom and an unimpressed expression. He was older than Ash, older than the other guy too. He was probably a manager.

"You're going to clean up this mess, son."

"Yes, sir." Ash swept up the nails, his chest heaving with anger. "Nails are unsatisfying to throw anyway." He finished what he was doing and handed the broom and dustpan back. "I'm sorry for the mess."

After paying for the box of nails he had destroyed, and an additional three boxes of the nails he actually needed, the manager asked him to not come back for a month. It was a good thing he had kept out some of the cash Elliot had given him. The rest was tucked neatly into his get-away stash. Not that he'd ever *get away*.

"A month is a very specific amount of time," Ash muttered as he walked to his truck. He paused. "Do I talk to myself now? I guess so. I talk to freakin' cats, so why not?" He then noted that a woman was in a nearby vehicle, listening to the radio with the windows down. They made awkward eye contact for a moment. She quickly rolled the windows up and locked the door.

Ash groaned loudly. He tossed the nails and his backpack into his truck cab. "If these walkie-talkies don't work, I'm going to take that as a sign that the universe is officially against me!" Ash shouted to no one in particular.

The next day he was feeling a little better. He *had* humiliated himself in a hardware store, then again in a parking lot. He *had* talked to a cat, which made no kind of sense. He *had* bounced off the county line like a tennis ball off of a racket. But, he had a plan!

If he ever saw that girl again.

Which might never happen.

Gotta stay positive! Ash told himself, as he packed the walkie-talkies in his backpack and headed out of the shed. It was Saturday, a day of possibilities. Anything could happen.

Ash was supposed to be working on the house. Ash was always supposed to be working on the house. But occasionally he slipped off on his own errands. Abby rarely took much notice of his comings and goings. Once a month, she checked his progress on the house. She'd done that the week before, so he knew she wouldn't be by for a while.

Today he headed to the graveyard. There was a spring in his step. He hummed to himself. His backpack bounced between his shoulders. Of course, she might not show up. But then again she might. Ash was living on that chance.

At the gate, Elliot was waiting for him. Ash's gait slowed.

"Ashes, ashes, we all fall down." Elliot sang it out, like a greeting to Ash. "What's got you in such a good mood, dear brother?"

"Oh nothing. Just thought I'd clean the place up a bit," Ash replied casually. There was no way he was going to tell Elliot about Neveah.

"Hmm. I thought you might have a little friend meeting you," Elliot said coolly.

"A friend? In a graveyard?" Ash laughed outwardly, but the hair on the back of his neck raised.

"Sure, why not? I met the most interesting girl in the woods the other day. Short brown hair. She was on a horse. Lovely girl." Elliot smiled. It was the smile of a crocodile in the Nile. Ash felt his blood chill. "You never know who you'll run into around here, Ashes." Elliot said this over his shoulder as he walked away. He was laughing, and Ash could hear it ringing in his ears long after Elliot was gone.

Neveah

The next morning, Neveah's mind was still reeling from her discovery. Her father had killed a man. Or ordered someone else to do it. Either way, he was responsible. Neveah felt no love lost over Conner. He had threatened her, snuck into her room. He was vile. But worth murdering? It was incomprehensible.

Neveah looked around at her beautiful home. She thought of the pretty dresses in her closet, her expensive shoes, her camera even. Was all of it bought with blood money? She felt sick. *I have to get out of here!*

Neveah grabbed her camera. She set it back down. She grabbed it again. However it was bought, it was too late to undo it now.

Out of her room, down the stairs, almost to the den, "Neveah dear, can you come

to the den?" It was her mother. *Almost made it.* Neveah squared her shoulders and went to her mother.

A woman was standing with Neveah's mother, a woman she had never seen before. She was tall and clearly Native American. She was beautiful, with long black hair that fell to her waist. She wore tasteful clothes in earth tones, and a strange woven pendant on a necklace. Nothing about her was out of place, yet somehow Neveah felt she would look just as natural in a painting from a hundred years ago.

"Neveah, this is your new tutor. Her name is Ruth. She has agreed to help you with school and prepare you for your entrance exams into college."

Ruth's gaze turned to her and Neveah had the strange feeling that Ruth could see right through her, as if she were no more than a piece of gauze stretched across the doorway. Ruth's mouth quirked up on one side. "It's nice to meet you, Neveah. I look forward to working with you."

"It's nice to meet you too," Neveah answered mechanically.

"Your mother tells me that you are quite accomplished in your studies already." Her peculiar gaze slid to her mother, then back to Neveah. "We shall see."

Neveah felt nervousness welling in her gut. She swallowed hard and looked to her mother. "I'll do my best," she said, looking back at Ruth. "When do we start?"

Ruth smiled. "I'll be back in the morning. We can start with history. Do you know much history about Native Americans? My one condition for my services is that I require all of my pupils to learn about Native American history," she paused, gesturing to herself. "For obvious reasons."

"I look forward to learning about it then," Neveah said. The tension in her body was slowly loosening its grip. Ruth seemed harsh, tough, but fair. At least, Neveah hoped that her estimation of Ruth was correct. Otherwise it was going to be a long year.

🖈 🖈 🖈

Neveah was gone again a few moments later. She considered taking Sunbeam with her but decided against it. The last thing she wanted was Sunbeam munching on the flowers on Ash's families' graves.

The grass in the fields had turned from green to yellow recently. Fall was settling its rich colors all over the land. Neveah did not take as much time to take in the view though. She found it hard to keep from breaking into a run. Would Ash be there? The anticipation of possibly seeing him filled her from head to toe.

There, in the distance was the vine-covered fencerow. And something was dangling from the gate. Neveah's brow creased. What could it be?

A walkie-talkie was hanging from the gate handle by a string. A note was stuck to it. *For N. From A. Channel 6.* Neveah was smiling as she flipped the walkie-talkie on and turned the dial to 6.

"Hello?" She said into the speaker. Would he answer? There was the sound of static, then nothing as she let her finger off of the button. Peeking inside the gate, she saw that the graveyard was empty. She took out her camera and settled in the grass, the walkie-talkie laying in her lap.

"Hello?" Neveah snapped up the walkie-talkie.

"Ash!" She said, a little too loudly. "Is it you?"

"Yes! You got the walkie-talkie! Awesome!" He answered, his voice sounding peculiar, as if he were talking through a tin can. She laughed out loud.

"This is so cool!" She said.

"I'm glad you like it." His voice sounded pleased. "I'm glad you came back, too."

"Shouldn't we have code names or something?" Neveah asked. "Isn't that what truckers do?"

"We aren't truckers."

"It might be fun though!" Neveah answered quickly. "Also, aren't we supposed to say 'over' when we're done?" Pause. "Over."

"Maybe it will be fun. What is your code name, then?" Ash said. "Over."

Neveah thought about it a moment. "How about... oh! Rapunzel!"

"Rapunzel?" He asked, surprise in his voice. "I guess that makes me Cinderfella."

Neveah

Ruth was tough. Neveah began her daily studies with a rigorous schedule of Native American history. Then math, math, math til she wanted to die. Then grammar, followed with writing, and just for fun, writing about Native American history. She'd never seen a textbook or met a tutor with so much knowledge about Native American culture and history. It went above and beyond anything she'd ever seen. Of course, she couldn't think of a time when she'd had it taught to her by an actual Native American. Neveah assumed that was the difference. Certainly it seemed personal to Ruth at times. Neveah noticed that Ruth's fingers seemed to linger on the glossy photos in the books she brought. Ruth spoke of these people as if she knew them, remembered them somehow.

Neveah was fascinated, but also totally weirded out by it.

And it wasn't all about Native Americans. Ruth taught her a

thoroughly astonishing amount about world politics and history. Neveah had no idea that there were just so many people in the world, and therefore did not have a grasp of how many contrasting viewpoints existed. Not everyone thought like she did, and there were more opinions than the two opposing opinions she overheard when her father watched the news. It was astonishing! Neveah soaked up the knowledge like a sponge, like a drowning man takes in air.

Everyday, Ruth left Neveah's head spinning. The core subjects she knew well, and demonstrated to Ruth happily. But suddenly there was geography and civics and world history and current events. People floundered and struggled across the globe? Neveah had no idea. It made her own problems seem small by comparison.

Neveah stumbled upstairs, her head tired but her body restless. She looked out the window in her room and saw the fields in one direction, the forest in another. The sun was setting low. Throwing the window open, she took in the fresh evening air. It blew her short hair back and washed the scent of field and forest over her.

"Rapunzel to Cinderfella," Neveah spoke into the walkie-talkie, lingering at the window.

"I'm here, Rapunzel," Ash answered. It was their nightly ritual. "Are you investigating tonight?"

Neveah was always investigating. She had already flipped on her laptop. "Yeah. I'm kind of at a dead end though. I just can't find a tag for this woman anywhere."

"Maybe you need to use Facebook or Twitter or something."

Ash's voice crackled over the small speaker. Of course he was right, but she didn't think she could get away with it.

"My Dad will find out. I can't use my name," Neveah answered.

"You could make up a name," Ash said. He sounded like he was working on something while he was talking, distracted. He often sounded that way. Neveah had asked him once and he said he was flipping a house. *Whatever that means.*

"Somehow I don't think I can make a profile as 'Rapunzel,'" Neveah answered drily.

"Well you would have to make up a realistic name. Or I guess you could use mine." Neveah imagined Ash rolling a house around an empty lot while he talked to her and giggled.

"Ash...ummm...I don't actually know your last name. Or anything other than your first name and some random stuff we've talked about. Won't I need your birthday and stuff like that?" Neveah said, starting and stopping awkwardly.

"Well, it would be a Facebook account, not an application for a bank loan. It doesn't matter if you make stuff up. But if you're that worried about it, I can help you. We'll have to meet somewhere with the internet though."

Neveah slapped the laptop closed. *Meet in person!* They hadn't done that since they had first met. Her heart stuttered in her chest. The last time was exhilarating and embarrassing and overwhelming. She'd dissected every word of it over and over in her mind since. Anxiousness and excitement warred within her.

"Ok. I'm not sure where though. Or ...well, I don't know when I will be able to sneak away. My mom is on high alert."

"Most nights I'm here, at this house I'm working on. You can come here, I guess. I've been using the neighbor's wifi for weeks. Don't tell them that though!" Ash answered with a laugh.

Neveah's hands shook while she took down the address.

"Just use the walkie-talkie when you think you can get away." Ash's voice was calm. Neveah heard that voice in her dreams that night. *I'm going to see him again!*

Ash

For the next few days, every time the walkie-talkie buzzed, Ash jumped out of his skin. Would this be the time that she was telling him she was coming? Actually coming to see him? It seemed impossible. Sometimes, Ash convinced himself that she wasn't even real and that he was imagining the conversations they had over the walkie-talkie.

I mean, I do talk to cats. Imaginary girls can't be a big leap on the crazy scale. Ash thought as he set another tile into the bathroom wall. As if summoned by his thoughts, Creature came wandering into the bathroom. She looked around the room, appraising his work it seemed.

"Hello. I was wondering if I would ever see you again," Ash said. It was meant to sound like one of his usual greetings, but inside he was terrified that the cat would answer him back. He was even more terrified that she wouldn't.

"You're getting quite adept at laying tile. I remember the first house you did this in. It didn't look this nice," Creature said calmly. She sat primly, in a way that only cats seem to do.

Ash was quiet for a while. *So she really does talk.* He wasn't exactly comforted.

"Don't tell me you've forgotten that I talk. We had a rather important conversation, if you'll recall," Creature said, her ears flickering.

"Oh I recall, alright," Ash answered, forcing his attention back to the tile and adhesive. "I'm just not sure if this is real or I'm losing my mind."

"Oh it's real. You'll just have to take my word for it, I suppose." Creature licked her paw in an absent-minded fashion. "So when are you going to meet the young lady again?"

"You know about that?" Ash asked, his eyes widening as he turned to look at her.

The cat's head tilted to one side. "Oh, young Ash. I know a great many things." He swore that she grinned then.

"Are all cats like you, secretly?" Ash asked.

"Why are you so certain I'm a cat?" Creature said matter-of-factly, then turned and left.

"What does that even mean?" Ash called after her. *I'm never going to get used to this.*

Creature had explained his family curse to him that day, and little else. He still didn't even know what to call her. "Creature" suddenly seemed a rude thing to call a talking feline.

He returned to his work. One tile, another, another after that. There was a rhythm to the work that was soothing to his mind.

Buzz, buzz.

"Rapunzel to Cinderfella." The tile slipped from his fingers and cracked against the floor.

Ash composed himself and reached for the crackling walkie-talkie. "Cinderfella here. How goes the investigation, Rapunzel?" Ash hoped his voice wasn't wavering.

There was a longer pause than usual.

"I don't think I can come tonight." Ash felt disappointment heavily, as he had every other night that she had contacted him. "And I can't talk tonight either. But I wanted you to know, so you didn't wait around for me or something." A pause. "I don't know if you would do that anyway, but it seemed rude not to tell you."

Ash debated telling her his instant thought: he definitely would have waited. Instead he said, "Thanks for letting me know. Have a good evening, Rapunzel."

Elliot

Ash was always getting in the way. Elliot spotted his step-brother leaving the graveyard. Ash's head was low, his shoulders hunched up. He looked like a kicked cat. *Pathetic, as usual*. He couldn't imagine enduring the treatment that his step-brother took from their family. Elliot would have retaliated in a most violent fashion had he been put in Ash's position. Ash merely carried on. It was a mystery.

Lately, Ash had been the source of some good information for Elliot though. Ash had been talking to the girl. Elliot had been listening. They didn't know, of course. And those silly code names. Who would be fooled by them? Cinderfella? Ridiculous!

But Elliot was learning a great deal. Ash was unexpectedly good at teasing information out of Neveah. She had figured out about her father's nefarious dealings and was investigating him herself! Ha! Elliot laughed out loud thinking about it. William had no idea that his sweet little girl was on to him! Elliot revelled in the knowledge.

Soon though, Elliot realized that Ash was going to be in his way again. While Elliot was certainly not an expert on romance, or most emotions for that matter, even he could see that something was building between the two. Elliot could not allow this to continue. Neveah was his. Not Ash's. He began to formulate a plan.

The Face loved a good trick. Could Ash get The Face to go along with a trick on Ash? When they played tricks on the animals in the woods, the animals tended to not survive them. Would it be the same with Ash?

All good tricks needed some kind of bait. What would lure Ash away? Elliot knew Ash would be easily lured away by Neveah. But The Face couldn't be trusted with her. No, he needed something else. He would continue to lurk around his step-brother until he found something. Surely there must be something else he cared about.

Elliot was perched in his normal spot outside of the house Ash was working on. He often sat under windows or in nearby trees to listen in on Ash's conversations. The walkies were silent tonight though. Neveah had told him she wouldn't be able to talk tonight, but foolish boy had the walkie-talkie propped up next to him anyway. Elliot did not understand these sorts of actions. He felt the grip of boredom squeeze him as he lounged in the tree. This often happened when he was following someone, but he was accustomed to it and shook it off. If he became too lax, The Face would take over, and he would remember nothing.

The Face was watching as well. Elliot could sense it, looming at the back of his consciousness. It peered out of Elliot's eyes like windows on a house. This, too, Elliot was accustomed to.

Ash was nailing in drywall. A boring task to watch. Ash paused in his work and looked over his shoulder. Something had come into the room with him. It was just out of Elliot's line of sight. He inched forward on the tree branch.

"There you are. I didn't expect to see you again tonight," Ash said.

"I didn't either," said a feminine voice. "No secret rendezvous with the girl tonight again, I take it?"

Elliot's weight made the branch bend lower as he slunk forward carefully. He felt The Face crowd forward in his mind. It was intent on whoever was in the room with Ash. Who could it be? The branch tipped just low enough for Elliot to see. Ash was talking to...a cat?

The Face roared within Elliot's head. His body bowed and he lost his grip on the branch. He was falling, disoriented by the wild shrieking within his mind. He landed on his back with a hard thud. The impact rattled through him, he felt it in his back and limbs with a shock. He couldn't remember the last time he'd fallen. Elliot fought to his feet, urging The Face to silence. It would not be silent. Elliot's body was being pulled to the cat, and he urged it away. Elliot fought The Face for control of his body. The Face was desperate to get to that cat. Elliot was desperate to hang on to his consciousness.

Elliot lost.

Elliot woke up to darkness. His eyes adjusted after a moment and he realized he was still on the ground under the tree he'd fallen out of. The house next to him was dark and silent. How long had he been lying there? He got up and looked around the house. Ash was long gone. It was late. What had happened after he blacked out?

And more importantly, why did that cat enrage The Face so? He recognized the cat, of course. It was the same one that had followed him through the woods before. He had seen it a few times over the years. Had The Face really not noticed it before?

He did not know where to look for answers. Closing his eyes, he could feel The Face still there, but deep within his mind. It was as if The Face was asleep. Elliot probed The Face with his mind. He imagined he was opening a package. What would be inside? The Face stirred, turning this way and that. He could feel it stretching and bending away from him. Could he penetrate its mind the way it did his?

He pushed harder. The Face awoke. He could sense it there, watching him.

"Let me in!" Elliot said out loud. His teeth were clenched and small beads of sweat were forming on his forehead, his neck. The Face smiled at him. It was an unkind smile, a mocking smile.

Suddenly Elliot could see a large fire. It was as if he were standing inside of it. He could smell it, feel its heat. He saw the billowing smoke above him and hear its wild roar. Listening a little closer, there was screaming somewhere nearby. The fire was consuming people, homes, animals. Elliot felt their loss of life.

And rising above all of this, there was that familiar laughter. Elliot recognized The Face's voice, laughing madly in the midst of all of this fire and death.

Elliot was back outside the house. The coolness of the night assaulted his hot skin. He could no longer hear the fire, the screaming, but he could still hear The Face's laughter. He had gotten what he wanted, he'd seen something inside The Face.

He still knew nothing.

Neveah

Neveah knew that she needed to talk to her mother. Would she be able to say what was on her mind though? What if her mother didn't know about her father's activities? It would break her mother's heart. She pushed open the back door and walked outside. There was the scent of pool chemicals and roses on the air. As she drew closer to her mother's rose garden, she could hear something. Probably Jillian's pruning shears.

She hesitated before turning onto the gravel path that led between long rows of rose bushes. She could see the trellises at the back of the garden, covered in thick vines and blooms.

Jillian was seated under one of those trellises. Her back was to Neveah, there were no shears in her hands. The noise, could it be that she was crying? Neveah was taken aback. She'd never seen her mother cry, didn't even know she had the ability.

How silly, Neveah thought. *Everyone cries. Don't they?*

Neveah turned to go back into the house. It could wait. Her shoe scuffed on the gravel. Jillian's head turned to the sound.

"Neveah? Is that you?" Jillian's voice was strong. Neveah would not have suspected she had been crying just a moment ago.

"Yeah. It's okay, Mother. We can talk later. I know how much you..." She paused. She had been about to say, 'need to cry.' Instead she finished, "love gardening."

"It's okay. Come sit with me a while, dear." Jillian patted the seat next to herself. Neveah walked forward and perched uneasily on the bench under the trellis.

"Mom, are you ok?" Neveah rarely called her 'mom.' She didn't know why she chose to now. Jillian was quiet for a moment.

"Did you know that you almost had a brother once?" Jillian asked. "A few years before you were born, I carried him."

It was Neveah's turn to be silent. She had no idea. "What happened to him?"

"He died." Jillian's voice was flat. Her eyes were distant. Neveah suddenly realized how little she knew her own mother. Did anyone really know her?

"What did you want to talk to me about, dear?" Jillian asked. Her eyes focused on Neveah in the same manner they assessed the roses in bloom. It was as if she were looking Neveah over for signs of blight.

"I wanted to tell you..." Neveah's hands twisted in her lap under her mother's scrutiny. She couldn't say the words. "I wanted to say that I really like my new tutor. Ruth is really great. Thank you for hiring her."

"There's no reason to fidget so, child," Jillian said calmly, eyeing Neveah's hands. "I'm glad you like her. Mostly I'm glad for a tutor that can keep up with you." She snapped a leaf off of one of the vines. It held the slightest yellowing. Neveah would have never spotted it in the riot of greens and reds.

"Me too." Neveah felt cold, and wrapped her arms around herself. She stood to leave. "Mother? I'm sorry. About your son." Neveah walked away.

Jillian stayed behind. As Neveah left the garden, she heard the definite snipping of Jillian's shears.

Elliot

Elliot knew that he still needed his mother. He snickered to himself when he walked into his room. She had clearly been snooping again. He decided that he would pretend he didn't notice for now.

"Oh Mother dear," Elliot whispered to himself. She was no better at rummaging through his room secretly than conducting her illicit affair with William. He wasn't supposed to know about that either.

Elliot was thinking more and more about the girl in the woods, Neveah. He had become transfixed by her. He found himself dreaming about her short hair, her petite frame. He daydreamed about her when he was at school. He awoke with her on his mind, and fell asleep imagining her small hands. He knew he needed her.

And for that to happen, he needed his mother. One side of his mouth quirked up at the thought. She was not likely to enjoy her participation in the matter.

All that much better for Elliot.

The first step was to unsettle his mother. That was easy enough to do. She was a silly woman, easily upset. And he knew her secrets. He had not forgotten a single one over the years. But did she know any of his? Unlikely.

He went to his closet and pulled down a small metal box from a top shelf. He kept a few select items there. When his mother spied on him, she always checked this box. She assumed it was a collection of his treasures. It was really only the treasures he allowed her to see. He wasn't foolish enough to hide the real ones here in his room.

He reached into his pocket and pulled out a heavy metal lighter. It had *WW* engraved in curly letters on the side. William was a vain man, and this was one of his signature lighters that he always carried. *Gaudy things*, Elliot thought. He set the lighter in the box.

Replacing the box on the shelf, he left the room in search of his little family. Gerald was sitting at the dining table with some homework spread out before him.

"Ah brother. Homework, is it?" Elliot asked, plucking a banana from a fruit bowl.

"Mmhmm," Gerald muttered, not looking up from his work. There was a pause while Elliot stared at his little brother.

"What do you want, Elliot?" Gerald asked. He paused and looked up.

"What makes you think I want something?" Elliot smiled.

"Elliot, you're my brother. I know when you want something. Spit it out, I have a lot to do here," Gerald said with a sigh. Elliot laughed. It was true. Of anyone, Gerald probably knew him the best.

"I'm just in a good mood today. Can't I have a look at my dear brother?"

"Fine. Don't tell me. Can you loiter somewhere else though?" Gerald turned back to his work. Elliot slid into the chair next to his brother, peeling the banana slowly. He pulled his pocket knife out and slowly cut off a piece of the banana and ate it. Gerald looked up and glared at him. Elliot laughed.

"Fine, fine. I'll leave. Maybe later we can go for a walk together. We haven't done anything together in a while, have we?" Elliot patted Gerald on the shoulder. Gerald didn't bother to hide his confusion. He looked at where Elliot had touched him and raised an eyebrow. Elliot smiled again and went back to his room.

He knew the seed had been planted.

Later that evening, the three of them ate dinner together. Elliot noted with satisfaction that Gerald and his Mother were exchanging furtive glances. Yes, Gerald had reported Elliot's strange behavior to their mother. What a good little brother! Elliot laughed out loud.

"What is it?" Abigail asked, wiping the side of her mouth with a napkin.

"Oh don't you worry, Mother," Elliot said, still chuckling. "I believe you will find out
soon enough what is so funny to me." With that, he slid back his chair and tossed his napkin on the table. He left the house and then waited out of sight.

"You're right," Abigail said to Gerald. "He is in an unusually good mood. What is he up to?"

"I really don't know, Mother," Gerald said. "But you know how he is. He probably caught a squirrel or something."

There was silence. Elliot imagined them sharing a look. Neither of them approved of his peculiar proclivities.

"No, no. This is different somehow," Abigail said. He could hear the clinking of dishes as she cleared the table.

"Yes. It is. He wants us to know this time," Gerald said. Once again he had proven the more observant of the two. Elliot felt something akin to pride for his little brother.

"You're right. But what?" Abigail asked. "I'm going to look in his room."

"Be careful, Mom. I know he leaves the house for hours, but sometimes I think he is just lurking outside, watching us."

"Oh that's nonsense. Why would he be watching us?"

Elliot smothered his giggles.

He had heard enough. He took a leisurely walk through the woods around their home, circling back to look in on Ash. His step-brother was generally very boring to spy on. He only went to school and worked, and rarely spoke or did anything interesting at all. But Elliot needed to kill some time so that his poor mother would have a chance to find her lover's lighter in his room. He really wanted her to brood over it for a while before he came home.

Ash was out working. Again. Elliot sighed and decided to make his way to Ash's worksite. He walked at a brisk pace, the evening air sticking to him unpleasantly. Elliot disliked the heavy humidity that sometimes plagued this area. He much preferred the cold of winter. Even the few snowfalls they experienced were welcome. The snow seemed to muffle all sound, which was to Elliot's advantage.

It was not a long walk for Elliot to get to the little house Ash was engaged in renovating. He could see a light on in the front room, and hear the sounds of drywall being torn out. Nasty work, Elliot thought. All sorts of dead things in the walls of old houses. Mice and roaches and who knew what else?

He peered in a window, and there was Ash, steadily working away. Ash was smiling however. Elliot couldn't remember the last time he'd seen his step-brother smile. His eye twitched. Ash was unlikely to be happy about finding a dead mouse in the walls. Ash must be talking to Neveah again.

"I'm serious! My horse is my best friend!" said Neveah. Elliot noted the walkie-talkie in Ash's hand.

"I guess I can't say anything. I'm sort of friends with a cat," Ash said into the walkie.

"I love cats!" Neveah's voice was distorted by the walkie-talkie. She sounded as if she were laughing from the bottom of a well.

"I just can't believe someone like you doesn't have tons of friends," Ash said, pausing in his work.

"Well, I never really meet anyone. I'm mostly alone at home," she sounded less cheerful this time.

"I'm sorry," Ash said. He, too, was no longer smiling. "I'll be your friend."

Elliot almost laughed out loud. What a sweet little moment for his step-brother! Ash had managed to surprise Elliot.

On the other hand, it was becoming painfully aware that Neveah was becoming attached to Ash. This was unacceptable. Elliot did not worry himself too much, a plan was already in motion to push his step-brother out of the way.

He stayed for a little while longer, listening to the two talk on their walkie-talkies. Elliot judged that enough time had passed for his mother to find the lighter. He walked back home.

Abigail was waiting for him when he got there. She sat at the table, the lighter in one hand.

"Elliot, we need to talk."

"Oh? What's wrong, dear Mother?" Elliot asked.

"Where did you get this?" Abigail asked, setting the lighter on the table between them. Her voice was firm. Elliot was a bit surprised. His mother rarely took such a direct approach with him.

"Ah that. It was a sort of present. From a friend of mine," Elliot answered. It was the truth, actually. He took out his pocket knife and trimmed his fingernails while his mother stared at him.

"A friend?"

"Yes." Elliot did not meet her eyes.

"How do you know this friend?" Abigail asked.

"Oh I've known him a while. I couldn't really say anymore how we met," Elliot answered. His mother's aggravation was palpable. He continued to fiddle with his pocket knife.

"How long is 'a while'?" Abigail asked, picking the lighter back up.

"Since…" Elliot pretended to be thinking it over in his mind. "I guess just before the fire. That's when he gave me that lighter."

The fire. Elliot did look at her then. The color was draining away from her face. His poor shockable mother had never suspected anything. It was time for her to know the truth.

"Yes. It had to have been just before the fire. How else could I have started it?" Elliot smiled at her across the table, knife in hand. Abigail's hand clenched the lighter, the other hand going to her throat.

"No, Elliot."

"Oh yes, dear mother," Elliot said, he flipped open the knife and stuck the point of it into the table. He stood from his chair and leaned across to her. "Oh yes."

Abigail was pale enough that Elliot could see a vein throbbing in her temple. She had gone still, like squirrels do when they are threatened. He laughed. He allowed himself a full, loud laugh. How could she have never even suspected him? But he could see now that she had not. It had never crossed her little squirrel mind that he had started that fire.

He laughed and laughed. In his mind, The Face laughed as well. It had loved that fire, had kicked its heels up in delight. The memory of it still filled The Face with mirth.

Abigail actually fled the room. He could hear his mother's

bedroom door slam home and the lock turn. She had taken the lighter with her.

"Well that went well," Elliot said to The Face.

Ash

Ash ducked out of class, but not quick enough.

"Mr. Price! Please stay." It was Mrs. Nelson's voice, and there was no questioning it. Ash sighed. He knew what this was about.

"Yes, ma'am."

He turned and waited for the classroom to empty out. The other students parted around him like a school of fish around a rock. Gilly grinned and winked at him on his way out of the classroom. Always helpful, that one.

"I assume you know what this is about, Mr. Price." She peered at Ash over her gold glasses.

"I think so, yes," Ash answered. Mrs. Nelson smiled broadly.

"Well it's not."

"Excuse me?" Ash answered, thinking he had misheard. She laughed.

"Your grade is fine. You're comfortably passing! No! I heard about the dollhouses you make! I have a granddaughter who would love one. I wanted to know if you would make one for me in time for Christmas."

Ash was silent. In shock. "Yes. Of course!" Mrs. Nelson laughed again and patted Ash on the shoulder.

"You've been working hard and it's paid off. I believe that you are going to graduate on time, Mr. Price. Don't worry."

Ash smiled. He felt relief loosen his chest.

"Well, how big of a dollhouse do you want, Mrs. Nelson?"

🡕 🡕 🡕

Gilly waited outside the classroom, still grinning. "You going to get stuck here another year or what?"

"None of your business, you jerk," Ash answered, shouldering his backpack.

"Is that any way to talk to your best friend?" Gilly held his arms wide.

"You're not my best friend. You're a pain in my side."

"I'm your only friend. That makes me the best one." Gilly fell in step beside him as they walked out of the school. "Don't be mad at me just because you are going to be a super senior."

"I'm not going to be a super senior. My grades are fine." Ash reached his truck in a few long strides. Gilly leaned against the hood, tilting his head like a parrot.

"Then what?"

Ash smiled at him. "Another order."

"You've got to be kiddin' me! More of those dollhouses?" Gilly spat on the asphalt. "I can't believe you have sold so many of those stupid things!"

Ash didn't answer. He threw his backpack into the truck and slid in himself. Gilly shook his head and patted the side of the truck as he walked away.

"My only friend," Ash said softly to himself. "Indeed."

✦ ✦ ✦

Ash had the walkie talkie propped against the doorframe while he worked to install kitchen cabinets. They were a nuisance to install alone, but he had done it enough times to manage it without complaint.

Not much anyway.

"Come on, you stupid thing," Ash muttered, hoisting an upper cabinet on a stand. He'd built a stand to prop the cabinets on, so he could then climb on a ladder and screw them into place. It would have been much easier if another person just held the stupid thing for him, but there was no one else.

Drill, drill.

Buzz, Buzz.

"Cinderfella? Are you there? Over."

Ash set the last screw and climbed down. His hands shook slightly. He told himself it was from the drilling. He lied.

"I'm here Rapunzel. How's the investigation going tonight?" His voice sounded shaky to his own ears, he hoped it did not to hers.

"I thought I saw something. A ledger, maybe. But I don't know if I can get to it. It's in his office." A pause. "Over."

"A business ledger? Like, a record of where his money is going?"

"Yeah."

"That would be a big something. Do you think all of his information will be in it? Not in another somewhere else?" Ash prayed that she would not start investigating outside of her own home. She took enough risks trying to search his home office. Who knows what trouble she could get in elsewhere?

"I don't think so. He always says that his home office is his only real office." Another pause. "Of course, it wouldn't be the only thing he's lied about. But enough about that. I don't want to talk to you about my dad. What about you?"

"I sold another dollhouse today." Ash still couldn't believe how easy it was for him to talk to her. Would it be this easy if she were standing in front of him, instead of a voice floating through the air?

"That's amazing! I wish I could see one!" She sounded so excited. Ash marveled at that a little.

"Maybe before I deliver it, you could come see it? I don't know if they are that great really, but people keep buying them from me. I guess they are alright."

"A real wooden dollhouse? I bet they are wonderful!"

Ash felt as if a balloon were being blown up inside his chest. There was a fullness that he didn't recognize. He thought about some of the things he'd like to say to her: I miss you, I wish I could see you again, Do you think of me as often as I think of you?

Instead he said, "Maybe. Maybe you'd like them."

Neveah

"Maybe. Maybe you'd like them," Ash said.

Neveah had looked up about a million pictures of dollhouses on the internet, wondering if Ash's looked like any of them. Were they simply wooden boxes with little door and window holes? Ash seemed like a guy who liked simple things. He'd once told her he wished he could just go visit another county.

Or were they elaborate affairs with wallpaper on the walls and shingles on the roof? He also seemed like the kind of person who paid attention to details. He never forgot anything she told him about her investigation.

Ugh, the investigation. It was going nowhere. She knew that she needed to try a new tactic. Internet searches were leading her to nothing. Mentally she reviewed what she had seen on TV shows and read in books. Since she didn't have a CSI forensics team to help her look for clues, a computer hacker friend to dig up evidence from her father's computer, or even a disreputable associate to question under a hot lamp, she was left with few options.

Over the past weeks, her fear and shock had turned to anger and a thirst for justice. He needed to answer for his sins. But how? She just couldn't figure it out.

"Cinderfella, I have to go. I will try to talk to you again tomorrow though." Neveah felt deflated, but knew that her mother would be back soon.

"Goodnight, Rapunzel." Ash's voice was soft over the walkie-talkie.

"Goodnight." She turned it off and slid it back between her mattress and box springs.

It was only moments later that Neveah's mother came into the room.

"Hello, Neveah. What are you doing sitting in the dark? You'll strain your eyes that way."

"I was just looking out my window at the sky. It's really clear tonight." Jillian walked to the window and peered out over her daughter's shoulder. "So it is."

There was a companionable silence that passed between them. Ever since Conner had broken into her room, Neveah's mother seemed subdued. Did she know all of the things that Neveah had learned over the last couple of weeks?

"Do you know how I chose your name?" Jillian asked. It was an odd question.

"Not really." Neveah turned her head so that she could see her mother's profile out of the corner of her eye.

"I grew up very poor. Did you know that?" She paused, her eyes searching the sky as if for answers. "When I was small, my mother told me that all good things began and ended in Heaven. When I learned that I was pregnant, I felt that only good things could begin with you. Your name is Heaven spelled backwards." She ran a hand over Neveah's hair, smoothing it out as she did so. "Well, almost. I flipped the e and a so it would be a little easier for people to say correctly!" A rare smile crossed her lips.

Neveah leaned into her mother's hand slightly. She knew very little about her mother's past. She soaked up the words, committing them to memory. She had always thought her name was odd, very non-traditional. She had assumed her father had chosen it. Jillian was very traditional about most things.

"Mom, are you happy? Is this a good life for you, I mean?" Neveah held her breath, waiting for an answer. Jillian only paused, again looking out of the window.

"You make me happy, Neveah. Don't ever forget that." She kissed Neveah's head and turned to leave. She paused again at the door, but then continued walking away. Was she going to say more? Neveah guessed she would never know.

Ash

"So what are you going to do when you graduate?" Neveah had asked him. Ash threw his roll of duct tape across the room thinking about it. It was a perfectly normal question, but one he had absolutely no answer to anymore.

Ash had answered, "I'm not sure anymore." He had quickly changed the subject. It was maddening. He couldn't tell her the truth. Neveah would toss her walkie-talkie in a lake and never speak to him again. He wouldn't blame her.

He imagined the conversation in his head:

"What are you going to do when you graduate?"

"I'm going to bounce repeatedly off of the county line like a mosquito on a door screen, hoping that one day I'll be able to get through and leave."

"Cool, cool, cool. I meant more like, are you going to join the army or something?"

"Well, you know, you have to be able to leave the county to participate in the military."

"Yep, makes sense. Well, I gotta go. Probably not going to be able to talk again tomorrow, or like, ever. Bye!"

Ash knocked his head against a bare wall stud. What was he going to do?

Ash's head snapped up. He knew what to do! He needed to find that cat!

Ash gathered his tools and loaded them into the truck. He would quit early tonight. He was going on a cat hunt.

He sat in the truck, engine idling. How does one go about finding a cat?

"I should have thought this through more," Ash said to himself.

"Yes, you should have."

Ash jumped. Looking around, he discovered the cat in question casually deburring a paw in his floorboard.

"How did you get in here?" Ash asked. "Nevermind. I need to talk to you!"

"Well, here I am."

"I need to know how to end the curse." Ash tried to sound convincing. He squared his shoulders and gave her his best I-can-do-it look.

"You'll likely have to kill someone. Are you ready to commit murder?" Creature said, not looking up from her paw.

"What? Murder? That's crazy!" Ash said.

"Crazier than a curse that's lasted for over a hundred years?"

"A hundred years? How could you know that? How old are you?" Ash asked, his I-can-do-it look quickly melting away.

"Older than a hundred?" Creature said. "It doesn't matter. I have to find him first."

"Find him? Find who?" Ash asked. "Can you start from the beginning or something?"

"Look, you have a very specific curse. There is a Creek entity of legend roaming around here. He needs to be killed. Again. That's how you end the curse. But I can't find him." The cat was serious, sitting up and looking at Ash with her full focus. "And believe me, I've tried."

Ash paused for a while. "Are you cursed too?"

"In a manner of speaking. I owe your family a debt. I'm stuck here until I can repay it." She jumped up on the seat next to him. "Now. That's enough questions for now. All you need to know is that I'm looking for Rabbit. When I find him, rest assured that you will be the first to know." With that, she jumped out of the truck and was gone into the night.

"Rabbit?" Ash asked. He called out the window, "I'm cursed because of a bunny!?"

Chapter Four

Creek Woman

I had never known such loss and pain. I knew that Big Man-Eater was viewed by the world as a monster, but to me he had been kind and loving. I missed him keenly. I was angry, deeply angry. Rabbit had killed my husband on a lark. It was a cruel joke. Even now I can hear his laughter echoing through the trees. A cold hatred filled my heart. I vowed to avenge my husband's death. Rabbit would know my wrath if it was the last thing I did in my inexplicably long life.

I returned to the village. Whites had begun settling nearby and my clansmen were wary of them. We were a people who were unused to strangers. They distrusted the whites, and were often confused by their ways, which were unnatural to us. In the beginning, the whites traded with us and peacefully farmed the land they bought from us.

I was shocked to find that I was treated much the same as the whites. I was not as strange as the whites, but they didn't know me either. Most of my original relations were dead and gone. Their ancestors did not remember my name or how I was related to the clan. I had emerged as from a myth. I was known only as Big Man-Eater's Wife.

I settled at the edge of the village and traded some of my belongings in exchange for the labor of building my home. Slowly I reintegrated into the rhythms of village life. Slowly the clan accepted me back as a true Creek woman.

The years went by and I made friends with some of the women in the village. Together we gathered the corn, squash and beans. I was there when the White Potato Clan formed and split away. I was there when the tensions over land ownership rose with the whites. And I was there, patiently waiting, when Rabbit came back, causing mischief.

My clan had learned a trick to growing the sweetest corn around. Rabbit loved corn and began stealing from our fields. The women were distraught. The elders gathered. No one wanted to earn Rabbit's ire, but we needed the corn. How did one trick a trickster? Especially one who had lived for so long?

I volunteered a plan and it was accepted by the village. Together we formed a body out of tar. Our Tar Baby, we called it. We set it by the field as if it were a true man guarding our harvest.

And then we waited.

After some time, Rabbit returned to the field to steal the corn. He saw the "man" and approached carefully. Rabbit was and is not afraid of men. He loves to trick them as much as anyone else. Rabbit began talking to the man, joking as always. But to his chagrin, the man did not answer. After a few attempts, Rabbit became angry at the silent man and punched his face. Rabbit's fist stuck fast in the Tar Baby's face. Angrier still, Rabbit kept hitting and fighting and kicking until all four of his limbs were stuck in the Tar Baby. Rabbit was trapped.

I emerged from my hiding place in the corn field. I wrapped Rabbit up with the Tar Baby in thick folds of burlap. I hauled his squirming, shouting form to the river and threw him in. I watched the sack, and Rabbit with it, sink under the deep water and laughed. I laughed and laughed and danced. My beloved Man-Eater had finally been avenged! Rabbit was dead!

Neveah

"I need to get in his office." Neveah set the walkie back down on her desk and continued to type away on her computer.

"I thought you said you weren't allowed in there?" Ash's voice crackled back to her.

"I'm just going to have to sneak in anyway."

"Have you ever done anything like that? How will you do it?" Ash's voice sounded, well *concerned* didn't fully cover it.

"I've snuck *out* of the house plenty of times. To go ride Sunbeam. It can't be that much harder, can it?" She hoped she sounded confident and reassuring, the exact opposite of how she felt.

A long pause.

"Please be careful. Who knows what he will do if you're caught."

"I'm his daughter. It's not like he'll kill me off or something." Pause. "I don't think."

Neveah let out a big breath. He was right. What would her father do if he caught her? She used to think the worst that could happen to her was losing Sunbeam. Now though? Now she knew that her father was a murderer, all bets were off.

Neveah checked the word count on her paper. She was almost

to 2,000 words. She needed to come up with 100 more words on the Trail of Tears or Ruth was going to march around the front yard with her head on a pike, she was sure of it. Ruth was the toughest tutor that Neveah had ever had. She was also, despite it all, her favorite.

Neveah had never been so enthralled with her studies. Or so exhausted.

"Do you know anything about the Trail of Tears?" Neveah asked Ash over the walkie.

"Uh. It was a bad deal. Lots of people died because of the cold. Weird to think about it being that cold in the South, isn't it?"

Huh. Neveah had never thought about that before. She'd never seen more than a few inches of snow or ice in Arkansas. Yet most of those Native Americans that died during the Trail of Tears died due to exposure and starvation. Her fingers went to the keyboard and she was able to fill out another 150 words. Perusing the paper, she believed Ruth would be pleased.

"Ash, do you never have homework? I'm always doing homework. You're never doing homework." When Ash answered, it sounded as though he had been laughing.

"I have a ton of homework I should be doing! I'm barely passing my classes, if you want to know the truth. I just also have to finish this house or Abigail will eat my liver."

"So when do you do your homework?"

"If I don't drop dead asleep when I get home, I work on it. Or I try to do it during lunch. Or sometimes about five minutes before it's due." The laughter was bleeding out of his voice and being replaced with something more negative. "I really need to pass my classes. I have to graduate this year."

"And somehow in between this you make elaborate dollhouses for customers?"

"It's a pretty slow trickle of customers. But yeah, I do." Pause. "I know it's crazy. I just don't see any other way around it. Abigail means for me to finish this house, and there will be another when I'm done. I have to pass my classes to graduate or I can't leave. I have to have money when I graduate or I won't be able to go anywhere."

Somehow she knew that he had set down his tools. Somehow she knew that he was looking around whatever room he was in and wishing he could be anywhere else.

"I'm sorry, Ash." *Woops!* "I mean, Cinderfella." They weren't supposed to use their real names on the walkie.

"Don't be sad because of me. I'll figure it out."

Neveah

Beep, beep.

Neveah's eyes flew open. She hit the alarm on her watch and listened for a moment. There was no noise in the house. She had set the alarm for 3 am when everyone should be asleep.

"Rapunzel engages in super secret spying in order to save the Queen," Neveah whispered to herself.

Quietly she slid out of bed and put on her soft-soled tennis shoes. Grabbing her camera and flashlight, she headed for the door. She turned the knob slowly, feeling the latch release. Pausing with the door cracked open, she listened again for any noise.

Silence.

She moved herself into the hallway and padded as quietly as she knew how downstairs. Pausing every few steps to listen, she could discern no movements in the rest of the house. Neveah's father had hired a guard, but he was supposed to stay outside. As long as she avoided windows, she should be safe.

As she passed the kitchen, her footsteps seemed to echo loudly. It made her wince with every step. Once further toward the den, she was thankful for the thick rugs her mother had insisted on.

Finally her father's office. William was a man of elaborate tastes. Even his office door knob was heavy and ornate. An interlocking filigree pattern was on the door's knob and the oversized lock panel had a lion's mouth fashioned on it. She turned the heavy thing slowly with one hand, looking around for the security guard all the while.

It was locked. The handle would only turn a quarter of the way, then stopped hard. She tried it twice, three times, then a fourth time. There was no give. Neveah didn't realize that the old-fashioned doorknob even locked properly anymore. There must be a key.

Neveah stretched up on tip-toes and felt around the doorframe. Maybe it would be hidden away there? Her fingers met with nothing.

Neveah felt the tension bleed out of her shoulders and chest. Nothing. She would have to postpone her search of his office until she could find the key.

"Locked!" It was Ash on the walkie-talkie. The next evening she recounted the whole tale to him. Her crushing defeat. Her calamitous failure.

"I *know!*" Neveah groaned over the walkie to him. "I couldn't believe it!"

"What will you do now?"

"I guess I have to find that key. Don't you think?"

"I think...I think you should be careful pulling the lion's tail." Ash was always cautioning her where her investigation was concerned. Did he worry about her?

"Right now it's irrelevant what I want. I have no idea where that key is." Neveah ran her fingers through her short hair. "I was so close! Agh!"

"Maybe he sleeps with it around his neck?" Ash said, a chuckle in his voice. "Maybe he wears it sewn into his shirt?"

"Sewn into his shirt? That'd make it awfully complicated to open the door twice a day," Neveah answered, laughing despite herself.

"Wherever it is, it's probably somewhere close to him. He wouldn't risk losing it, if all of the evidence is in there."

Ash was right. She knew her father was careful. He would have that key close at hand, where he would never miss it, never lose it.

"Ugh! Enough, enough! I want to talk about something else. Something that doesn't make me want to pull my hair out!"

"Hmm, well I'm working on a dollhouse right now."

"What! You aren't flipping houses tonight?" Neveah still only had a vague understanding of what "flipping a house" meant.

"I begged off tonight. I convinced Abigail that I was going to fail high school if I didn't catch up on some homework." A pause, "Which, by the way, is the truth. I'm trying to hustle up and finish this thing so I can actually do homework."

"I bet Abigail loved that."

"Oh yes. But she doesn't want too many questions asked about me. If I flunk out, someone is bound to notice." Ash said this with a laugh, but Neveah felt a clenching of her heart. How could his step-mother be so callous towards him?

"So does that mean you're at your house then?" Neveah hoped, hoped, hoped.

"Yes. Yes, it does. If you think you can get away..." His voice trailed off.

"Yes! I'll be there in, like, ten minutes!" Neveah practically threw herself out the door and down the hall. She breezed through the house in a blur, calling over her shoulder to anyone listening that she was going to take Sunbeam for a run. If there were protests, she did not hear them. She was already gone.

Neveah had taken Sunbeam, even though the distance was not great to the little graveyard where she had met Ash. She didn't want anyone to notice Sunbeam still in her stall while Neveah was supposed to be riding her.

Suddenly the gate was in front of her, and she slid from Sunbeam's back.

She paused before opening the gate. Neveah looked back at her horse. The horse, of course, had nothing to say. Neveah ran her fingers through her hair to straighten it and then opened the gate. Her hands only shook a little.

Ash was waiting inside the graveyard. His hands were in his pockets and he looked nervous. Was he nervous? Neveah certainly was. They had only met the one time before. What if it was awkward now?

Ash smiled. She smiled back, and felt immediately connected to the boy she'd spent so many hours talking to over the walkies.

"Hi," Ash said. He fidgeted where he stood. "So, what are you going to do with your horse?"

"Oh. Umm. Can she stay in here? I can tie her off so she doesn't eat the tulips."

"Yeah. That works." Ash helped her shut the gate behind Sunbeam. The horse happily munched on the grass, oblivious to the nervous teenagers around her. Neveah stroked her neck and took a moment to catch her breath.

"Are you ready?" Ash's voice sounded unsure. Neveah smiled at him and nodded.

He held his hand out to her.

She took it.

She felt the color rising in her cheeks and neck. They were touching! She was holding hands with a boy! Neveah suddenly wanted to squeal and tell someone, anyone, what was happening.

She followed him out of the opposite gate and into a spacious open yard. A few yards on the other side was a shed. It was like any other outbuilding that someone might use to store Christmas trees and lawnmowers, old family heirlooms that no one wanted or anything else that people kept but rarely used. This was his house?

There was a front door, which faced the graveyard. There was a small window. He opened the door and then they were inside. It was small and cramped. A single bed on one side, a desk on the other, stacked high with books and papers, small tools and wood glue. The back wall held a sink and small table topped with a microwave. A mini fridge. Another door which must have led to a bathroom was to the left.

"It's not much, I know," Ash said.

Neveah didn't say anything. Instead, she took in the dollhouse.

It was beautiful!

She had imagined the possibilities, but was still surprised. The dollhouse was six rooms, each one lined with wallpaper and flooring. Was that felt? The roof had individual shingles carved into it. There were bricks and siding details she would never have imagined possible.

The little chimney could not have been more realistic if it were chugging smoke!

"Ash! This is amazing!"

"Really? You think so?" Ash said, relief evident in his voice. "I've been working really hard on this one. It's the biggest one I've ever been asked to make."

"I can't believe the detail you have put into it! Did you etch out individual bricks? Holy smokes!"

Ash shrugged. He was blushing.

"What do you have left to do? It looks finished to me." Neveah asked, meeting his eyes for the first time since they had left the graveyard.

"Uh, well I usually make a little mailbox for the front door. I'm having a bit of trouble getting the hinges to work though."

"Hinges? You have tiny mailbox hinges? Where did you even get them?" Neveah couldn't imagine any hardware store carrying what must be the world's tiniest metal hinges.

"Well, 'hinge' might be overstating things. It's just something I make with wire." He turned to his desk and picked up the 'hinge.' It was tiny, lying in his large teenaged boy palm. She peered past him to where he had been working and saw the pieces of the mailbox there.

For the first time, she noticed how much taller than herself Ash stood. Standing this close together in the tiny house, it was very apparent. At only five-foot-one herself, almost everyone was taller. But

Ash suddenly loomed gigantic. It made the contrast of the tiny mailbox seem almost ridiculous.

"Well I was going to offer to help, but I think I would just mess up what you've already done." Neveah slid backwards from him. Maybe he hadn't noticed how small and mousy she was.

"Actually, I would rather have your help with my English paper, if you're willing." Ash rustled through a stack of notebooks on his desk. With his back turned, Neveah inspected him a little more carefully.

Ash was definitely tall, it wasn't her imagination. All the hours of working meant that he was well muscled through his shoulders and arms. He had dark hair that curled at his temples and blue eyes the same color as a lake in winter. He had what her mother would call "the awkwardness of youth." Jillian had said as much about her enough times. And Ash was thin at the waist. Thin wrists, thin neck. Neveah's hands went to her own neck in reaction. She felt no extra flesh there, but surely Ash was too thin for someone of his size?

Neveah glanced down at herself. Would she appear fat in comparison? The dressmaker her mother hired always commented on her thin figure. Could that have been a lie to make her feel better? To continue working for them?

Ash was looking at her oddly. Had he spoken to her?

"Sorry, what did you say?"

"I said, I'm supposed to be writing a paper about Romeo and Juliet. Have you read it?" Ash asked.

"Oh!" Neveah laughed, "Yeah. I've read it. Great stuff. I guess. If you like everyone dying at the end anyway."

"They die at the end?"

"Oh no! You haven't read it all?" Neveah felt like an idiot. A fat idiot.

"Well, that's part of the problem. I need to finish it. Then I need to write about it. I'm kind of in a mess." Ash pulled at a curl behind his ear. It looked like a nervous habit. Neveah felt heat in her body and blushed. *Need to focus, need to focus.*

"I guess we could read it. How much do you have left to read?" Neveah asked. *That's right, volunteer to read a romance with a person who makes your head spin. Good plan,* Neveah told herself.

"All of it?" Ash winced like he expected her to shout at him.

"I guess we should get started then!" Neveah said. She looked around for a place to sit. The bed? Did they have to sit on the bed together? Ash must have seen her distress.

"Do you want to sit outside and read it?"

"Yes!"

Ash

Need to focus, need to focus. Ash kept reminding himself he was supposed to be thinking about Capulets and Montagues, not Neveah Winters sitting so close to him. So close he could touch her. *Focus!*

Neveah was reading the play to him. It was easy to love the story because she seemed to love it. It was evident in how she read it with such enthusiasm. He found that Shakespeare wasn't so bad, even funny at times, as long as Neveah was reading it to him.

Neveah's horse had been happily munching on the grass for a little over an hour now. Ash could see that the sun was setting. It was starting to get cold. He shrugged out of his jacket and handed it to Neveah. She settled it around her shoulders without stopping. The jacket looked huge on her.

Everything must look huge on her. She was so tiny! He felt like an ogre towering over her and hoped he didn't look like one too. While she read, she tucked her hair behind her ears. She had short brown hair that curled only a little, much less than his own. He noticed that she had small feet and small hands. When he had held her hand, his own could wrap all the way around hers.

He had held her hand! He still couldn't believe he had been brave enough to offer. He was astounded that she'd agreed. Her green, green eyes had twinkled when she took his hand. It was the closest thing to magic he'd ever known.

Well that wasn't true. There was the bouncing-off-an-invisible-boundary thing. And the talking cat thing. And the family curse thing. Okay, he'd experienced some magic before but this was the best so far.

Neveah paused and looked at the sky.

"Do you need to go?" Ash asked.

"Yeah, I think I do." She wasn't smiling. She closed the book and handed it back to Ash. They both stood. Ash fiddled with the book. He didn't want to say goodbye. And he didn't know how. Did they shake hands? Did they hug? Would he accidentally crush her if he hugged her too tightly?

Neveah gave him back his coat and then wrapped her arms around herself. She looked at the ground, then her horse.

"Well, it was good to see you again," Ash said.

"Yeah. It was," Neveah answered.

"Maybe we can do this again sometime?"

"I really hope so." Neveah met his eyes then.

This was the moment. He was supposed to do something. He could feel it. But what?

"Do you need help with Sunbeam?" Ash asked. That probably wasn't it.

"Um, not really." She started towards the horse. She was so close...

Ash reached out to her.

She went to him. They embraced.

It was so simple. It felt natural. He could feel her arms around his waist. He could smell her hair.

"I don't want to go," Neveah whispered.

"I don't want you to go either," Ash whispered back.

She let go. "I'm sorry."

"What are you sorry for?" Ash asked.

"I...well we barely know each other, right? And here I am..." Neveah was blushing again.

"Here you are...what?"

"I just don't want you to get the wrong idea about me. About what kind of girl I am." Neveah was twisting a ring around her finger.

"What kind of girl you are? You're the best kind. You're the most amazing girl I know!" The words tumbled out of Ash's mouth.

Neveah's eyes were big and round. Ash suddenly felt very stupid.

"Do you really mean that?" She asked.

"Yes?" Ash answered, wincing. Surely he had done something wrong.

Neveah smiled. It was a big smile, the kind that starts at your toes and works its way all the way up until you can't smile anymore. Maybe he *hadn't* done anything wrong?

Neveah jumped into the saddle. She seemed really small to be on such a big horse, but she looked comfortable there.

"I really have to go. But I will come back, if I can." She turned her horse. Ash opened the gate. Just outside the fence she turned and said,

"You're the best kind, too, Ash."

And then she was gone.

Elliot

William was a little bit trickier to handle than Abigail. Elliot knew this. Before he attempted to corner the big man, Elliot would need a bulletproof plan. He sat high in a treetop and thought it over.

He could convince his silly mother that he started the fire that had killed Nathan. That was simple enough. He certainly had circumstantial evidence that William had been involved, by giving Elliot that lighter at least. However, William would deny, deny, deny. He would not feel threatened that Abigail had seen the lighter.

No, Elliot would have to blackmail William in another way altogether.

Fortunately Elliot had something in his pocket. He pulled out the photograph and looked it over again. When he'd taken this photo, Elliot had been about to play a trick on William, not for the first time. But he had accidentally caught William in the middle of covering up a murder.

Elliot smiled. His foiled trick was going to turn into his advantage.

The Face had convinced Elliot to sneak into William's house, and put a snake in his bed. It was a favorite prank that Elliot and The Face had used on any number of people over the years. Elliot had caught the slithering creature and stuffed it into a dark bag. He had snuck to William's house, and was lurking under his office window, waiting for a chance to sneak inside. A commotion inside convinced Elliot he would not be able to sneak in any time soon. As was his nature, he stayed though, listening and learning about his long-time mentor.

"I want him dead." It was William's voice, calm and authoritative.

"Of course, sir. Where is he?" Elliot recognized this voice as William's security man. Elliot had seen him lurking around enough places to know him.

"I have him tied up and gagged in the den. I never want to speak of this matter again, is that understood?"

"Yes, sir."

Elliot rushed to the back door and hid where he would have a good view. Just in time, he pulled out his phone and snapped a few pictures of William's men dragging a man out, bound up like a dead pig. "Always be prepared for an opportunity," was the first rule of life that William had impressed on young Elliot. He had taken it to heart.

Now it might be William's undoing.

The day after Elliot had taken those pictures, the man had been found dead. Conner something was his name. It had been in the papers, and therefore was now public record. He supposedly drowned in the lake. Elliot smiled to himself. Yes, a judge and jury would be very interested in these pictures that Elliot had.

Elliot hopped down from the tree and made his way to the forest clearing where he often met with William.

He hummed a tune as he stepped lightly through the underbrush of the forest. He suspected William would be quite angry when Elliot presented his photos. The Face was taking notice now. The Face normally liked more straightforward tricks, without the use of modern technology and certainly without threats of things like courts. However, he could sense that a creature was about to be trapped and it had whet The Face's appetite for trickery.

Elliot could see William's broad shoulders and back waiting in the clearing as he approached. He paused to savor the moment. This was the moment just before the trap was sprung on an animal. Elliot felt a rising anticipation that made him almost lightheaded. His limbs felt light, and his heartbeat sped up.

"Hello, William!" Elliot called out, stepping from the foliage into the clearing.

"Hello, my boy!" William answered. He was in a good mood. All the better!

"I'm glad to see you today. I have some matters I'd like to discuss with you." Elliot paused to look around. It was unlikely William would agree to these friendly meetings after today. He tried to take in the feeling of it. Would he miss it? William was something like a friend, and the only one Elliot had.

"Oh really? A business matter?" William asked, his interest piqued. Elliot's mouth curved up in a smile. He knew then that he would not regret this trick.

"More of a family matter actually."

William frowned. They did not speak of their families to each other.

"About your family, specifically," Elliot said, then waited. He carefully placed his hands in his pockets. He wanted to appear at ease.

"My family is no concern of yours, Elliot. I thought I'd made that clear." William was squaring his shoulders. He reminded Elliot of an animal, trying to appear bigger to scare off a competitor.

"It might be now," Elliot said. "I think going forward, whatever I want to be my concern, will be my concern."

William's eyes narrowed. "Spit it out, boy. Whatever it is you're wanting to say."

Elliot smiled. He had always appreciated William's straightforwardness, even in the face of danger.

"I have proof. It is proof that you were involved with a murder and it is enough that I could take it to any police station and most likely get you arrested," Elliot said. He did not move his hands from his pockets, did not move a single muscle of his body.

"What proof could you have?" William asked. He did not, Elliot noticed, try to deny that he had murdered anyone.

Elliot pulled the picture from his pocket and threw it at William's feet. The man frowned at him before bending to pick it up. He unfolded the paper slowly, and then crumpled it in his big fist.

"I assume this isn't the only copy?"

"William, you insult me by asking that."

"What do you want?"

Elliot looked up at the open sky above them, squinting at the sunshine. He pulled his pocket knife out and idly snapped the blade open and closed. William did not move, but watched him like a cat watches a mouse.

"I want Neveah," Elliot answered simply.

William's coolness was lost instantly. He roared like a wild beast and flew at Elliot. The two men grappled on the floor of the forest clearing.

William was large and strong. Elliot was also strong, but could not hope to match him. Instead, he used his wile and speed to avoid being pinned. Elliot was quick to dance out of William's hold, always spinning just out of reach. While William moved to his feet, Elliot jumped on his back, and wrapped his arms around his neck.

Had it not been for the knife, this would have never worked. William stilled the moment he felt the press of the blade against his throat. Elliot smiled.

William knew better than most what Elliot was capable of. Regardless, Elliot reminded him.

"Be still or I will skin you alive and hang your innards from the treetops," Elliot whispered in William's ear. "And if that doesn't concern you, just think what I will do to your little girl if you're dead!"

"What do you want with her?" William's words were pushed out through his gritted teeth.

"Oh don't worry, my dear friend," Elliot said, his smile back on his face. "I won't hurt her. No, she is special. But I must have her. She will be mine. No one can touch her, no one can have her but me."

Elliot felt William's body tense with his words. But he was pinned. What could he do?

"I'm going to let you go now. But remember our arrangement. I will have her. And if you try to keep her from me, I will take these pictures to the police. And while you are rotting in a jail cell I will kill your wife and take Neveah for myself anyway. Do you understand?" Elliot said the words slowly, pressing the knife in as he spoke. He felt the hot wet of blood on his hand. The sensation filled him with pleasure, and he pushed back the heady flood of emotion to focus.

"I understand," William answered. Elliot let him go and backed away quickly. William turned to look at him.

"If I catch you, I'll kill you," William said, then left.

Elliot watched him go. He looked down at the blood, William's blood, sliding down his hand and arm. It wasn't much, but enough for him to feel the heat of it. His body filled with heat and his head felt light. He licked the blood from his fingers and laughed.

The Face laughed with him.

Neveah

Neveah took her laptop under one arm and grabbed notebooks with the other. She headed out of her room and down to the dining room. Ruth would be here any minute and she needed to finish writing in a few notes on her latest assignment. On the way, she considered grabbing a croissant out of the kitchen to snack on.

She hovered in the doorway only a moment then backed out into the hallway to listen. Her parents were in the kitchen speaking in hushed tones.

"Haven't you noticed how she's been acting lately?" Jillian asked. "Something is different."

"I haven't noticed anything unusual. She's a teenage girl, teenage girls are strange at times." William answered in a hurried voice. There was a long pause. "Obviously you've noticed something so what do you think it is?" He asked with a sigh.

"I don't know. What if she knows something?" Jillian asked, her voice tight. Neveah held her breath, praying they would reveal something to her.

"Know something? What is there to know, Jillian?" William's words were careful, his tone menacing. Neveah imagined her mother taking a step back away from him.

"I only meant, after what happened with Conner, she might need to be reassured." Jillian's tone was icy enough to freeze fire.

"He will not bother us anymore. I took care of that."

There was a long pause.

"Does your daughter know that, though?" Jillian's tone was flat and emotionless.

"I certainly left that newspaper announcing his death out in the open for her to find. Surely she's observant enough to have seen it." William's tone was matter-of-fact. Neveah's stomach dropped into her

137

tennis shoes. William had left that newspaper out for her to find intentionally?

Neveah turned away from the kitchen and rushed back to her room. Once there, she dropped her notebooks and laptop and buried her face in her pillows.

She was no detective, uncovering mysteries! He had been leading her along all this time! How could she have been so stupid! Her father had been deceiving everyone for years, how was a stupid teenager supposed to compete with that?

There was a knock at her door and she hurriedly wiped her face with her shirt.

"Yes?" Neveah asked, her voice shaking slightly.

Ruth's head popped in. "Ah here you are. Am I interrupting something?"

"No. No, come in," Neveah said, turning to pick up her things. "I'm sorry. I was headed downstairs to meet you."

"Little one, what's wrong?" Ruth asked, her smooth dark face creasing with concern.

"Oh, it's nothing," Neveah said. She shook her head and struggled to regain her composure.

"Well, that's clearly not true. However, if you do not wish to speak of it, I won't force you," Ruth said in her oddly formal way.

"I..." Neveah began. "Have you ever felt like someone betrayed you, tricked you in some terrible way?" Ruth sat at the edge of her bed, a look of deep thought crossing her face.

"Yes. More than you might imagine." She looked at Neveah. "It is a difficult thing to overcome."

"But do you? Overcome it, I mean? Eventually?" Neveah asked. Surely Ruth would know.

"In ways, yes. In other ways it shapes the rest of your life." In her eyes was sympathy. "But that's not always a bad thing either."

They sat in silence for a moment. "I hope you are right."

↗ ↗ ↗

"Your tutor sounds mysterious." Ash said over the walkie-talkie. He was back at the house across town, working hard.

"Um yes! She is *so* mysterious!" Neveah responded. "I love it, actually."

"I tend to find those types sort of frustrating. You never get a straight answer."

"I will try to not be too terribly mysterious then," Neveah said, giggling to herself. "Have you read any more Shakespeare?"

"Yes. It's not as interesting as when you were reading it though," Ash answered. Neveah blushed alone in her room. She held the walkie talkie close to her, cradling it in her hands like a newborn kitten.

"Do you think you'll be able to write your paper, though?" Neveah asked.

"I think I'll muddle through." A pause. "I wish we could meet again."

"Me too." She sighed, looking at the time. "I have to go."

"Ok. I'll be here tomorrow, if you can talk again."

"Ok." Neveah suddenly felt the words on her lips, *I love you*. Shocked by this, she blushed deeper. "Ok, I'll talk to you tomorrow!" Neveah blurted the words out quickly and threw the walkie talkie away from herself.

"I need to get out of here!" Neveah whispered to herself. She grabbed her camera and headed for the door.

Down the steps two at a time, and down a hallway. She heard the bathroom door shut and looked over her shoulder.

The door to her father's study was standing open. He must have left it open while he went to the bathroom!

Neveah hesitated only a moment. She dashed into the study and headed for the desk. Flipping on her camera, she quickly snapped pictures of everything there. She reached for the first drawer and pulled it open. Down the hall, she heard the toilet flush.

Quickly, quickly! She pulled out what was on top and flipped it open. A list of names and phone numbers. She snapped a picture and shoved the notebook back into the desk drawer.

Neveah headed quickly for the door. Her heart in her throat, she met her father as he was coming back in the room.

"What are you doing in here, princess?" His expression suspicious, he was blocking the doorway. Neveah forced a smile on her face, willed her voice to be steady.

"I was looking for you, silly!" Neveah injected as much brightness into her voice as she could muster.

"Well here I am. What can I do for you?"

"Oh. Um." Neveah's mind raced. "I was going to see if you would get me a new sd card for my camera. This one is full already."

"Again? I feel like I have to buy one for you every month." He was smiling and shaking his head though. "I'll order one tomorrow. Anything for my sweet princess."

Neveah smiled and danced sideways out of the room. He didn't wait for her to go, but headed on to his desk. She paused to listen. Did he notice anything moved? Was he suspicious? There was no noise. She treaded down the hallway, through the den and out the backdoor.

Then she stood with her back against the side of the stables, hidden from the view of the house. She finally stopped to catch her breath. Her heart was pounding in her ears. Her hands were sweaty. She counted blades of grass for a moment to stop her head from spinning.

The camera! She flipped it back on and scrolled through the pictures she had taken. Most of them would require some considerable zooming to read the words. The last picture of names and phone numbers gave Neveah hope though. Surely there would be something useful there? Surely. She closed her eyes and hoped.

Elliot

"I think it's time I paid my dear friend a visit," Elliot said out loud to himself. He was in the car with his brother, Gerald.

"What friend?" Gerald asked. He was just pulling into the driveway of their home. School was finished for the day and they had the evening to themselves.

"I have friends, brother," Elliot said, laughing.

"I've never seen any." Gerald answered, shrugging. "Are you sure this friend is real, Elliot? You're not just seeing things or something?"

"Do you think I'm mad?" Elliot asked, sincerely amused at the idea.

"We both know you aren't like other people. I don't know if that makes you crazy or what," Gerald answered. He had parked the car and was looking at Elliot seriously.

Once again Elliot felt something like sympathy for his little brother. Poor Gerald actually cared for him, cared about his well-being. It must be exhausting.

"Don't worry, little brother. This friend is very much real," Elliot said and got out of the car. He had no backpack or books to put away, so he struck out into the woods without going into the house first. When he looked back, Gerald was standing in the driveway watching him leave.

It was only a matter of moments before Elliot was approaching the Winter's estate. He considered his options for entering the house. By now, William would be in his home office, working away at some new mischief. It was one of the things Elliot continued to appreciate about him. William worked hard at his criminal activities, throwing himself on his work like a lion on a wildebeest.

Neveah must be in her room, Elliot could just make her out at her window, her head bowed over a notebook, writing furiously.

Jillian, William's wife, was outside in her rose garden. Elliot found her to be a cold and peculiar woman. She was obsessive about those roses, and seemed oblivious to her very obviously criminal husband. Did she really not know what he got up to?

Elliot walked in through the front door. Everyone else was outside or locked in their rooms. The cook was hard at work in the kitchen, the groundskeeper gone for the day. Elliot had spotted the security guard William had hired watching over Jillian. He smiled to himself and eased his way up the stairs towards the bedrooms.

He paused outside Neveah's room. He could just make out the sounds of notebook pages turning, a little sigh from her, the sound of shuffling feet. He breathed in the air around her room, savoring it. Then he could hear her voice on the walkie-talkie.

"Rapunzel to Cinderfella, are you there?"

Instantly, Elliot's anger rose. His vision darkened, his teeth bared, it was an act of considerable willpower on his part to smother the feelings and move on down the hallway. He would take care of that little problem another time.

Elliot slipped into William's bedroom, and then into the on suite master bathroom. He had noted that William often took a shower at the end of his work day and redressed for his time at home with his family. Elliot slipped into the shower and waited.

It was some time before Elliot finally heard the soft footsteps of someone walking into the bedroom. It was Jillian, she came into the bathroom, washed her hands, reapplied some of her makeup, and left. Peering out of the shower quietly, Elliot could see part of her back as she unzipped her dress and began changing into something else. He pulled out his phone and snapped a picture. Then he slipped further down into the tub and closed his eyes. He imagined William discovering him here with his naked wife. Elliot smiled to himself, suppressing a laugh.

Not long after Jillian left, William entered. He was standing in the bathroom, removing his cufflinks and tie. Elliot pulled open the shower curtain slowly, and smiled.

"Hello, William."

To his credit, William did not jump or cry out. He merely stopped what he was doing, his eyes sliding over to Elliot in the mirror's reflection.

"What do you want, Elliot?" William said, placing his hands carefully on the counter.

"I think it's time I met Neveah. I want you to see to that," Elliot said simply. He stepped out of the shower and crossed to the doorway.

"That's it? You've been lurking around in my bathroom to tell me that?" William turned finally to Elliot, one eyebrow quirked up. "You could have sent me a text message for that."

"I wanted to make sure you got my message," Elliot answered. He paused, maintaining eye contact. He wanted to make sure William got his other message: You can't keep me away from her .

William nodded. "I will contact you soon." Then he turned back to the mirror, reaching for his razor.

Elliot chuckled at that and left. He easily slipped back down the hallway, this time exiting through a window in a front room, a parlor maybe? The security guard was facing the opposite way and Elliot slipped by and back into the dark cover of the forest. He laughed to himself.

"I believe William got my message, don't you?" Elliot asked The Face. The Face had been watching all along. In a moment, Elliot realized The Face was disappointed. All that, and there was still no snake in William's bed.

Neveah

It was another dead end. Neveah stared down at the list, willing meaning into it. She had looked up every name on the list online and found nothing. Even using a fake Facebook account had turned up nothing for her. The numbers attached to them could really only be traced further by paying a fee, something she was unable to do without a credit or debit card of her own. She had tracked down a phone book even, and found none of the names listed there. What had she expected though? Criminals didn't register on a website. They didn't post mugshots of themselves online with tags saying, "Muscle for hire!" Neveah shook her head; it was a wild goose chase.

Neveah set the list aside. What else could she do?

"Rapunzel to Cinderfella, are you there?" Neveah laid facedown on her bed, her hands dangling off of the edge.

"I'm here. How is the investigation going?" Ash's voice echoed across the invisible air between them.

"Badly. Very badly," Neveah answered, rolling over on her back. She looked up at the ceiling, counting lines as she had countless times before.

"I'm sorry. Are you stuck again?"

"I have a list of names, and I can't find anything about any of them."

"What are the names?" Ash asked.

"You want to hear all of them?" Neveah asked, surprised.

"I doubt I'll recognize any of them, but maybe. I don't know. It's worth a try, right?" Ash said, his voice sounded unfocused. He was probably working on that house again.

"Okay, well here it goes. Nathan Sexton, Conner McFadden, who we know is dead. Umm... Silas Morgan, and Elliot Fisher." Neveah stopped to reach for a glass of water.

"Did you say Elliot Fisher?" Ash asked, his voice sounded suspicious.

"Yes. Why? Do you know him?"

"Elliot is my step-brother," Ash said.

Neveah paused, her glass midway to her mouth. "What?"

"I'm serious. Elliot is my step-brother. How does he even know your dad? He's our age," Ash sounded increasingly agitated.

"I have no idea. I've never seen my father working with anyone close to our age. Of course, I haven't seen many of the people he works with apparently." Neveah was rambling. She took her finger off the walkie-talkie.

"Listen to me. This is serious. Don't go looking for Elliot. He's dangerous. Promise me." Ash's voice had become intent. She could feel him staring at the walkie-talkie from across the distance.

Neveah blinked at the walkie. How dangerous could his brother really be?

"Ok," Neveah said.

There was a long silence between them.

"Is he really that scary?" Neveah asked, her voice small.

"Yes. I'm serious, Neveah. He's not the kind of person you want to be alone with. He's the kind of person who would set your house on fire and laugh about it later."

"You make him sound like a sociopath or something," Neveah said.

"I think he might be." Ash was dead serious. His quick and serious answers shocked her.

"Ok, I won't look for him," Neveah promised. "But what does that mean about the other names on this list?" Neveah looked down at the names written there. Were they all sociopaths? Was this her father's list of crazies? Was he keeping killers on retainer? She felt a chill down her spine. Her fingertips were cold suddenly, where they gripped the paper.

"Maybe it's good that you can't find any of those names?" Ash asked. She could hear sympathy in his voice. Neveah rubbed her temples. How had she gotten in this mess?

"I just want to know. Is my father really the kind of person who has people murdered? Is he really the kind of person who deserves to be put in prison? How can I live with someone like that?" Neveah asked. She didn't expect Ash to answer her.

"Well, I live with Elliot. Mostly I just try to not cross paths with him. I try to live a good life. I try to mind my own business," Ash said. "I don't know if you can do that though. He is your father, not a step-brother you can ignore."

Neveah put the list back in the notebook she'd been keeping, and stuffed it all back under her mattress.

"What happened to your father?" Neveah had been afraid to ask before. She felt that she could now though.

"He died. It wasn't long after he married Elliot's mom. There was a fire. Our house burned up. He got me out of the house. Then he went back to save the pictures of my mother. The house fell in on him before he could get back out again." Ash's voice sounded robotic, recounting the events.

"I'm so sorry, Ash. That sounds awful. How did you ever get past it?" Neveah asked.

"I'm not sure I have," Ash answered.

Neveah felt tears welling up in her eyes. She couldn't imagine losing either of her parents so horribly. Ash seemed so strong and patient and kind. How did he manage that after losing both of his parents?

"Losing my mother was harder in some ways. She died suddenly, from a sickness. I was really young and I didn't understand a lot of what was happening. But, my dad was a total wreck afterwards. He really struggled to keep his business running. Then he met Abigail." There was a pause here. "I don't know if he really loved her. I think he just thought that she needed him. And I think he thought I needed a mother." Neveah waited for him to say more, but he didn't. Instead the silence lagged on.

"You really loved your dad, huh?" Neveah said. Was that a stupid thing to say? She couldn't take the words back now. "I'm sorry. Of course you loved him."

"Yeah, I really did." Ash said. "I'm sorry. I didn't mean for things to get so serious. You don't want to hear about all the sad things that have ever happened to me or whatever."

"I don't mind. You listen to me worry and gripe all the time. I could listen to more of you, you know?" Neveah said.

"I am usually very boring," Ash said, she could hear the smile in his voice. "Mind-numbingly so, in fact."

"Ha. Ha. I doubt it!" Neveah answered. "I don't think you're boring anyway. How could any boring person make such cool dollhouses."

"I make dollhouses, not launch missiles into space. It's not that exciting." Ash was laughing now. Neveah felt relief.

They talked for some time that night. Neveah was relieved to hear him laugh again. But that night as she was lying in bed, counting the lines in the ceiling again, she thought about what he said about Elliot. She felt a chill despite the covers piled on her bed. Was Elliot really that dangerous? And how was he connected to her father?

Ash

Ash had to sand down the old wood floors of the house. He had several rooms left and was tirelessly pushing to get it all done tonight. There was a little black walkie-talkie nearby that likely accounted for his fervor. Would she contact him tonight? He never knew for certain, but he always hoped. And if he wanted to actually talk to her and hear her talk back, he needed to finish sanding.

The heavy sander hummed loudly under his hands and his mind wandered, as it often did, to his uncertain future. He couldn't leave the county. What an absurd obstacle to overcome. He had to finish high school, which was proving difficult enough. He had to finish this house, to keep Abigail off of his back, which was taking longer than expected. The house was in much worse condition than they had originally believed. And he had to continue making his dollhouses so that when he graduated, he would have enough money to leave. Why

150

hadn't he started a simpler side business? Like making mailboxes or something easy? No piece of his life could be allowed to slip, or he would fail.

And now, he had to figure out how to end a 150-year-old curse, so he could leave the county? It seemed wildly unfair to add this to his already too-long list of responsibilities.

Not to mention the mysterious talking cat was turning out to be difficult to get answers from. One might assume she would be more forthcoming, but one would be wrong. She was maddeningly vague and withheld much more than she gave. But, the cat was his only link to this curse. Had he not bounced off of the county line like a human ping pong ball, he'd never have believed it himself.

There were some things about it that did make sense though. He'd been wracking his brain ever since and he could not remember a single time that his own father had left the county. How had they avoided doing that for so long? Surely there must have been a reason to leave at some point?

Ash paused in his work and leaned against the wall. How had his father never thought to mention this to him? He must have known. Nathan had been such a loving father, but sometimes thoughtless. Had he been waiting to tell Ash when he was older? Of course his death had been unexpected, he might have planned to do a great many things. Ash resolved to ask the cat about his father the next time he saw her.

The hair on the back of Ash's neck stood up unexpectedly. He turned to the doorway, which was empty. He knew the feeling well.

"Elliot, I know you're there," Ash called out. "What do you want?"

Elliot's grinning face appeared in the doorway. "How do you know I'm here? It must be our deep brotherly connection!" Elliot laughed.

Ash moved towards his tools. He suddenly wanted to have a hammer close at hand. Elliot perused the room as if he were at an art museum, casually taking in the scene. He whistled, his wide brown eyes dancing around the room. "Looks like this house is a lot of work, dear brother."

"Yes, Abigail was not pleased," Ash answered.

"I'm sure she wasn't." Elliot stared at Ash for a long time.

"What do you want, Elliot?" Ash finally asked.

"Do I need a reason to visit you, Ashes?" Elliot feigned shock.

"You usually have one," Ash answered, his tone dry. Elliot laughed again. His mocking grin back on his face.

"I suppose I was going to tell you about my little trick today. It was so fun, I thought you might be interested!" Elliot's eyes were shining, he was like a little boy in a toy store. "I found a cat, you see. A black cat. I've always heard that if a cat falls, it will always land on its feet. But from how high? I wanted to know." Elliot paused, cocking his head as if listening for something. "Yes, yes I always have wanted to know. So I took the cat to the cliffs."

Ash felt a dread in the pit of his stomach. A black cat? Surely it wouldn't be the same one?

"It turns out that the cat did land on its feet. I think all four feet might be broken though, shattered to pieces. It yowled like you wouldn't believe when it hit the bottom! It was funny…" Elliot smiled at Ash, his eyes twinkling with delight, "It was funny because when it cried out, it almost sounded human!"

Ash heard his words like hammer blows to his chest. It was Creature, he knew it in his soul. Oh what would he do? He must get to her, save her, if he could! Elliot was waving to Ash and walking out the door.

"What cliff?" Ash asked.

"Oh you know the one. I showed it to you once before, if you'll remember. When we were younger. It's quite a ways out in the woods. You had better hurry if you're going to get there tonight, dear brother." Elliot said. He was so sure of himself, it was maddening. Elliot had known Ash would react this way, it was probably why he had done it.

↗ ↗ ↗

Ash knew exactly which cliff Elliot was talking about. Elliot had dangled him off of it by his foot when they were younger. An experience like that tends to stick out in the mind. He had driven to the edge of the woods, and now he rushed through the trees with a flashlight in hand. The sky was darkening quickly, he'd be lucky to even find the cat.

What am I going to do if that cat dies? Ash thought it a thousand times in the drive to the forest. He thought it a thousand times again as he stumbled through the trees. It was more than that though. He held a genuine affection for the animal. She had been his companion for a long time before he learned that she could speak. She had accompanied him many times to the graveyard to visit his parents. She had, in fact, been with him when his father died in the fire. What would he do without that cat? He closed his mind to the question and focused on putting one foot in front of the other.

The forest became wilder before it cleared out at the top of the cliff. His legs were sore from pumping up and down the hilly terrain, sliding past trees on his way down and pulling at them on his way up. Now he was at the top of the cliff. It was not a direct fall down, but only jutting rock was between the top and bottom. It would make for a hard fall indeed. He shone his flashlight down, looking for the cat on one of the ledges. He surmised the drop from where he stood to be close to 70 yards. How could anyone survive that, cat or human? The light did not reach all the way to the bottom. It would take him all night to go the easier way down. He was just going to have to manage the drop.

Ash slowly climbed down. He hadn't brought a rope, but he was strong. He prayed that he would be able to negotiate the cliff face. What other choice did he have? Without her, he would never learn how to break the curse and if that happened he might as well die here anyway.

His foot stretched down, searching for a foothold. Then the next foot. It felt painfully slow. Whenever he reached a small ledge, he would search for the cat.

Finally, he found her. Looking up, he must have climbed down 30 yards. The black form was curled up and not moving, a few more feet below him. It was so dark, the cat was just a smudge darker than the rock around her. Ash called down to her, but there was no response. His chest tightened; he could hear his heartbeat in his ears. *Oh no, please no!*

He edged closer to the black form, his feet feeling for footholds. He leaned down as far as he could and could just touch her fur. She did not stir. Ash pushed down a feeling of panic. His feet slid on the rock. He scooped the cat up, praying he could carry her safely back up the cliff.

The rock beneath him began to give. He felt it come away from the cliff face with rising horror. He held on with one hand, his other cradling the broken feline. His feet braced against the rock, he felt the moment it began to slide away. Then everything was moving. He held the cat close and prayed, prayed to anyone listening, *Please! I need to live!*

Chapter Five

Creek Woman

Peace quickly became a thing of the past. Tensions with the whites rose and rose. They were always hungry for more land. They brought their missionaries to turn the minds of our young ones. They brought their farming equipment and tore down our trees. They captured our animals and domesticated them, an unnatural process to us.

Inevitably war broke out. The "Red Sticks," they were called. Creek rebels who sought to return our people to older ways, they began raiding and fighting with the white settlements, including Creeks who had converted to European ways. Of course, everyone knows now how that ended. The Creeks were soundly beaten by Andrew Jackson at the Battle of Horseshoe Bend. Many of our villages were burned down. Many women and children died of starvation, or exposure afterwards. Our men were shackled and enlisted to fight our neighbors, imprisoned, or executed. It was a terrible time for the Creeks, as well as our fellow Natives.

And then our land was sold to the Whites. At first wholesale, then piece by piece. We were cheated, we were betrayed by many of our own blood, we were destitute. With no means to feed ourselves, our hunting grounds taken, we had no choice. The Creeks started emigrating to Indian Territory.

We took boats upriver, but were forced to walk from New Orleans to what is now Oklahoma. Through winter, through rain, with babies strapped to our backs and elderly towed on flatboards, we walked those horrible miles. Our belongings often had to be abandoned on the roadside, because they couldn't be ferried across rivers. We nearly froze to death and starved. In compensation, each man was given a brass kettle and a rifle. It was meant to be a means of survival.

It was a joke. Worse than any joke that even Rabbit would have played on us.

I had packed what I could and left with my kinsmen. It was 1829. I had been conditionally accepted by my clan, but tensions with all things foreign had cast a shadow of doubt on me as well. I represented a time and way of life that was being forgotten. The old traditions were being set aside for new ones. Old beliefs had made way for Christianity and the white Jesus. Where could I possibly fit in with this new era of Creeks?

Then, the cholera came for us. En route, many died. Once we arrived, many more died from the disease. Our bodies did not hold the keys to fighting this white man illness. The Creeks, a proud and mighty people, had been brought low by the foreigners. So, like the many legends of our people, we tried to change our shape. We sent our children to the Christian schools. We learned agriculture. We moved forward.

I was asked to leave. My strange eternal youth had been noticed by the Whites. There was no explanation for it. I myself, did not know why I had not aged in so many years. But there was no denying that I had a magic about me, and magic did not fit in with the Christian worldview of the Whites. I left quietly.

Elliot

It took Ash less time than Elliot expected to reach the cliff. He had almost been too late. Elliot had made himself the perfect perch just out of sight of the cliff face to watch. He felt the excitement rising in his body like a madness. The Face also watched closely, giddy. It was a heady feeling, it filled him like a hot air balloon. His plan was coming together.

Ash was shining his flashlight down the side of the cliff. Did he really think that dinky thing would penetrate the settling dark? Elliot laughed to himself. Ash hadn't brought anything to help traverse the cliff's face. Elliot watched with interest as Ash slowly lowered himself down with nothing but his own strength. The work Abigail subjected him to must have made him strong. Elliot was surprised that Ash was able to go down this way. But slowly, one foothold and handhold at a time, Ash made the descent.

Elliot saw the moment he spotted the cat. He held his breath. Would the ruse work? It was just a black cat. Elliot had not caught the cat that Ash knew. He felt it was too much of a risk to trap the animal that enraged The Face so much. He might get lost in the gaps and never come back. No, this was just some stray he'd lured from a diner trash can. But it was all black, and female. In the dark, it would be easy to mistake one cat for the other.

Ash scooped the cat up in his arm and adjusted his weight to climb back up. Elliot's hands twisted in his lap. This was the moment he had worked so hard for. Would it work? Ash had fallen for the decoy cat.

Elliot felt the rumble deep in the earth. It shuddered the tree he was perched in and he knew it had worked. He watched with glee as the ledge holding Ash and the cat began to break away from the cliff face. It all slid downward in a cloud of rock dust. Ash was lost in it. Elliot's smile stretched across his face almost painfully. His eyes were wide, taking in every detail of the moment.

Ash was gone!

Elliot laughed to himself and jumped out of the tree.

"A lovely night indeed!" He said to The Face. He could feel its grin mirroring his own. He headed back through the forest towards home, whistling all the way.

Ash

Ash felt as if a tiny person with a hammer was inside his head pounding on his brain. It was a moment before he could push the feeling away enough to open his eyes. His body felt heavy, as if weighed down by rocks.

His eyes flew open. His body *was* weighed down by rocks. The cat was smashed against his side. He knew that no creature in that position could be alive. His heart suddenly felt weighed down by rocks as well.

His legs were pinned well and truly. He could wiggle his toes though, which he thought meant he hadn't lost circulation. He wasn't sure though. There was a large boulder pressing up against his side, the cat jammed between them. The arm on that same side was also pinned, and he could feel nothing there. There was no pain in his body, but he knew this must be shock, and would not last.

"If there's a God, can you please help me?" Ash said aloud, his voice croaking on rock dust in the process. He coughed, and it was painful. His body began to register pain in his head, his legs, his arm. He pushed with his free arm against the surrounding rocks, hoping to free another limb. He was able to push some of the weight off of his legs, but not free them. He felt the rocks around him shift again.

What do I do? Ash closed his eyes and tried to think of something. He had no phone to call for help. He was miles from any home or business. He had no tools to help free himself. Just himself, a dead cat and a flashlight.

The flashlight!

Stretching out his free hand, he felt around for the flashlight. Maybe if he flashed it enough times, someone would see the light? It was a long shot, but his only shot at the moment. His hand felt the handle and he pulled it close. His eyes had trouble focusing on what he was holding, though it was close to his own face. It was definitely the flashlight, but it looked broken. He tried to flip it on, but no light came.

Ash suppressed the urge to cry, to shout, to give up.

The pounding in his head couldn't be ignored. It seemed to worsen. He felt as though he could hear Indians pounding their war drums inside his head. It rose to a fever pitch and he knew he would black out soon. He struggled to hold on to consciousness.

His vision was swimming. The night had turned inky black, and the rocks were beginning to blur. And what was that? He thought he saw hair dangling down from the sky, black hair, as dark as the night. He tried to look up, and there were dark green eyes looking at him. The eyes seemed worried. He tried to form words, to ask for help, for anything. He could not. The darkness took him and he knew nothing else.

Neveah

Ruth was a mystery. The woman seemed so strict at times. She was a demanding tutor. She brooked no excuses from Neveah and set the bar high. Neveah, for the first time in a long time, was scrambling to keep up. So it was quite a shock when she heard Ruth talk to her mother about leaving the house for further studies.

"Neveah is an intelligent girl. I believe she would benefit from a more intensive research project. I will propose some local historical options to her, but they will require her to leave the house. I will accompany her and supervise, of course." Ruth wasn't really asking. Jillian seemed equally surprised. Neveah heard the long pause, waited for Ruth to backstep or rephrase the request, but she didn't. She merely waited in the silence, daring Jillian to tell her no.

Jillian relented.

Neveah was then informed that there was a bit of history to the local hospital, and that Ruth was taking her there for her research. Jillian insisted on her personal driver taking them to the hospital. Did Ruth even have a vehicle of her own? Neveah had never noticed one in their long driveway while she was there. Neveah half believed that Ruth materialized from thin air in time for their lessons, then poofed back out when they were over. How ridiculous! She must have a car.

Neveah watched out the window of the backseat as the car slid out of their estate and onto the main road. She had not been this far in a car in a very long time. She glanced at Ruth, who seemed smug. Ruth reminded Neveah of a cat just then, very pleased with herself.

"Am I really supposed to research the history of the hospital?" Neveah asked.

"Of course. I expect a full report at the end of the month," Ruth answered quickly. Her mouth quirked ever so slightly. "However, I doubt it will take much of your efforts to make the full report. You might have some time to visit a friend while you are there. If you are careful, and quick." Ruth's expression was so serious, Neveah would have believed she were carved from wood. She gaped at her tutor.

"Visit a friend? What friend?"

"Haven't you wondered where he's been?" Neveah blinked. Had she heard Ruth right?

"What?"

"He didn't answer the walkie-talkie last night, did he?"

Neveah's eyes bugged open wide and she spluttered, actually spluttered.

"Ash is in the hospital? What happened?" Neveah's mind whirled. "How do you even know about that?"

"I know a great many things, young Neveah." Ruth turned to look out of her window and said nothing more for the remainder of the drive. Neveah's head spun with the implications and she missed much of the view from her own window.

The current hospital was a clean modern building, that sprawled across the ground with no apparent pattern. The driver pulled the vehicle to the front entrance, and Ruth and Neveah walked inside. Neveah hardly registered the details of the place as they walked. Ash was in the hospital? There must have been some sort of accident. Her heart raced, her mind worried. Was he ok? What happened to him?

Ruth walked purposefully through the building and led her away from the busy open foyer. The hallway became emptier and quieter as they walked. Ruth's long black hair swayed back and forth and the heels of her boots clicked against the tile. It was the only sound in the hallway now: *click, click, swish, swish.*

Finally there was another doorway, it seemed to open to the outside. Light flooded this back hallway. Ruth pushed open a door and they were back again in the bright light of day. Neveah took in a deep breath of fresh air, shaking off the smell of sickness and antiseptic. Ruth had stopped and was pointing.

"That is what you are here to research."

There was a massive white building. It was five stories tall, the lowest level made of brown stone. The upper four were whitewashed. It was orderly, obviously designed with a purpose. The windows were dark. It looked abandoned.

"What is it?" Neveah asked.

"It is the old hospital. And your task is to learn what happened there, when and why it was important," Ruth answered. Her words were short.

"I have a month to learn this?"

"Yes. I expect no less than 5,000 words on the subject," Ruth answered.

"5,000? I could write that in a week if I needed to," Neveah blurted out in surprise.

Ruth paused for a moment. Her eyes were on the distant building. She turned and placed a hand on Neveah's shoulder.

"I know that. You could write a thorough report in no time and we would be done with this endeavor. Then we would have no excuse to come here. However, I have a motive in this as well." Ruth's eyes met Neveah's, and she realized how troubled Ruth looked. "I know you want to spend time with Ash. I want you to. He needs your help. He's had a terrible accident, but it's important that he keeps up with his school work. If you will agree to help tutor him, I will make excuses to your mother for us to keep coming here. Do you agree?" Ruth asked.

Neveah's mouth felt thick for a moment. What did Ruth know of Ash? What did she know of Neveah's relationship with Ash?

"Yes. I agree," she answered slowly. Ruth's hand squeezed her shoulder. As quickly as the moment had come, it was gone. Neveah was soon following Ruth's swaying hair and clicking boots down hallways again. In a matter of moments, she was standing in front of a patient room with the name 'Price' scrawled across the whiteboard next to the room number.

"He's in there. I will wait right outside," Ruth gestured towards a bench in the hallway. "And Neveah?"

Neveah spun on her heel to look at Ruth. "Yes?"

"His injuries are significant. Try to brace yourself." With that, Ruth shoved a book into her hands and shooed Neveah into the room.

Neveah took a deep breath and pushed on the door handle. The room, like many hospital rooms she'd seen in tv shows, was mostly white and green. There was a window that let in a lot of bright light, which pleased her. She would hate to think he was stuck in a dark room alone.

Ash was lying on the bed, an IV feeding into his right hand, and a pulse monitor clipped on his finger. A bandage was wrapped around his head, and a cast was set on his left arm. She could see the bulge of boots on both feet as well. He was covered in a blanket that seemed too thin to her. Surely he was cold in this place? Neveah put her arms around herself, feeling the chill suddenly.

Ash was asleep. How long had he been like this? And why was he alone. Ash had said there was no love lost between himself and his step-mother, but surely at a time like this, she should be here? He had no other family.

Neveah perched on the edge of the seat next to his bed. It was cold. Ash's eyes looked purple, his cheeks too pale. Neveah was not sure what she should do. She couldn't tutor an unconscious person. Neveah looked down at the book Ruth had given her. *Romeo + Juliet* by William Shakespeare. How had she known?

Neveah flipped open the book to the place she had left off reading the last time she had seen Ash. She cleared her throat and suddenly felt self-conscious. What if someone walked in on her? She pushed the thought away and began to read aloud.

A small shadow crowded in on the sunlight. Neveah turned to look out of the window and found that a black cat had settled there. Was that Midnight? The cat was looking in on Neveah and Ash as if she were about to ask to be let in. Neveah smiled and continued reading.

Ash

Ash could remember his mother. She had died when he was young, but he could still remember her. She had long hair and green eyes. He could remember that she would sing to him at night. Her voice

166

was high and sweet and he fell asleep to it night after night.

He sensed light. It pushed against his eyelids. He felt the heat of it. It seemed a struggle to open his eyes. He felt that he was laying down in a bed, but it didn't feel like his own bed. He lifted his eyelids a little.

White hands were reaching for him. They held his hands. A soft voice whispered, but he couldn't make out the words.

Mother? Have I died? Ash looked a little harder. Surely heaven would not hurt. Suddenly his whole body hurt. He felt it from the top of his head down deep into his feet. Those white hands were not as white as his mother's had been. The voice was different too. No, he was definitely alive.

"Ash, can you hear me?" The voice was instantly familiar.

"Neveah?" Ash lifted a hand to rub at his eyes. He felt the tug of a needle and realized an IV was in his hand. He looked around again. He was in a hospital bed. He could see more bandage than skin when he looked down at himself. "What happened? How did I get here?"

"Well, we don't know exactly. A woman called in to 9-1-1 and reported finding a body at the base of a cliff in the forest. A rescue team came out and found you, but not the woman who reported it. Do you know who it was?" Neveah asked.

Ash remembered the black hair, the green eyes. "I don't really know. I kind of remember someone." He tried to sit up. Neveah reached out to help him. "How bad is it?" He asked, gesturing to himself.

"Um, well. It's not good. I've been asking the nurses, but I'm not even supposed to be here. They can't tell me much. I think you broke some ribs and your arm and also maybe your legs?" Neveah said this in a rush, biting her lip as she talked.

"What?" Ash asked. "God, I'm a wreck!"

"Ash, what were you doing out there?" Neveah asked, her small face creasing with worry.

"Well, it's kind of a long story," Ash paused. "Actually it's not, I went to rescue a cat."

Neveah gaped at him. "Excuse me?"

"Okay, maybe it is a long story," Ash said. "But trust me, it was important."

"Well that explains one thing at least," Neveah said. She pointed to the window. There, perched on the ledge outside of the window, sat the black cat. As if she knew she was being discussed, she turned and grinned at Ash.

"I think they have me on drugs," Ash said. Cats didn't normally grin, did they?

"Most likely, yes," Neveah answered quickly, staring at the cat.

Neveah

"Most likely, yes," Neveah answered, still inspecting the cat.

"So what are you doing here?" Ash asked. "Not that I'm sorry to see you. I can't imagine anyone I'd rather have here, actually." Ash's pale face suddenly bloomed with color. Neveah imagined her own did as well.

"Well that's kind of a long story too. Or maybe just a strange one." Neveah flipped the pages of the book nervously. "My new tutor has me here doing some research on the hospital. But she gave me way too much time to finish it and told me I could use my extra time to help you."

"She did? Who is she?" Ash asked. Neveah told him her name and described what she looked like. He shook his head. "I don't know anyone like that. How could she even know who I am?"

Neveah shrugged. "I didn't know she knew you until we were on our way to the hospital."

"Well, whatever the reason, I'm glad you're here." Ash smiled a small smile. Neveah felt lost in it for a moment. Suddenly she realized what she had meant to do all along. She stood quickly and headed for the door. She stopped before leaving.

"I just realized, I need to tell someone you're awake!" Neveah rushed out of the room. Ruth was gone. A nurse was passing by and Neveah reached out to stop her.

"Please! Someone needs to come in here! He just woke up," Neveah said, her voice hushed but hurried. The nurse nodded and rushed to the nurse's station. Neveah bounced on her heels, waiting for someone to come back.

A moment later another nurse, the one from the day before, bustled around the corner and met her eyes.

"I'm going to need you to wait out here for a moment." The nurse was stern, but not unkind. Neveah nodded and perched on the edge of the bench in the hallway. Where was Ruth? She twirled her thumbs and bounced her heels. How long would they need her to wait?

Where is Ash's family? Neveah was still mad about that. He had told her that the relationship between himself and his step-mother was pretty cold. Still, she was shocked to find no one here visiting except herself and a cat.

Neveah took a deep breath to still herself. She wasn't his family. She might not be allowed back in today. She suddenly realized that her messenger bag was still in the room. She couldn't leave without it! Her mother would notice that for certain!

It was only a few minutes until the nurse emerged from the room. Neveah bounced up on her feet instantly. "Can I go back in?"

The nurse nodded. "But only for a few minutes. The doctor will want to check on him soon. So be quick about it, girl!" The nurse was grinning as Neveah rushed past her into the room.

Ash was sitting upright in bed. The cat in the window was gone, Neveah noted.

"I guess I need to clear out of here. The nurse said a doctor was coming to check you over." Neveah reached for her messenger bag and held it in front of herself.

"Okay," Ash said simply. They were both quiet for a moment. "Do you think you'll be able to come back?"

"Apparently Ruth intends for me to," Neveah answered, shrugging. "Oh and she said I need to help you with your homework. That's the reason she's doing this, I guess."

"Homework? Well, I definitely have plenty to catch up on, even without laying around this place for who-knows-how-long." Ash rubbed absently at his head. There was a bandage there, which worried Neveah.

"I don't know if it'll be tomorrow or what. I'll come back though. Maybe I can sneak your walkie-talkie to you? Where is yours?" Neveah asked.

"Um, well, it's probably in my backpack. Don't worry about that. I don't want you to get in trouble over me," Ash said quickly. "Besides, Abigail will probably have to bring it to me soon. So don't get caught sneaking around my place, okay?"

Neveah nodded. Ash looked relieved. Was he really so worried about her getting in trouble?

"Well, I guess I'll go then." Neveah slipped the strap of her bag over her head.

"Yeah, okay," Ash said. He looked as nervous as she felt.

Before she could change her mind, she leaned forward and kissed his cheek lightly. Ash beamed at her.

"Bye!" Neveah said and rushed out of the room.

Neveah stepped out into the hallway with her heart pounding loudly in her ears. She felt embarrassed. Surely anyone looking at her would know what she had just done! The nurses passed by without looking at her. She calmed herself. That's silly. No one here knows what I did, or cares! She thought to herself.

Someone cleared their throat to her left. Neveah turned to see

Ruth sitting on the bench. She raised her eyebrows at Neveah. "Have a good visit?"

Neveah blushed down to her toes. Did she know? Neveah prayed, *please God, let the ground swallow me right now!*

Ruth smiled and stood. "I think that's enough adventure for today. Don't you?"

Neveah didn't answer, just followed Ruth out of the building and into the waiting car.

Ash

Ash didn't know how long he had lain in his hospital bed unconscious, but judging by how his body felt, it must have been a while. He felt like he hadn't had a bath in days, and it was unpleasant to say the least.

Ash could not have been more pleased to wake up to Neveah in his room, reading him Shakespeare. Honestly, she could have been picking her nose, and he would have been happy to see her. But, he was also relieved when she left the room. He was worried she could *smell* him.

The no-nonsense nurse that bustled into the room to look him over had a name tag swinging from around her neck that read "Beverly." She patted him congenially after she checked all of his vitals.

"I'll be right back with the doctor. He's going to want to look at that head of yours," she said, then left the room in a flurry.

Neveah came back in to get her bag then.

Ash was totally shocked when she darted forward and kissed his cheek. He wanted to put his arms around her, to touch her, but it didn't seem like the right time. Neveah left the room as quickly as she had come, leaving a pleasant trail of perfume behind. Of course she smelled as great as she looked!

He didn't have long to wait for the doctor. This, as much as anything, made him realize his injuries were serious.

"How are you feeling?" the doctor asked without preamble.

"Okay, I guess," Ash answered. The doctor checked over the vitals written on a clipboard, then took out his stethoscope. After listening to various places on Ash's chest and back, he clicked his tongue and started feeling Ash's head with his cool fingers.

"Tell me if anything hurts," the doctor said.

"It all kind of hurts. My head is pounding, actually."

"Anything else hurt?"

"I kind of ache everywhere. My legs feel terrible. I can't really feel my arm though. Is that normal?"

The doctor sat down in the chair next to Ash's bed. The nurse busied herself with adding in notes on his clipboard.

"You've had a pretty serious accident. Several large rocks fell on and around you. Quite frankly, I'm surprised you lived through it. We have mended you up as best we can. You have two broken ribs, your left arm is broken at the ulna and radius, Both of your legs have serious fractures below the knees. And we are going to do a CT scan and x-ray on your head to decide how serious the damage there is. You definitely have suffered a concussion though. It's going to be quite some time before you recover from all of this. It's going to be some time before you don't feel discomfort and pain from your injuries. I'm sorry, but I want you to know what you are facing." The doctor was serious, his forehead creased, his mouth tight. Ash kept noticing a mole on the doctor's left cheek while he talked.

"How long do I have to stay in the hospital?" Ash asked. It was the only thing he could think to ask. "I need to get back to school."

"We will know more after your scans, but it will at least be a few more days. We need to keep you under observation that long."

Ash nodded his head, trying to take in all the doctor said. Had he said his name? Ash couldn't remember. His head was throbbing, and suddenly it was all he could think about. He put his working, non-bandaged hand to his forehead.

"We are going to keep you on a regiment of painkillers for the time being. Those ribs are going to be uncomfortable for a while. There's not a lot we can do to help with those bones except manage your pain. We've reset your arm and legs though," the doctor gestured for the nurse. "When did he last have the painkiller?"

"Two hours ago, Doctor."

"In another two hours, make sure he gets another dose." The doctor stood and left, pausing only to nod to Ash.

The nurse hovered at his side for a moment, dithering. "Your mother has been called. She knows you're awake now."

"She's not my mother," Ash answered. Why had he said that? It didn't matter.

"What do you mean?"

"She's my step-mother. My parents are both dead." The words felt heavy in his mouth, like they had only passed a few days ago. He felt so, so tired.

"I'm so sorry," the nurse said, then left the room.

It was only a matter of time before Abigail came to visit him. He had a few hours reprieve, which he mostly spent napping, and then she was there. He knew she was there before she even opened the door. He could hear her calling to the nurse and asking for an update while she was in the hallway.

Hearing her voice made him wince. He was sitting up and holding his head when she finally came into the room.

"Asher! You're awake!" Abigail said. Her hands flew around as she spoke.

"I assumed that's why you're here, Abby," Ash said. He knew that she did not like being called Abby. He did not know why he baited her now, but he couldn't seem to help himself. She frowned at him from across the room.

"How are you feeling? Are they treating you well here?" She asked. She looked out the window and saw the cat. When had the cat returned?

"The doctor kind of explained things to me. The nurse has been nice, she checks in on me a lot. I guess I've been here a while though. I'm not really sure what all happened, honestly," Ash said. It was hard to focus on what he was saying. He wanted to lie down and go to sleep again.

"Well, what on earth were you doing out there to begin with?" Abigail asked, her hands didn't seem to know where to settle. They went to her hips, then together in front of her, then back again.

"Abigail. I'm sorry. I don't remember everything that happened. I went out there to rescue a cat though. Elliot told me-"

"Elliot? What does he have to do with this?" Abigail said, her hands stilled.

"He threw a cat off of the cliff. It was a cat that I know. Or I thought it was anyway. I went to rescue it. When I got down to it, the ledge gave way, I guess. That's all I remember. I don't even remember being rescued," Ash said. He eased back on the bed, if only he could rest for a moment. Maybe then he could remember more.

"So all of this," Abigail gestured to him and the hospital room around them, "is because of a cat?" Ash could tell she was not impressed.

"I'm sorry, Abigail. I didn't know all of this would happen," Ash said. He closed his eyes. He just needed to close them for a moment.

"Ash! Asher, are you listening to me? I need to know," He fought to open his eyes. Abigail was pale, standing at the foot of his bed. "I need to know what Elliot told you."

"What? Why do you want to know about that?" Ash couldn't understand her. Why did she look as if someone had walked over her grave?

"Just tell me!"

"He told me where the cat was," Ash said, then closed his eyes again. He couldn't open them anymore. He was instantly asleep, leaving Abigail alone.

"Oh God, Elliot. What have you done?" Abigail said to no one.

Neveah

If Neveah thought the visits to the hospital would slow down her regular studies with Ruth, she was sorely mistaken. Ruth left her with just as much to do as ever. She sat in her room working through her trigonometry homework, praying to get done in time to go ride Sunbeam. She looked out the window at the sun beginning to set and knew she wouldn't make it tonight. Neveah sighed, the pencil in her hand sagging a little.

"I'm sorry, Sunbeam. I don't think it's going to happen tonight either." Neveah hadn't been able to ride her horse in several days, and she missed it. Sunbeam, aside from Ash, was her only friend.

There was a knock at her door. Jillian stepped in.

"Are you almost done with your homework, dear?" Neveah's mother asked. Her tone was mellow. Neveah was instantly suspicious.

"I should be done within the hour. Is everything ok, Mother?" she answered.

"Well, your father wants you to meet someone. Why don't you take a break and come downstairs," Jillian said the words carefully. Neveah felt a tightening of her chest. The last time her father had introduced her to someone was Conner. Conner, who had later slipped into her room with a knife. Conner, who was now dead. She was instantly seized with the fear of this new stranger.

"I'll be down in just a minute then." Neveah set down her pencil and went to her bathroom. In the mirror, she saw her fear reflected back at her. She tried to smooth away the frayed feelings.

"It's probably nothing," Neveah told her mirror self. "No reason to get bent out of shape. No reason at all." She washed her hands, and smoothed down her hair. Jillian was waiting for her in the hallway. To Neveah's surprise, as they made their way into the den, Jillian put her hands on Neveah's shoulders. It was a supportive gesture, one Neveah couldn't remember her mother ever giving.

In the den stood her father. He was big man, and he always seemed to fill any room. He had a fire roaring on the hearth and it made the room quite warm. It was still a bit early in the year for fires. It was a moment before she realized there was another person in the room.

He stood up from the sofa, and turned towards her just as her father did. He had auburn hair that looked dark in the firelight. He had dark eyes. He was tall and his smile seemed somehow wrong. She knew she had seen him before.

The woods! He had happened on her and Sunbeam in the woods that day! The day she had learned of her father's affair. Instantly Neveah was filled with the urge to leave the room.

"Neveah, I would like you to meet Elliot Fisher," Her father was saying. *Ash's step brother!* Elliot's head bobbed in acknowledgement. Jillian's hands tightened on her shoulders. She didn't want to touch him, and prayed he wouldn't extend his hand to be shaken.

"It's nice to meet you, Neveah," Elliot said. His words were oily smooth. His eyes followed her like a cat eyeing a mouse. Jillian almost pushed her across the room.

"It's nice to meet you, too," Neveah answered, the words almost choking her. Her stomach clenched. She looked to her father for guidance. How could he possibly be connected to Elliot?

"I've known Elliot for a while now. He is just a year older than you. Maybe the two of you could become friends. That would be nice, don't you think?" William was looking at Elliot now. Elliot nodded his agreement.

"I'd like that very much," Elliot said. He was smiling, but it did not touch his eyes. Neveah swallowed hard. She could almost hear her mother's voice telling her not to show fear. She straightened her spine. *Get it together, girl!* Neveah told herself.

"How did you two come to meet?" Neveah asked, her eyes tearing away from Elliot and turning towards her father.

"I believe we met originally at a charity function. Elliot's mother is very active in the community," William answered smoothly. Elliot said nothing.

"Surely you are too young to work for Daddy?" Neveah asked, looking back at Elliot. His eyes met hers. There was amusement there.

"I am, I suppose. We have a unique relationship. I guess," Elliot looked to Neveah's father. "I guess you would say your father is my mentor."

"Yes, that puts it nicely," William answered.

"Why are we just now meeting you, then?" Jillian asked. She was talking to Elliot, but William was the one to answer.

"Oh, you know me, darling. I don't mix family and business much. I know Elliot more in my business dealings. It wasn't until recently that I realized he might benefit from meeting our little family." William was smiling, but his words were steel. So Elliot wanted to meet them? Why?

As if he could hear her thoughts, Elliot said, "Please don't be alarmed, Mrs. Winters. I wouldn't hurt a fly." He smiled, as if he had told a particularly funny joke.

"Well, it's good to finally meet you then," Jillian said smoothly. "I wish however, that my husband had given us some notice of your coming. Neveah has some other responsibilities detaining her this evening. I hope you will forgive us for cutting this meeting short." Jillian nodded to Elliot and then turned to Neveah. "Say goodbye to our guest, dear. Then you need to get back to your studies."

Neveah nodded her head to Elliot and attempted to smile. "It was nice to meet you. Have a good evening." She smiled at her father and then left the room. Jillian walked to the hallway with her. Under her breath she whispered, "Don't leave your room until I say so."

Neveah's back stiffened, but she kept walking. Her mother had never given her a cue like that before. Whatever had set Neveah on edge, had obviously done the same to her mother. This, more than anything made her nervous.

She reached her room and locked the door. Instead of finishing her trigonometry, she clutched a pen knife and perched by her window, watching the driveway for a leaving vehicle.

She remembered that day in the woods. He had known who she was then. What did he want with her? And why was her father allowing him to come around?

And what about him made her feel so threatened? Even Sunbeam had shied away from him. Reliving their conversation in the woods, she could think of nothing threatening in what he said. It was unnatural, this reaction he caused in her.

"Who are you, Elliot?" Neveah asked out loud. She was determined to find out. It was not much longer when she saw Elliot stride away on foot. Once out in the driveway, he turned, looking in Neveah's direction, and smiled. Neveah shuttered her window quickly, praying she hadn't been seen. How could he know which room was hers? She gently turned one louvred blind open to peek outside.

Elliot continued his walk in a leisurely fashion. Then, instead of following the road, he ducked into the woods and was gone. She felt a shudder go down her spine. She gripped the pen knife harder. Something about him was not right.

Neveah opened her bedroom door quietly and went to the staircase. Downstairs was utter silence. Neveah slipped into the hallway to listen. Creeping closer to the den, she waited just out of sight. There was the sound of tight voices speaking low. Then suddenly she heard her father's voice.

"Do you think this is what I want? It's not! Of course it's not!"

"She is our daughter! Not some bargaining chip! Or have you forgotten that as well?" This was Jillian's voice, shrill and out of control. Neveah had never heard her mother's voice like that.

"I haven't forgotten, Jillian! I just don't have a choice!"

"You always have a choice!" Jillian fled the room. Neveah had but a second to dive out of sight. Her heart was pounding, hearing her mother walking past her in the hallway. She had just made it into the kitchen, and was crouched behind the island there. She heard her father throw something. It crashed and hissed in the flames of the fireplace. It startled her. She was unaccustomed to either of her parents losing control like this.

It was a matter of moments before William too left the den. He stopped in the hallway. Neveah peered carefully around the side of the island. Did he know she was there?

Neveah could just spy William standing in the kitchen doorway, his back to her. His right hand went to his inside jacket pocket. Out came the heavy ornate key to his office door. So that's where it was! Neveah didn't dare breath. William turned the key over in his hand, then continued down the hallway. She heard the heavy knob turn, then the door close behind him. Neveah breathed again.

Easing her way back to her room, she reviewed what she had overheard in her mind. Her father had made a choice, a choice that made her mother furious. A choice that involved Neveah. What could it possibly be? She assumed it was to do with Elliot, as he had only just left.

And William had said he didn't have a choice. Was it possible that Elliot, a teenager like herself, was blackmailing her father? The idea seemed incredulous.

Once again, Neveah wished she had more information.

She slipped out a notebook from between her mattress and box spring. She had been keeping notes on what little she knew of her father so far. She quickly added the overheard conversation and a few notes about Elliot. They had been very vague about how they had met or what they did together. Neveah couldn't help but believe that this was intentional. Her pencil tapped against the notebook as she thought it through again. She quickly added another note: *Elliot saw me in the woods. He already knew who I was*. She tried to remember the date, and wrote down that as well. Maybe one day she could give the whole thing to the police.

Is that really what she wanted? For her father to go to prison? She couldn't contemplate it any further and shoved the notebook back in its hiding place.

She resolved to talk to Ash about it. Maybe he could help her. Sunbeam certainly wouldn't be able to help and she really didn't know whom else she could possibly trust this information with. Besides, Elliot was Ash's step-brother. He seemed the most likely person to ask.

Elliot

"Please don't be alarmed, Mrs. Winters. I wouldn't hurt a fly," Elliot said. He couldn't help but grin at his own cleverness. He looked at William, who was frowning at him. William understood the rouse.

William's wife made excuses for Neveah and ushered the girl out the door. Elliot was amused by her hasty retreat. He had seen the moment she had stiffened her back, practically heard her thoughts as she had decided to face him bravely instead of cower.

"I'm sorry again for the short meeting, Elliot," Jillian said, turning back into the room.

"Quite alright, Mrs. Winters. I came here on short notice," Elliot nodded politely. "Besides, William and I can carry on well enough ourselves."

"Yes, dear. We'll be alright here." William said, dismissing her with a wave of his hand. Jillian's jaw clenched, her back stiffened. She turned on her heel and left.

"I think that went well, don't you?" Elliot said. "You have a lovely family, William."

"Cut the bullshit, Elliot. You know as well as I do that this was not my idea," William answered. He had poured himself a drink from a crystal decanter, and sipped at it now.

"There's no reason to be surly about it, though," Elliot responded quickly. He walked to the side table with the decanter and took out a glass for himself. "After all, we're going to be family soon. It's only right that we all meet."

"Get out."

"Excuse me?" Elliot asked, quirking an eyebrow up. He rubbed his finger around the rim of the glass.

"I kept up my end of the bargain. You met her. You are getting what you want. Now get out of my house." William did not turn from the fire as he spoke. Elliot chuckled. He set the glass back on the side table and headed for the door.

"Lovely time, as usual, William."

Elliot noticed Jillian fuming in the kitchen as he passed by. She did not look at him, but instead beelined to the den behind him. He let himself out the front door.

In the driveway, he turned and looked at the second story window. It was dark, but he could just see the outline of Neveah, watching him. He smiled at her. The window was quickly shuttered. He laughed out loud to himself, and headed for the woods. In a moment he was gone, but he was certain he had left a longer-lasting mark on the Williams's estate.

The forest embraced him indifferently. There was a sudden silence all around, as if the animals of the place sensed him and fled. He smiled to himself, imagining William facing his unhappy wife.

"Things are lining up nicely for me," Elliot said out loud. The Face appeared in his mind. It emerged there cloudy, as if it were still under lake water. He could depict a short muzzle, animal eyes. The Face sneered at him. It was unhappy with his newest trick. It did not play to The Face's tastes. It cared little for human relationships, and was restless.

"I know, I know. But I believe a new trick is in order to celebrate. Don't you?" Elliot said smoothly. "Yes, a new trick. Ash is, after all, still in the way. This time we need to get rid of him for good."

The Face was appeased. He could sense the shift in mood instantly. "What kind of trick did you have in mind this time?"

Rather than speak, instead Elliot's mind was suddenly filled with smoke and bright flames. Elliot chuckled to himself. "Yes, I prefer setting fires as well."

Elliot was lost in a gap. His last memory was seeing Neveah open her window and look out.

Ash

Ash woke up and there was sunlight again. He looked around, and noted that his backpack was in the chair next to him, along with a stack of books. Textbooks. A note was on top and he reached out to pick it up.

Ash! Everyone at school heard about what happened! I'm glad you're okay. What were you doing out there alone, man? I would have totally gone rock-climbing with you. Here's your homework. See you later, Gilly.

Ash put the note down and smiled. Of course Gilly would think Ash had been out on a cliffside after dark just for fun. He flipped through his backpack and noted the handouts from classes stuffed inside. That was not what he rummaged around for though. He opened the back pocket and felt around at the bottom. It was there! He pulled out his walkie-talkie and smiled. He could talk to Neveah again.

There was a large round clock in his room that said it was 11:00am. She would be working with her tutor right now, he supposed. He sighed, setting the walkie aside. He pulled out his small copy of *Romeo+Juliet*. It was inevitable that he would have to read it. It was much easier with Neveah reading it to him, but he knew he couldn't wait on her forever. He flipped the book open and began to read.

Beverly, his nurse came in.

"You're awake! Good!" She said. She had a cheerful disposition, smiling in the sun that spilled in from the window. "I've got food for you, kiddo." Beverly hummed as she set a tray before Ash, adjusting the side table to sit in front of him on the bed.

"Do you know yet how long I will be here?" Ash asked. He couldn't imagine how much school he'd missed in the last week already. Beverly chewed her bottom lip for a moment.

"I'm not really supposed to tell you this, but I will anyway. The doctor technically could discharge you now." Beverly's eyes darted to the door and back.

"Then why hasn't he?" Ash asked, his voice lowering to just above a whisper. Beverly seemed to be in a mood for telling secrets.

"When your step-mother came in, asking questions, she made it pretty clear that she wanted you back to work as soon as you got out of here. The doctor says the best thing for your recovery is serious rest. She argued until she was blue in the face, I tell you! I've never seen anyone like that! So I think he's keeping you here as long as he can so you can get some of that rest. I don't know how long he can keep it up though," Beverly winked conspiratorially, then set a fork and spoon on the side table.

Ash settled back against the bed. Had Abigail really thrown such a fit? He was surprised. He had assumed she would nod her head to the doctor, then take him home and do what she wanted. Ash's forehead creased. His head began to ache again.

The doctor had literally told him not to think too much. An impossible order, Ash thought. He had nothing else to do! He jabbed his fork into the baked chicken that awaited him and tried, *tried* not to think.

Elliot

Elliot crawled on his belly through the forest floor. It was peculiar, the feeling he got from stalking prey in the woods. He had heard other people talk wistfully about "feeling home." He assumed this was akin to what they spoke of. It seemed the most natural place for him to be, just out of sight of his next victim.

A deer was before him. He felt the tickle of thick underbrush against his bare arms. There was a heavy smell of wet earth. It had rained the night before, and the ground still held much of the water. The deer bent her head and nibbled at the yellowing grass. He moved forward a few inches, careful not to snag on the thistles around him. The deer raised her head, he paused. The doe looked around, her big black eyes shiny in the sunlight leaking through the canopy. He imagined the brown head and those black eyes between his hands for a moment. He could imagine the weight of the animal as he took it down. He focused on the moment ahead of him. Elliot's muscles tensed, ready for action. He was so, so close to her.

The deer ran.

Elliot sighed, disappointed. It was no wonder she had spooked. He heard someone crashing through the woods, like a wrecking ball through a storefront. Elliot moved to intersect the intruder. He found a good hiding spot behind a stand of trees, clumped thicker than the rest. He could just see between them, without being seen.

There, clumsily wading through the thick foliage that grew to waist height was a balding man in a suit. Elliot almost laughed out loud at the ludicrousness.

It was William's security guard! What could he be up to out here? Elliot intended to find out. It would be easy enough to follow the big man through the woods.

Elliot had not been following very long when the man stopped to rest. He had hacked his way ungracefully through a half mile of forest, thick with foliage that had only sharpened with the fall. It was deceptive, how tangled a person could become in vines that no longer bore their leaves. The man mopped his forehead with a handkerchief he produced from his pocket. Sweating, he leaned against a tree and looked around. Elliot was perched above him, in the tree. He noted the man's expression. Even Elliot could see that he was not enjoying his foray into the woods. The man looked at his watch and swore. So he needs to be somewhere on time? Elliot mentally took notes as he watched.

The man trudged on. Elliot realized that he was headed for Elliot's own home. The wheels began to turn in his mind.

He should have guessed. Elliot had threatened not only William's authority, but his precious daughter. He would not give up without a fight. Elliot knew this man had already been hired once to kill adversaries. But did William really believe this man had a hope of besting him? It was laughable.

Elliot sprinted ahead of the man, The Face already thinking of ways to trick the man. Elliot was thinking, too.

At home, his mother was in the kitchen, making notes at the table. Gerald was playing a video game in the living room nearby.

"Mother, dear. I think it's best if you and little brother leave for a while," Elliot said without preamble. Her head came up, her eyes unfocused for a moment.

"What? Leave? Why?" Abigail asked, the words coming slowly as she processed his statement.

"Just trust me. You won't want to be here." Elliot stood firmly; his hands crossed over his chest.

"Elliot, what is going on?"

"Mother, a friend of mine is unhappy with me. He has sent someone to deal with me. I'm going to deal with him instead. Do you really want to know any more than that?" Elliot answered, his eyes meeting hers.

Abigail searched his face for a moment. She seemed to come to a decision. She squared her shoulders and set the pen down.

"Gerald, grab your coat. We're leaving." Abigail's voice was firm. Gerald's game could be heard in the silence between them. "Gerald! Now!"

Elliot heard the controller being thrown down, then the thud of his brother's heavy steps coming.

"Where are we going?" Gerald asked, his tone whiny. "I was almost to the next level!"

"It doesn't matter. We need to leave."

"But why?" Gerald might have been a toddler at that moment, on the verge of throwing himself in the floor.

"Because I have company coming over, dear brother. It's likely to get unpleasant," Elliot answered for his mother. He met his brother's eyes, letting The Face come forward enough to show there. Gerald stepped back from Elliot. He turned and walked out the door. Abigail grabbed her coat, and Gerald's, and left quickly behind him. At the door she paused, her hand on the doorknob.

"Elliot. Please. Don't go too far," Abigail's voice was just a whisper, but Elliot heard her clearly. He could sense her fear as well.

"Get out!" Elliot roared back at her. She scurried away like a kitchen mouse. It was only a moment before Elliot heard the engine start and the car drive away.

"Good. Now to make the house ready for our guest," Elliot said to himself. The Face smiled, showing teeth.

Neveah

It was late, very late. Neveah should have been asleep, but instead she was counting the lines on her ceiling again. She had had another nightmare, waking in a cold sweat with a vague memory of glinting knives and blood. Now, she thought again and again of Ash's words about Elliot. Now she had met him, in her own home. When she remembered his eyes looking at her, she felt a chill all over again.

Neveah rolled over in bed, determined to shake off the uncomfortable feeling in her gut, and sleep.

A scream pierced the air.

Neveah sat bold upright in bed. It was her mother, screaming in her bedroom. Neveah grabbed her penknife from her nightstand, and ran down the hallway. The door to her parent's bedroom was standing open, and her mother was backed to the doorframe, sobbing. Her hands were over her mouth, trying to muffle the sound, it seemed. Neveah had never seen her mother so afraid before, and the vision of it shook her. What could she do with a penknife to whatever had turned her brave mother into this?

Her father was there too, ushering them both away. Neveah broke free and ran to their room.

"Neveah, no!" William called.

On her mother's vanity, the mirror was clouded with large words. They said, *Remember our agreement!*

Neveah edged closer to the words, dark in the moonlight. They were written in blood.

Neveah gagged, and backed away. Her back hit the doorframe, jarring her. She dropped the penknife. She bent to pick it up, and noticed drops of blood on the floor. William jerked her upwards, hauling her out of the room. Before he could block her view, she looked up. She screamed.

Suspended from the chandelier over their bed, was a body. It was the security guard. He had been gutted, like a pig.

Chapter Six

Creek Woman

I found my travels alone to be difficult. I was beset with troubles. I was a woman who had survived a long time, and was not easily overtaken by difficulties. However, when my horse fell sick and died, I struggled to carry my belongings and myself through the heavy snowfalls of deep winter.

Then I, myself, fell sick. I feared that I had caught cholera, like so many of my clansmen. I was struck with a fever and could not possibly carry on as I had. I found a den in a hillside and collapsed inside on the hard dirt floor. During my time as Big Man-Eater's wife, I had learned something of the magic of my ancestors. I wrapped myself in illusion, so that no one would see me. I prayed to the Creator that the illusion would hold, even if I fell unconscious.

It did not. Now I believe that my Creator allowed the illusion to slip, because otherwise I would surely have perished there.

A pack of wolves found me. They sniffed the air of the cave opening and bayed to each other. "Something is here!" their cries seemed to say. I usually felt no fear of animals, but did not know these creatures. I was weak, and often predators seek to consume the weak.

I was surprised when their howling summoned a man. He was dressed heavily in furs. I felt that I could trust him when I saw that he wore a rabbit-skin hat. In truth, I was so weak with the fever that I had no choice. He carried me on his back to his home. He made me a pallet by his hearth and warmed me with a fire. He fed me broth spoonful by aching spoonful. Slowly, my health returned.

One morning, I awoke, my head clear for the first time in uncounted days. I realized that a baby was crying.

"Is there a child here?" I asked, my voice weak. The man returned with a babe in his arms. The infant could not have been more than a few months old. I reached out and stroked the soft hair on the babe's head. It was dark, like my own.

"I'm Joseph," the man said. "And this is my son, James. It's good to meet you, miss."

I couldn't remember a time when a white man had spoken to me with respect.

In time I recovered. As I recovered, I learned much about Joseph and the rhythms of his life. He had loved a Native woman, an Osage. Then she died, bearing this child, his only son. It was clear that he needed the help of a woman. It was clear that he would love this Osage woman forever, and was not looking for love again. But in my heart, I still loved Big Man-Eater, so I understood. I began to believe that I had found a place for myself. We could raise James together, expecting nothing that the other couldn't give.

For three beautiful years, that's what we did. James was happy and healthy. He grew with every changing season. I taught him the ways of my people. I taught him as much about the ways of his mother's people as I could. Joseph taught him of his ancestor's homeland across the great ocean, and the ways of the forest. Together they hunted with the wolves, and we were never short of food. It was a happy time in my life, the happiest since Big Man-Eater's passing. I laughed at the days to come; I could imagine no hardship that our peculiar family could not overcome.

Ash

It seemed an eternity before Neveah arrived. He had grown accustomed to her bi-weekly visits. Soon, he would have to be sent home, and he dreaded the days as much as he hoped for them. He was desperate to leave this bed, this hospital. He was anxious to get back to school and catch up so that he could still graduate in time.

When Ash thought about giving up his visits with Neveah, though, he felt unmoored from life. What would he do without her there, reading his English assignments to him and scolding him for not finishing his math? He half believed that she would disappear, like a dream fades with morning.

He sighed, looking at the clock. She was usually here by now. Where was she? Ash was just beginning to truly worry when he heard her voice in the hallway, muffled by the closed door. There was a longer-than-usual pause. Then the handle turned and she was there.

Something was wrong, Ash knew it instantly. Instead of bursting into the room full of life and color, Neveah looked nervous, her mouth tight and unsmiling. It was like looking at a balloon slowly deflating.

"What's wrong?" Ash asked. Neveah's big eyes grew watery when they looked at him. What he wouldn't give to be able to get up from this stupid bed!

"Something terrible happened!" Neveah answered finally, the tears slipping over and down her cheeks. She dropped her messenger bag where she stood and cried, big tears rolling down her petite face.

"Come here, sit," Ash said, ushering her forward, and trying to edge his left leg over, so she could perch next to him. She did, rubbing her face with her hands.

"Oh Ash! I'm so scared!" Neveah said. Ash couldn't remember Neveah ever being scared.

"What happened?" Ash asked, taking one of her hands into his own.

"Ash, it's Elliot." Neveah's green eyes looked into his. Hearing that name, his body suddenly flooded with ice.

"What do you mean? What did he do?" Ash's voice was stony.

"Daddy brought him home, to meet me. It was so strange. I felt so...uncomfortable. Daddy never brings anyone home with him. The last time he did was Conner." Neveah's free hand pulled at the hem of her long shirt. "And I remembered what you had said. 'Don't be alone with him.' I didn't know what to do. But then Mother ushered me out and it was over."

"And? And did Elliot do something?" Ash asked. Of course he had. Elliot was always doing something.

"Then, it was late, the middle of the night. Mother started

screaming. Screaming, Ash, like nothing I've ever heard. I've never seen her flinch even, and she was screaming like a mad woman!" Neveah's hand gripped his, hard. "There was a body, Ash. The security guard. He was hanging over their bed. He had been...I don't know...gutted. Like an animal! It was horrible!"

Ash went cold down to his fingertips. A man gutted like an animal. Elliot was the only person Ash knew who could do something like that.

"But Ash," Neveah said, her voice soft. "That's not all. There were words, written on Mother's mirror. They said, 'Remember our agreement.' What do you think that means?"

Ash didn't know what to say. How could he comfort her? His step-brother was a madman, and for some unfathomable reason, he'd become involved with Neveah's family. What could he do? What could any of them do?

Ash looked out the window, and saw the black cat watching them closely.

"I don't know what to do. I think I know who does though," Ash heard himself saying. Neveah followed his gaze to the cat in the window and raised an eyebrow.

"Are you talking about the cat?"

Elliot

Elliot was pleased with himself. The Face grinned back at him in his mind and he knew that it was also satiated. Gutting a man had been an exciting new experience and they had both reveled in it. He sat in their backyard, remembering the sensation of sliding the knife into the man's warm gut.

Gerald slid open the back door and leaned out to look at Elliot.

"Here you are." Gerald shut the door behind him and sat in the grass next to his brother. Most of the grass was dead, winter had finally come.

"Here I am, little brother."

"Mom says Ash is coming home soon. Not that it matters to me one way or the other." Gerald began pulling blades of grass and tearing them into little strips.

"Does it not?"

"What do you mean?"

"I thought Ash's wellbeing might, in fact, matter to you. He is our brother of a sort. You seem to care about that kind of thing."

Gerald paused. Elliot waited. He knew when his brother was sorting out his thoughts.

"Elliot, that kind of thing matters to most people. If I died, I wonder if you would feel anything at all. If Mom or Asher or anyone you know died, would you feel anything?" Gerald did not sound angry. Elliot rolled the idea around in his mind, imagining what it would be like to lose Gerald.

"When Father died, I felt...relief," Elliot paused. "If you died, I would feel something. Not relief. Something else. I honestly can't say more than that."

"Well, I suppose that's a start." Gerald threw down the strips of grass and stood. "I came to tell you that Mom wants you to leave Ash alone for a few days. Evidently your little trick with that dumb cat really messed him up. So I'd steer clear of him for a while or Mom might actually kill you."

Elliot smiled. "I'll take that into consideration, little brother."

Neveah

Ash told her that he wouldn't be in the hospital much longer. They were going to release him soon. After five weeks of holding onto him for scans and "observation," the doctor finally had no more excuses. Neveah could hardly believe he'd been there this long. Ash must be so excited to get out of bed.

But that also meant no more secret tutoring sessions while she was "researching" the old hospital.

And Rapunzel is sent back to her tower.

Neveah was proud of herself. She had still managed to get her research done. The old hospital had once been a tuberculosis sanitorium and had been instrumental in treating the populace of the entire state. It had happened around a hundred years ago and...

And she genuinely could not care any less. Neveah researched, made notes, even took pictures, but all the while her mind was straying back to the boy in the new hospital.

Or the body swinging above her parent's bed.

Neveah closed her eyes and counted to one hundred. It helped calm her down and think of other things.

Neveah tapped her pen against her notebook. She really needed to take all of this research and turn it into a paper. She looked across her desk. She had a red pen laid out.

Remember our agreement! It had been written in red, red blood.

Neveah threw the red pen across the room. It bounced harmlessly against a wall and rolled to a stop a few feet away from her.

"Neveah, what are you doing?" Jillian's voice burst in on her thoughts. Neveah stood quickly, dropping her notebook from her lap onto the floor.

"Mother! Nothing!" She stooped to pick up the notebook and the handful of pens that had found their way to the ground as well. Neveah gripped the pens so hard that they pressed into her palms, leaving little imprints when she set them down.

"Neveah. Come sit with me." Jillian guided her by her shoulders to the bed and they sat, hip to hip.

Neveah felt like a bundle of shattered nerves. Almost everything reminded her of that horror scene in her parent's bedroom. And if it didn't remind her of that, it reminded her of when Conner had come into her room. She struggled to sleep, to eat, to do anything really. Sitting next to her mother, she longed for comfort.

"I know things have been difficult lately," Jillian began. "Since the incident."

Neveah almost burst out laughing. *The incident* was her mother's term for having a man slaughtered like livestock and strung up over her bed. It was such an inoculated way to view a horrible event that it bordered on the ridiculous.

"'Difficult' is kind of an understatement, Mother," Neveah said, staring at the red pen on the floor.

"I know it's hard. I know it's easy for a thing like this to occupy your mind every waking moment," Jillian gripped Neveah's shoulder. "But you have to come to a decision. You can either succumb to this one horrible thing, let it eat at your mind and define the rest of your life. Or, you can decide to put it behind you. You can resolve to move on and let it stay in your past."

Neveah tried to wrap her head around what her mother was saying. It seemed impossible. Could anyone really do that? Just *decide* to move on?

"Is that what you've done all these years, Mother?" Neveah asked. She turned and looked at her mother. She let the emotion and vulnerability show on her face instead of hiding it like usual. Would she turn away? Would she deny what Neveah referred to?

Jillian met her eyes and did not flinch.

"Yes."

Neveah flinched instead. So her mother knew about her father. Jillian knew about the awful things he did. She had, apparently, just resolved to let it not bother her and that was enough.

"I don't know if I can be like you," Neveah said simply.

Ash

The day had finally come. Beverly had been fussing over Ash all day. His doctor, Dr. Henderson had checked in on him, promising to return when Abigail came. Ash had crammed what he could into his backpack and hoped Neveah could come see him before Abigail got there.

It wasn't meant to be.

Abigail whirled in with a flurry of paperwork, demands and the faint scent of floral perfume. Despite their strained relationship, Ash had always been impressed with her ability to charm and take center stage of almost any room.

This room was a little harder than usual. Beverly and Dr. Henderson had not forgotten her uncharacteristic fit at the beginning of his stay. They answered her questions, but peered at her sideways out of their eyes with suspicion.

"We are releasing him from the hospital, Mrs. Fisher, but Asher still needs lots of rest," Dr. Henderson said, looking at her over his glasses.

"Of course, doctor!" Abigail smiled at him. He did not look convinced.

"He shouldn't return to his normal activities until his legs have mended better. We are giving him crutches to walk on. He can't carry anything more than his backpack though. His right leg mended quickly, but both legs are still tender."

Abigail nodded, and flipped through the discharge paperwork that Beverly shoved into her hands.

"And his left arm is going to take even longer to heal than the legs. It was broken in two places. It's going to be several weeks before Asher can handle a power drill or do any kind of manual labor. Do you understand?" Beverly and Dr. Henderson both stared at her hard. Abigail's eyes grew large.

"I wouldn't dream of it!" She placed a delicate hand at her throat. "I'm no monster, after all."

In his bed, Ash rolled his eyes.

"I'll be okay, Dr. Henderson," Ash said to them. Beverly helped him up from the bed.

"You'd better be," Beverly whispered under her breath. Ash suppressed a laugh and leaned forward on the crutches.

"Can you walk on those?" Abigail asked, eyeing him as he teetered beside the bed.

"I've been practicing walking with them in the afternoons." Ash smiled at her as he gained his balance. "I'm not very fast though."

✦ ✦ ✦

After a happy goodbye to Beverly, and a slow awkward walk to the car, Ash finally left the hospital. During the car ride home, Abigail and Ash did not talk. Instead, he looked out the window and thought about Neveah. Would she come to the hospital and find his empty room?

Winter had begun settling in. The countryside was dead and brown. He thought, *this may be all there ever is for me.*

Abigail pulled into the driveway in front of their home. She turned off the engine, but didn't get out. Instead, she sighed and sat with her keys in her lap.

"I think I know what Elliot did."

"You do?"

"Maybe not the exact details, but I gathered that this accident was more or less his fault."

Ash didn't say anything. It was true. He hadn't given any thought to whether or not he would tell Abigail. It was unlikely that she would do anything about it. What *could* she do? Elliot was uncontrollable.

"If you want to stay in the house with us while you recover, I will let you. I don't know what he'll do though. It's up to you."

Abigail got out of the car and walked into the house. She didn't offer to help her injured step-son or send anyone else out to do the job. Ash thought for a moment about going into the house. He imagined that his treatment inside wouldn't improve.

"At least in my shed, I might get to talk to Neveah," Ash said, thinking of the walkie-talkie in his backpack. Decision made, he slowly made his way to his shed and slept the rest of the day away.

Neveah

Ruth had come and gone for the day, a swirl of dark hair and kind eyes. She had prodded Neveah through a grueling trigonometry lesson and a rigorous history lesson about the Peloponnesian Wars. Neveah was beginning to suspect that Ruth was purposely giving her more difficult work to distract her from her recent traumas.

It wasn't working. Between the letters and numbers on the page, Neveah saw drips of blood. When her gaze became unfocused, in her mind, she could see the words that had been scribbled on her mother's vanity mirror. It was a living nightmare, and she felt terrified all the time.

Not helping the matter, Ash had gone home. She no longer had the brief solace of her meetings with him. Neveah couldn't know for sure, but she felt certain that if only she could see him for a little while, her fears would ease.

They had spoken briefly over the walkie-talkie once. Ash struggled to stay awake and so she had kept her fears and troubles to herself.

"It won't be like this forever." That's what Ruth had said before she left for the day.

"What could she possibly know about it?" Neveah wondered. She had a hard time imagining Ruth being afraid of anything.

Neveah was standing in the stables holding a rope. She couldn't really remember walking to the stables. She didn't remember making the decision to go riding. Did anyone know where she was?

Sunbeam nudged her in the chest with her nose. Neveah dropped the rope and hugged her horse's large head. The tears came quickly, overwhelming her in a moment. Sunbeam snuffed, but otherwise made no movement.

Neveah didn't manage to saddle her horse and go for a ride. She had cried for an interminable amount of time, then brushed Sunbeam down and gone back inside the house.

Elliot could be out in the woods, and the thought of encountering him again made her skin crawl. Some instinctual part of her mind had accepted that Elliot had butchered the security guard, even though no one had said so. She had no proof, just a clenching in her gut that wouldn't let her believe anything else.

The long cry left Neveah worn out, like a wrung out washcloth. She entered the house and she leaned against the door jam. As she rested her head, her father stepped out of his office and saw her.

"I was just coming to talk to you." William tried to smile, but even as tired as she was, Neveah saw that it was forced.

She didn't answer him. Neveah simply nodded and followed him down the hallway and into the den. On the way, she saw her mother still sitting in her father's office, her back straight and tense.

Neveah collapsed on a heavily cushioned chair in the den, William stood at the fireplace with his back to her. Whatever he had to say, she sensed that he did not want to say it. Finally he turned to face her with another forced smile.

"Neveah, princess. You know how I've always protected you." William's hands uncharacteristically fidgeted for a moment. Neveah sat up a little straighter in her chair.

"Yes?" Neveah said, an eyebrow raising.

"Well, to that end, I've made certain arrangements for you. Things I don't want you to have to worry about." William became very still.

"Daddy, what do you mean?" Neveah felt a panic rising inside.

"I wanted to make sure that you are safe. That you will always be safe.
And to do that, I need someone who will look after you." William looked away. "Always."

"Someone to look after..." Neveah's voice trailed off.

"I've arranged for you to be married." William met her eyes and she saw fear there. "It's for your protection, dear."

Suddenly Neveah thought of the words written on her mother's vanity mirror: *Remember our agreement!* Then she thought of her mother and father arguing about a choice he had made about her and she understood.

Her father intended to marry her off to Elliot.

Neveah could hear a rushing in her ears that sounded like the room had suddenly filled with water. The last thing she saw before she blacked out was her father's eyes, still full of fear.

Elliot

"She didn't exactly take the news well." William's voice sounded agitated over the phone. Elliot smiled to himself.

"I'm sure it was a shock. She'll grow accustomed to me soon enough. You'll see."

"I'm not sure I wouldn't rather die than let this happen." William's voice was surly.

"You'd better decide fast. If you don't make this happen, you definitely will die. And your wife. And if it pleases me, Neveah too." Elliot hung up the phone and laughed to himself.

He rose from his bed and wandered down the hall to the kitchen. His triumph spiked his appetite and he rummaged through the cabinets for something to eat.

A footstep in the next room. Elliot turned in time to see his mother enter the kitchen. She saw him and then took a step back. Her expression had been the same as if she had found a dead mouse in the kitchen.

Elliot could not remember his mother ever recoiling from him like that.

He turned to face her.

"Yes, mother?" Elliot did not smile when he said this. Abigail suddenly looked old to him, older than he'd ever considered.

"Nothing, Elliot. Nothing at all," Abigail said, then practically ran away. Elliot heard her shut the door and listened with curiosity to the lock sliding in place. He took a few steps towards her and stopped. What would he say to her, even if she opened the door?

Elliot glanced his own reflection in the sliding glass doors and it startled him. Where his own reflection should be, instead he saw something *other*. Turning, he realized that his face was changed. The place where his mouth and nose met bulged outwards in a grotesque parody of an animal muzzle. His eyes had gone almost completely black.

Elliot's back crashed against the wall as he stumbled back in shock. His hands felt his face, felt the changes. It was as if he were touching someone else's face, or someone's...muzzle? His fingers went numb, his mind struggling to understand.

The Face pressed forward in his mind and he understood immediately what was happening. The Face was taking over. It was forcing its shape onto him.

Elliot felt his own form being pressed down and away. Rage surged up in his chest and he screamed.

The Face just laughed at him.

Elliot leapt forward and smashed the glass of the doors with his bare hands.

Several minutes later, Gerald came home to find his brother bloody and unconscious amidst a pile of glass. The back doors were smashed to pieces. Gingerly stepping around the mess, he walked down the hall to find his mother crying in her room behind a locked door.

"Mother?" Gerald tapped on the door.

"Is he gone? Elliot?" Abigail's voice wavered.

"He's passed out in the kitchen," Gerald said. The door cracked open an inch. His mother's eye appeared, mascara running.

"Did he look...wrong?"

"Well he was pretty banged up, if that's what you mean," Gerald said, his brow creasing.

"That's not what I meant," Abigail answered. Her one eye looked haunted and it gave Gerald the chills. "That's not what I meant at all."

Ash

Ash knew something was wrong with Neveah from their brief conversation after he got home. He fought and fought to keep his eyes open but knew he wouldn't last long. The next day he waited and waited until time.

He tried to do homework. Gilly had dropped off plenty of it for him over winter break. He desperately wanted to catch up in time for school to start. It didn't seem likely though. Every time he started reading his English notes or looking through his algebra II textbook, he started to nod off.

Part of the problem was his medication. Dr. Henderson had insisted on sending him home with painkillers and made him promise to take them for at least another two weeks. Ash admitted that the pain from so many broken bones was significant, but it had tapered off quite a lot since his ribs had healed. Still, a promise was a promise, so he took the prescribed pills every morning and again at dinnertime.

Dinnertime!

That first day, Ash had hobbled to his shed and expected to not see Abigail or his step-brothers again until he could walk normally and work. That evening, Gerald had shown up with a tray of food, including a dinner cooked by Abigail herself. Ash was shocked.

"Abby made me dinner?" Ash had asked, dumbfounded.

"Well, I definitely didn't do it!" Gerald had answered. He was surly, as usual. Ash no longer took this personally. As far as he could tell, Gerald was always surly.

"Tell her thank you," Ash said, taking the tray from Gerald and settling it beside him in bed.

"Tell her yourself, cripple!" Gerald left as quickly as he had come.

This night, the second night home, Ash wondered if he would get another tray of food. He had a box full of ramen noodles here in the shed, but Abby was a good cook. He would welcome more of her food.

Just as Ash was reaching for the walkie-talkie for the thousandth time, Gerald barged into his shed. The two boys looked at each other for a moment. Ash blushed, having been caught with the walkie. It was impossible for Gerald to know what it was for, but he was embarrassed all the same. Gerald only grimaced, set the tray down and left again.

He paused at the door. "She said, 'You're welcome.'"

Ash smiled to himself and happily ate a plate full of baked chicken and mashed potatoes.

As he shoveled mouthfuls of food, he kept glancing at the walkie, willing it to buzz. It was in this state, propped in bed with a mouthful of chicken and glaring at a walkie-talkie that he heard a soft knock on his door. His brow creased. Gerald didn't knock. Was Abby coming to check on him?

"Who is it?" He called, his mouth still full. It was Neveah. His eyes grew round and he tried to quickly swallow his food.

"Can I come in?" She asked. Her eyes were big and her voice wavered in a way that made his heart ache, though he couldn't say why exactly.

"Yes! Come in!" Ash said, ushering her forward with his hands. "I'm sorry it's such a mess in here. I can't get around very well yet."

Neveah walked forward and perched on the edge of his only chair. It reminded him immediately of her visits at the hospital. She didn't seem to notice the clutter in his room, the plate full of food beside him, or anything at all really.

"Is everything okay?" Ash asked, sitting up on the edge of the bed to face her. Neveah looked around as if searching for something. Her eyes finally met his and he saw that she was shaking.

"Neveah." He reached for her, then hesitated, afraid she might fly apart at any moment. "I've never seen you like this! What's going on?"

Instead of answering, she began crying. Great wracking sobs that shook her whole body. He scooped her up in his arms as naturally as he would a child, but then did not know what else to do. Ash felt an overwhelming need to *fix it*. He just didn't know what *it* was.

After a while, Neveah seemed to calm. Or maybe she simply couldn't cry anymore, he wasn't sure.

"Daddy wants me to marry Elliot," Neveah whispered, her face still pressed to his shirt. Ash felt a numbness wash through him. He could no longer feel her warmth next to him.

"What?" Ash asked, praying that he hadn't heard right.

"Daddy. Wants me. To marry. Elliot," Neveah said, enunciating the words slowly, painfully.

"How can he even do that?" Ash exploded. He was sitting on the edge of the bed, the next moment he was standing reaching out for his crutches.

"No one can make you get married! What a stupid! Ridiculous! Barbarian idea!" Ash was shouting and thumping one crutch. He turned and saw Neveah. She was sitting there, her shoulders curving inwards as if she were about to cave in on herself. She wasn't listening to him. She was probably beyond hearing. If he was angry, and -he could admit it- scared, what must she be feeling?

"Oh God. Neveah, I'm an idiot!" He leaned his crutches back against the wall and sat beside her.

"What do we do?" Ash asked.

"I don't know."

Neveah

After her father told her the news, Neveah passed out. When she woke up a few moments later, her mother was there, holding her hand. Jillian had waved her father away and insisted Neveah go upstairs and be left alone. Neveah had immediately slipped out of the house and gone to see Ash.

In that moment, she couldn't imagine talking to anyone else.

It turns out that she couldn't talk, even to him. After telling him the shocking news, they had sat in silence.

What do we do? Neveah kept remembering his words over and over again.

Neveah had finally regained enough wit to go home. It was only a matter of time before someone came to check on her. She had snuck back in the house and crawled into bed.

It was now three days later and she had not left her bed since except to take an occasional shower to clean off the sweat.

Every night she slept fitfully. Her dreams were filled with images of bodies swinging above her bed, and Elliot's slippery smile, his clammy hands reaching out for her. She would wake, crying out and sweating, but so, so cold.

Jillian stayed by her side often. She didn't say much, didn't ask much either. Neveah was glad. She had no idea what to say, no inclination to speak at all, but she also did not want to be alone. Her mother sat beside her, making notes in a notebook or looking up things on a laptop that she teetered on her knees. Jillian frequently checked her daughter for fever and urged her to eat, but otherwise made no demands.

It had been three days and Neveah had not seen her father in all that time.

❧ ❧ ❧

Neveah had been lightly dozing, imagining for once the simple pleasant feeling of riding her horse in the sunshine. Her eyes suddenly snapped open, her mind instantly wide awake.

"Daddy." Neveah's father was standing at the foot of her bed. She did not smile. She did not ask him to sit down. She simply stared at him, her gaze boring a hole through the center of his person.

"Princess," William started. He fidgeted like a schoolboy in the principal's office, a most peculiar sight in such a large man. "Sweetheart, how long are you going to stay in bed?"

Neveah glanced at her mother, who had gone as rigid as stone. Whatever decisions William had made, Jillian clearly did not support them.

Neveah didn't grace her father with an answer. She simply laid back down in bed and turned her face from him. Out of the corner of her eye, she could see him clenching and unclenching his fists.

"I know this has been a shock, sweetheart. I know. But we can't let little setbacks get us down." William's voice started to grow authoritative as he spoke. "We are of a different class than most people. We have to live with certain realities. Certain expectations. We have to carry on in the face of these...inconveniences."

"William, that's enough. She's just not ready," Jillian's voice cut in. Neveah closed her eyes and willed the tears to stay in, to not fall.

"She's going to have to face this eventually," William growled at her mother. "We all are."

Ash

Ash was beginning to settle into a rhythm with his new existence as a semi-invalid. He woke every morning groggy from the medicine and hauled his tired self into the shower. He struggled through as much homework as he could until lunchtime. Ash usually had some kind of cold lunch that had come with the dinner tray the night before. Then he slept.

Ash was sleeping a lot these days. That was a good thing. When the painkillers began to wear off, Ash couldn't sleep at all. Instead, he would lay in his bed, imagining the roof collapsing on him. He preferred to sleep.

Around 6 o'clock, Gerald would wander in with a tray of food, a whirlwind of brusqueness and frowns. Ash was amused by these brief daily exchanges with his step-brother. The two had barely spoken in all the years they had known each other and shared a family. While Ash's father was still alive, the two had had little to say to each other. When Nathan passed away and Ash moved to the shed, they became like strangers. But now Gerald was forced to look at and speak to Ash, and it appeared to unsettle him greatly.

At first, Gerald practically threw the food at Ash and rushed away. Now he lingered in the doorway, taking furtive glances at Ash's shed. Ash did not push him away, he held no particular ill-will against Gerald. The two boys circled each other like animals that first meet in the forest, wary and sniffing.

"So this is where you've lived all this time?" Gerald asked on the third night.

"Yup." Ash held a meatball on the end of his fork, waiting to see if Gerald would say more.

"It's not so bad here, though. Right?" Gerald's usual surliness faded just enough to show...was that worry on his face? Ash was surprised.

"It is what it is," Ash shrugged.

"What a stupid answer! What does that even mean?" Gerald stormed away without a backward glance.

Ash shrugged again and continued eating his spaghetti and meatballs.

✔ ✔ ✔

The evening was the hardest part of every day for Ash, and the best. He spent the first part of it resting his broken limbs, his fingers itching to hold the walkie-talkie. The waiting was miserable.

Every night, after the sun had set and most of the world had gone to bed, Neveah would pick up the walkie on her end and talk to him.

"Cinderfella are you there?" Neveah's voice sounded tired to Ash, as it had every night since her visit and the unsettling announcement from her father.

"Hello Rapunzel. How did today go?"

"Mother never leaves my side now. She almost followed me into the bathroom," Neveah whispered into the walkie. Ash smiled, imagining her rolling her eyes and making faces at her mother.

"She's just worried about you. I'm kind of worried too," Ash said. "I still can't believe your father is supporting this."

"I don't think he likes it. Not that it matters." Neveah's voice was flat.

"I wish there was something I could do," Ash said, as he did every time they spoke now. "Elliot. Of all the people... It's unthinkable."

"Nevermind that he wants me to marry at all? I'm only sixteen!" Neveah's voice took on more life, even if angry life.

"I know," Ash said with a groan. "You're right, of course. The whole thing is crazy. Who arranges a marriage for their teenage daughter these days?"

"I don't know what I will do, Ash," Neveah said, forgetting their codenames. "I won't marry him. I can't. I'll do anything to get out of it."

Elliot

Elliot was sitting outside of Ash's little shed and listening again.

"I won't marry him. I can't. I'll do anything to get out of it." Neveah's voice crackled, but Elliot heard her all the same.

Between his hands he held his old pocket knife. He crushed it, breaking the joint between the blade and handle, blood seeping between his fingers. He barely noticed the pain.

It was Ash. She might consider the arrangement, if only she had never been allowed this ridiculous attachment to Ash. Elliot felt his blood thumping in his ears.

He rose from his hiding place and ran into the woods. He would have to do something about his step-brother, something once and for all. But he needed a plan first! The trees whizzed by him in a blur as he ran faster and faster, the cool night air calming him. The movement of his body eased his tension.

After running all the way to the lake, he stopped on the end of the fishing pier, peering out at the moonlight where it touched the water's surface.

The Face pushed closer to him then. Instead of feeling an intrusion, Elliot felt solace in its company. The Face understood him. It hated things that interfered with its tricks as well. The Face soothed Elliot's mind with images of a village burning. The two of them closed their shared eyes and felt the glow of that long ago fire. They took comfort in it. Elliot could feel lives slipping away in the fire and this soothed him as well.

"We need a new trick," Elliot said to The Face. His mind turned away from the fire and he once again looked out at the lake. Elliot sat on the end of the pier, his feet dangling over the edge. As he thought, his thumbs drummed the wood underneath him. The Face twitched, an almost imperceptible motion that snapped Elliot out of his reverie. The Face turned, ever so slightly, but Elliot followed its gaze.

Elliot looked down. The pier? The Face smiled at him.

Yes. The pier.

Chapter Seven

Creek Woman

I do not know how Joseph had become so bonded with the wolf pack. There were some secrets he chose to keep. In time, I learned much about him and his past. Eking out a life in the woods had made him a hard man. However he still held much sincerity and kindness in his heart. He showed his appreciation to me in unspoken ways: material for a new dress, a copper bracelet bought from a passing wagon train, and once, a pendant he wove from the rushes in the stream. My trust in him deepened with time.

I do not remember making a conscious decision to reveal to him my unusual past. At different times, I simply told him stories. Over the years, he began piecing together the truth. Finally he realized that I had lived such a long life, and asked me why.

"I don't know. I never have," I said simply.

"I thought you might die, when I found you," Joseph said one evening. "Now I wonder if it's possible."

"I'm certain it's possible. I just don't know how. If I knew that, maybe I would know how to end Rabbit's long life as well," I answered, as I sewed a new shirt for James.

Joseph had trouble swallowing the notion that a rabbit could cause so much trouble. He caught them all of the time in his traps and traded their furs for the goods we needed. I explained to him that this was no ordinary rabbit. It was The Rabbit, an entity of power and spirit.

"And are you one of those entities?" He asked, he had paused in cleaning his rifle.

"Maybe," I answered. It was the most honest answer I could give.

One winter day, Joseph came home, his cheeks red from the cold, but otherwise as white as the snow on the ground. "Please come!" He called to me, taking my coat and wrapping it around my shoulders. Together we rode his horse into the woods, little James bouncing between us.

There, amongst the trees, was the leader of his wolf pack. He was a large male with golden eyes. The tawny fur of his muzzle was red with another animal's blood, but the rest of his body was red with his own.

"Can you help him?" Joseph asked. I put my hands to the poor creature's body and willed what life I could into him. I did not know if I could save the creature, did not know if it was within me to heal another. But Joseph had saved me when this creature found me in the snow. I was determined to try to save the wolf now.

We were there for a long time. Poor James grew tired and cold, and cried to go home. Joseph did what he could to calm the rest of pack as they paced restlessly nearby. I wanted so much to save this beautiful animal, but knew in my heart that it wasn't working. Finally the sun dipped below the horizon, and it was beyond a doubt. The wolf was dead.

"What happened here?" I asked Joseph, as we returned to our home, heartsick.

"The wolves were tricked somehow." He answered. "His tail was tied to a horse, and he was dragged through the woods and over rocks on his back. I don't know how far, but enough to do the damage you saw." Anger and sorrow warred in his voice.

"Who would do such a thing?" I wondered aloud. James was asleep in my arms and I held him closer. "And why?"

I didn't have to wait long for the answer. The answer was waiting on our doorstep.

Rabbit.

Ash

Ash could finally trade his heavy duty painkillers for an over the counter one, which cleared his mind significantly. He no longer felt the urge to sleep all day long. The downside to this change was that he was restless with spending so much time in his shed. And the normal sounds of the shed creaking in the wind were unbearable. Every noise made him start, afraid that it would all come falling in on him.

Gerald still came by every evening with a tray full of food. At first, they exchanged the briefest of words. As the days pushed on, Gerald began to linger longer and longer until now he passed a companionable hour with Ash.

Ash was pleasantly surprised to learn that his step-brother was not constantly surly. It only seemed that way.

"It's Elliot," Gerald said one grey and rainy evening. "I know how he is. I know what he does. But he's my brother. I love him."

"I can understand that," Ash said, spooning chicken tortilla soup into his mouth. He just couldn't get full these days! "Family is important."

"Is it?" Gerald asked. "It seems like it is for other people. But with Elliot, I don't know. I don't think that kind of thing matters to him."

"Surely he loves you? He's your brother, he must," Ash asked, pausing his spoon midway to his mouth.

"I know how he treats you. I've seen it over the years. And he doesn't do the same things to me that he does to you, or to other people. He treats me differently even than he does Mom. But love me? I don't know if he knows how."

Ash did not know how to respond to that.

"And he's getting worse. That's what really bothers me," Gerald said. "Just a few days ago, I came home and he'd broken the back door to pieces. He was bloody, passed out. He couldn't even remember doing it."

"Good grief," Ash muttered. "There's no telling how much force it would have taken to break that door, you know."

"Yeah, well he sure scared the hell out of Mom," Gerald nodded. "She was crying in her bedroom when I came home. She said his face changed somehow. She said his eyes went all black like an animal. That's crazy, right? No one could do something like that."

And so Ash began to understand that Gerald wasn't surly, he was worried. Gerald was worried that his small family was going insane.

Ash could understand his concerns. Elliot wasn't like other people even at the best of times. Abigail wasn't much like other people either.

The other detail of his new life was that in the mornings, Creature visited him. Like always, she showed up one morning without warning and woke him up by kneading her paws on his chest as if he were a human cat toy.

"Ow!" Ash said, waking with a start.

"Oh sorry." The cat did not sound sorry. Ash rubbed his chest with one hand and propped himself up with the other. "How long have you been here?"

"Not long." She was sitting primly beside him on the bed, expectantly.

"What is it?"

"Oh nothing."

"You look like you want something. Like you expect something." Ash said, frowning at her. Her tail twitched ever so slightly.

"No. Not really." If her eyes were lasers, they would have born a hole through Ash.

"Are you sure?"

"Yes."

"Okay." Ash reached for his shirt and started heating up his breakfast. Creature followed him to his microwave and watched the plate spin around.

"Are you hungry?" Ash asked.

"Well, if you're offering, I suppose I could eat."

Ash cut part of his sausage and eggs and set it on another plate for her. She attacked it as if it were still alive, and the food was gone in a moment.

"You could have just asked, you know," Ash said between mouthfuls of food.

"I'm not sure you understand what it means to be a cat."

And ever since, she had been there, sharing his breakfast.

Neveah

Three days turned into two weeks and Neveah had barely left her bed. Jillian still kept vigil for most of the day, watching over her daughter with a peculiar mix of cold disinterest and loving attentiveness. At times she sat making notes on her notebook and typing on her laptop for hours without so much as a glance at Neveah. Other times, she sat at her bedside and held her hand, ordering a variety of foods to tempt her into eating more. Neveah had no idea what she was working on so diligently, and Jillian didn't offer to explain. Neveah was too tired to care, so instead she laid quietly in her bed and tried to think about anything except her life. A great aching hollowness had filled her, and it was the only thing she seemed to feel other than fear.

Ruth had returned as well. After postponing her lessons for a few days, Jillian decided it was best to return to life as normal. Or as normal as they could manage. From her bed, Neveah listened to Ruth read from books about Native American history, looked at flowcharts about the Krebs cycle for plants, and watched a movie about the origins of e=mc², among other things. Ruth patiently doled out knowledge, seeming undaunted by her pupil's lack of response. Every day, she finished her lessons the same way. She would put her materials in her bag, sweep her black hair over her shoulders and say:

"I'll be back in the morning, and I hope to find you restored."

Neveah never spoke aloud, but in her heart she said, "Me too."

How long could this go on? Neveah wondered it often. She would decide to get out of bed, to speak, to do her homework, to *do anything*. Then she would think of her father marrying her off to Elliot, she would think of Elliot's slippery smile and then she could no longer do anything except cry.

What did Jillian think of this? Neveah assumed her mother was unhappy with it by the way her back went as rigid as a wall when her father came to her room. She didn't seem to be speaking any more than Neveah where her father was concerned. But would Jillian really agree to marry her to Elliot? Neveah just couldn't understand how things had come to this.

A body swinging over the bed. Words written in blood.

Neveah squeezed her eyes shut. Fear. That's how all of this was happening. Elliot had threatened her parents in a way they never imagined. And to quiet the beast, they were giving him their daughter. It was shocking, but true. Neveah couldn't accept it, and so she continued to lay in her bed, praying that she would wake up to a new world where this wasn't true anymore.

❧ ❧ ❧

Ruth was reading aloud an account from Ponce de Leon's search for the Fountain of Youth, when Jillian stepped out of the room unexpectedly. The door to Neveah's room closed and Ruth closed the book in her lap. Neveah said nothing.

"I know you've been given a great shock," Ruth said, her eyes meeting Neveah's. "I know you feel tired and as if you cannot bear the future. But you must carry on, little one."

Ruth leaned forward and squeezed Neveah's hand.

"You've been handed a great burden. Sometimes, when we face these burdens, we find unexpected opportunities for joy. Try to remember that."

She opened the book and began reading again. Only a moment later, Jillian stepped back into the room. Ruth was reading as if she had never stopped.

Neveah thought about her words for the rest of the day and night. Was it really true? What joy could she possibly have from this?

That night Neveah had a dream. In the dream she was being fitted for a dress. The same seamstress her mother always called on was there, pinning the hem, her mouth full of pins. Jillian directed her to pin it higher in the front, and the woman crawled around to do so.

230

Neveah could see herself in a large standing mirror. The dress was full and beautiful, fit for a wedding. Looking at her own face, she saw that she was gaunt and sickly. Her hair was limp and dull.

"Mother, I can't get married like this," Neveah said. Jillian did not respond, did not even look up. She tried to turn, but couldn't because of the heavy dress.

"Mother…" Neveah said again, still no response. She looked at herself in the mirror again and saw that she was fading away. Her hands were already gone, her arms turning translucent.

"Mother!" Neveah cried out.

But it was too late, she was already gone.

The dress stood alone and empty, and no one noticed at all.

Neveah woke up plastered in sweat and breathing hard. Is that how her life was going to be? She was just an item to be bartered off by her parents? For the first time, Neveah felt something other than fear or a dull hollowness. She threw back the blankets and walked to her bathroom.

Neveah looked in the mirror to reassure herself that she wasn't actually fading away. She looked terrible. Neveah's skin was pale, her hair limp and dull, much like in the dream. Her nightgown hung from her skinny shoulders without any shape. Feeling her abdomen, she realized she'd lost weight.

"I can't keep going like this," Neveah said to herself. She turned on the shower and let the water get as hot as she could stand. Looking down, her fingers and toes were turning pink under the heat. Steam slowly built up until it was billowing out of the shower. She didn't care. It felt good to just *feel* something. Something other than fear or numbness.

"Unexpected opportunities for joy," Neveah whispered it to herself.

Elliot

Elliot waited in the den, a fire already going on the hearth. He eyed the decanter of liquor on the side table and decided to help himself to a glass. Elliot didn't particularly care to drink. He already lost enough time from his memory without the help of an alcoholic blackout. It was the kind of thing that William associated with manhood though. Elliot was swirling the stuff in his glass when William stepped into the den, calm and collected as a mountain in a snowstorm.

"Elliot. I wasn't expecting you until later." William poured himself a glass without commenting on Elliot's. They both knew he was underage. William had more pressing concerns.

"I know. I was in the neighborhood though." The two of them sat, peering at each other across their glasses as predators in the wild might.

"Is that so?" William raised an eyebrow. They both knew what he meant. He'd been snooping around the house again.

"I wanted to see how things were progressing here. Has she been told yet?"

"She has." Elliot was impressed to see William say this without any outward signs of distress.

"And when will she be mine?" Elliot set down his glass and leaned forward, steepling his fingers. William went still.

"In due time. She's quite young still." William set his own glass aside and straightened his blazer. "Too young to be married off yet. When she is eighteen, we can discuss it again."

Elliot smiled. "You're stalling."

"I don't think it's an unreasonable decision. She's only sixteen. No one would understand the decision to let her wed this young."

"I don't particularly care about weddings. I just want her," Elliot said. He rose from his seat and stood next to the fireplace. He turned so that he was looking down at William in his chair. "I know what this is really about. You think that if you delay this, that you will be able to avoid it altogether. You'll try to have me killed."

William did not try to deny it. He merely picked up his glass again and smiled.

"Didn't we already see how that went, William?" Elliot smiled back. The Face pressed forward, and Elliot fought to push it back again. *Not now!*

"There are others, you know. I have many contacts."

"William, you know as well as I do, none of them will matter. Do you really want your wife to wake up to another body in the bedroom? Maybe next time I'll put it in bed with her. Or maybe I'll put the next one in Neveah's room and watch it drip blood on her sheets.

What do you think?" Elliot leaned in close to William, pressing his smiling face into William's.

At first, William was silent, his face stony. "No, I don't want that."

"Then we have an understanding." Elliot leaned back, folding his hands behind his back.

"What are your terms?" William asked. He had trouble spitting out the words.

"Soon. I want her soon. If I have to marry her to ease your sense of nobility, fine. I don't care. But no more delays."

Ash

Ash was certain that he was getting his strength back. He no longer needed crutches for navigating around his small home, and had begun exercising when he could. At first, the awkward push-ups with his cast were too painful. Now he could manage them with almost no pain. His legs hurt him less every day. He had fewer and fewer headaches. It wasn't going to be long until he could go back to school.

It wasn't going to be long until he'd have to start working again.

Ash sighed. He hadn't heard from Neveah in days either.

"She'll contact you when she can," the cat told him that morning again.

"Do you hang out at her house too?" Ash asked, picking up a sandwich to eat. His appetite was insatiable.

"In a manner of speaking." The black cat seemed to smile then.

"What's your deal anyway?" Ash asked, tearing off a corner of the sandwich and putting in front of her to eat. "Do you have a house or something? A family?"

"I have a home, just like anyone else. It's not somewhere you can find though. And I suppose you are my family."

"Me?"

"I am inextricably linked to your family line. Do you think that happened without my involvement with one of your ancestors?" Her expression was very human and uncat-like at that moment.

"Involvement? You were, like... 'involved' with one of my ancestors?" Ash used air quotes, suggestion heavy in his tone.

The cat laughed. "Not like you are suggesting, but yes. We were close. I helped raise his son."

Ash paused. "So did you love him?"

She didn't answer at first. "Yes." She stopped talking and instead ate the sandwich. Ash thought he understood a little.

"It's hard. Losing people you love," he said. She didn't answer, which was answer enough for him.

There was a knock on the door. Ash turned to look.

When he looked back, the cat was already gone.

"Come in!" Ash said.

Abigail pushed open the door.

"You have a doctor's appointment today. I need you to get ready." She glanced around the shed. "Do you need anything?"

"I need to do some laundry," Ash answered. "Do you think you or Gerald could help me carry it in? I don't know if I can walk that far without crutches."

Abigail shrugged and left. Taking that as a yes, Ash started gathering his dirty laundry up and stuffing it into a linen bag. In a matter of moments, Gerald was there.

"Do you think the cast will come off today?" He asked without preamble.

"No idea. It would be nice to have my arm back though." Ash handed him the linen bag and grabbed his crutches. Gerald threw the bag over his shoulder and held the door open for Ash.

The sunlight hit his face and Ash realized he hadn't been outside in days.

"Oh man, the fresh air feels good!" Ash said.

"Yeah, you need to get out of there more. Between me and you, your room's getting a little...aromatic," Gerald said. Ash laughed, and Gerald smiled. Ash was beginning to like this new step-brother. He hoped this would continue even after he healed from his injuries but assumed nothing.

➹ ➹ ➹

A few hours later, Ash was getting his cast removed. The same nurse and doctor helped him, asking pointed questions about his recovery as they went.

"Are you working?" Dr. Henderson asked, looking at Ash over the cast.

"I already told you he wasn't!" Abigail said. Dr. Henderson waited for Ash to answer.

"I haven't done any work," he answered, nodding. "Truly."

"Good." Dr. Henderson inspected Ash's arm and made some notes on his clipboard. "I'm sending you home with a sling and a brace. You can go back to school now. I think you need to wait a while longer before returning to manual labor though." He looked at Abigail as he said the last part. She smoldered in her chair but said nothing.

"Thank you, Dr.," Ash said, smothering a smile.

⤲ ⤲ ⤲

Back in the car, Abigail sneered at Ash.

"I don't care what he says. In two weeks, you're going back to work. You look fine to me!"

Ash didn't argue. He was glad for the two weeks. When they pulled up in the driveway, Gerald was there waiting.

"Thought I'd help Ash back to his shed," Gerald said to his mother when they got out of the car. Abigail sniffed delicately and walked into the house alone.

"I'm going to pay for that later!" Gerald said with a smile.

"Don't get yourself in trouble for my sake," Ash said.

"Eh," Gerald said, shrugging. "It keeps things interesting. Besides, she doesn't do much to me. I'm not her problem child."

"I thought I was, all this time," Ash said.

"You? No. It's Elliot." Gerald pushed open the door to Ash's shed. "He's always causing-" Gerald stopped short.

"Oh."

It was Neveah. She was sitting on Ash's bed, waiting. Ash, Gerald and Neveah looked at each other awkwardly.

"I can go...I'm sorry!" Neveah said, shooting to her feet. Her camera fell out of her lap, clattering onto the floor. She stooped to scoop it back up. "Oh..."

"No. I'll go," Gerald said. He looked at Ash and winked. "He probably wants to see you more than me!"

Ash and Neveah both blushed, making Gerald laugh as he walked away. Ash came inside and pulled the door shut. Then he remembered Gerald's comment about his room, and propped the door back open.

"I'm so sorry!" Neveah's hands were on her cheeks. "I just came over here and I didn't think you'd be gone long, so I waited. I didn't think! Oh my gosh!"

"It's ok! I don't think Gerald will say anything to anyone." He took Neveah's hands in his own. "Don't worry."

Neveah's cheeks were still red, but she seemed to calm some.

"I'm surprised to see you though. I haven't heard from you in ages!" Ash said, hoping that changing the subject would ease her embarrassment.

"I know!" Neveah said in her animated way. "Mother has hardly left my side all of this time. I've...oh Ash, it's been a terrible time! This is the first time I've been out of bed, much less out of my room, in days!"

Ash nudged his bag of clean laundry to one side and settled down on his one chair. "I've been worried about you. I thought you might have run away."

"No. Nothing so brave." Neveah sat across from him on the bed. She took a deep breath. "But I've decided that I can't just sit around and wait for someone to climb up my hair and save me. I've got to do something!"

"Climb...your hair? Is that likely to happen?"

"Umm...it's sort of a metaphor...it means...oh it doesn't matter! What matters is that I snuck out to see you because I didn't know who else to talk to and I've missed you so much! I can't believe we haven't spoken in almost two weeks and-" Neveah stopped and blushed again. Ash smiled.

"I've missed you too."

There was that moment again. Should he kiss her? Hug her? High five her? Ash didn't know. His anxiety overwhelmed him for a moment. He knew he should say something, say anything.

Say something! Say-

"My cat talks!"

"What?"

Not that! Ash cringed. "My cat...talks. Yeah, I said that, didn't I?" He shrugged. *Too late to take it back now!* "Yeah, she talks. It's true. I'm not crazy."

"I didn't know you had a cat," Neveah said, looking around. Looking for the cat, Ash assumed.

"Well, she's not *my* cat, I guess. She's a cat that I know. She's...I don't think a talking cat can belong to anyone."

"Oh Ash. You've really stepped in it this time, haven't you?" said a voice from the window.

The cat in question was sitting on his windowsill. A window, Ash had sworn he had closed and locked. He heaved out a great sigh of relief. If Neveah heard the cat talk, he definitely wasn't crazy.

Neveah had gone still as a cornered rabbit. She was staring at the cat.

"You get used to it after a while," Ash said, gesturing to the cat.

"What do I say to the cat?" Neveah whispered, leaning toward Ash.

"Whatever you want, child," the cat answered. "It's not like you don't know me. We've gone on many walks together, if you'll recall."

"Midnight!" Neveah squealed. "It is you!" Neveah scooped the cat into her arms and nuzzled her face against the animal's dark coat.

"Oh wait! Is that rude for me to do?" Neveah asked, looking down at the feline in her arms.

"I suppose not. I'm still a cat for now."

"For now?" Neveah asked.

"Don't ask." Ash answered.

Neveah

"Don't ask." Ash said.

Neveah had expected a lot of things on her way to Ash's house, but the possibility of a talking cat had not made that list. Midnight jumped down from Neveah's arms and settled herself on Ash's bed.

"Actually, children, I believe it is time I told you both some things," Midnight said.

"Really? Now?" Ash said, his eyebrows raising. "After I've asked you a million times! *Now* is the time?"

"Would you like me to wait some more?" Midnight answered. Her tone of voice sounded so familiar to Neveah.

"No. I wouldn't," Ash said, on the verge of a pout. "Please tell me things."

Midnight smiled. Neveah had never known a cat to smile. Suddenly she remembered the black cat perched in the window of the hospital.

"That was you!" Neveah pointed.

"Probably. Yes," Midnight answered.

"In the hospital! You were waiting in the window every time I visited Ash!" Neveah kept talking, the words tumbling out of her mouth. "And, and it was you who led me to Ash in the first place!"

"It was?" Ash asked.

"And it was you...you...how do you know us? Why did you bring me to Ash? What's going on?" Neveah was still pointing and Ash was still frowning. Midnight seemed completely unperturbed.

"The two of you are linked in a most peculiar way. You were bound to meet eventually. I just sped things along. Before it was too late."

"Too late? What do you mean?" Ash asked.

"Rabbit. I think I have found him!" Midnight's form began to shift. It was so subtle that Neveah could hardly say when it started. Then suddenly, her tutor, Ruth was sitting on Ash's bed, eyes gleaming. "It's Elliot! He's Rabbit!"

Suddenly Ash and Neveah were both standing and shouting.

"Ruth!" Neveah shouted.

"Elliot?" Ash shouted.

Ruth said nothing but smiled at them both. "Yes."

Neveah looked at Ash. "This is my tutor, Ruth!"

"Well, she was my cat first!" Ash answered.

"And many other things and people even before that. Now sit down, both of you," Ruth said.

They sat. Ruth straightened her long skirt around her.

"One time in a movie I saw, this character could shape shift, but not her clothes. So every time she changed back to a human, she was naked," Neveah said in a rush. Ash and Ruth both looked at her, blinking.

"I'm sorry. I'm very nervous," Neveah said. Ruth smiled at her.

"I'm still the same person, little one."

"This at least explains why you talk," Ash said. "But please tell me. You think Elliot is a rabbit?"

"In a manner of speaking, yes. I believe Rabbit resides *inside* Elliot."

"There's a rabbit living inside of Elliot? What on earth does that mean?" Neveah said.

"You've got some catching up to do," Ash said and took a deep breath. "I'm cursed. Apparently, my whole family is. I can't leave this county."

"What? That's silly! Curses aren't real!" Neveah said. She waved a hand as if to say *you can't fool me!*

Ruth and Ash stared at her.

"Okay, I guess I did just see a cat turn into a person," Neveah said. "But, a curse? Really?"

"Believe me, I thought the same thing. But I can prove it."

"I believe it might be beneficial if I just began at the beginning. I will tell you a story, children," Ruth began. *"My story began long before all of this happened..."*

Elliot

Elliot knew that the gaps were growing. He couldn't remember whole days now. He pressed the worry down and tried to focus. He was holding a length of rope, and standing on the long fishing pier at the lake. Why was he there? What was the rope for?

Elliot felt The Face's presence looming in the back of his mind, subdued for now. He knew it would not last long. Elliot remembered going to see William, confronting the man, but did not remember leaving. He could remember setting a few traps in the forest, idly wasting some time, but not coming home or going to school the next day.

The Face and Elliot had been working together to devise a new trick. It was hard work. The Face had played so many tricks in its long life. And sometimes, Elliot got the nagging feeling that working so hard on a new trick was a waste of time. Would The Face really go along with one of his ideas? It seemed to want control of their body more than his cooperation. Still, he stayed awake at night trying to devise new ways to capture a person.

He turned and headed home. Elliot was so very tired. He wondered what The Face had been doing since his last memory. It was a long walk home, and he tried to remember as much as he could. William was furious with him. He thought about his long-time mentor, and felt a twinge. He might never have a friend again now. The Face laughed at him. Had The Face played a trick on him? Elliot was so tired, he was no longer sure.

He finally reached his own backyard, and spotted Gerald walking ahead of him.

"Little brother," Elliot said, without the usual smile and chuckle though. Gerald turned and looked at him.

"Where have you been?" He asked. Elliot did not answer. He didn't know, did he?

"Have you been visiting our invalid?" Elliot asked, gesturing towards Ash's shed.

"Yeah, just helping out a little," Gerald answered, his voice carefully neutral. Elliot saw his mouth begin to quirk up in a smile though.

"You're becoming friendly with him, aren't you?" Elliot stopped. Gerald stopped to look back at him.

"He is our brother, after all." Gerald turned to continue on to the house. Elliot felt an icy chill fall over his body. He looked back towards the shed. Gerald was befriending Ash now?

Elliot thought about the long conversations he'd overheard between Ash and Neveah. She clearly favored him. Then Elliot imagined Gerald having long conversations with Ash. Would he favor Ash over Elliot as well? The idea seemed unbearable. His hands felt cold, and his mind reeled. The Face seemed to watch with amusement.

"Elliot? Are you coming?" It was Gerald. He was holding the door open. There was concern written across his face.

Elliot realized that Gerald loved him. He would probably love Elliot no matter what. Elliot did not understand this, but believed it.

"Coming." He stepped through the doorway. Gerald regarded Elliot with an open curiosity.

"Are you okay?"

"Fine, little brother," Elliot smiled. Elliot patted his brother's shoulder, a rare contact between the two of them. Gerald met his eyes and seemed to search there for something. "I'm still me."

"Yes, I see," Gerald said, his mouth firming at the corners. "You're still you."

Elliot went to his room and collapsed on his bed. The fatigue was overwhelming him, something he rarely felt. In all the years he had shared his body with The Face, he was almost never tired, or even sleepy. It was peculiar. Others were not this way, he knew. He always viewed it as another advantage of sharing with The Face. Now he wondered if any of the advantages were real advantages at all. Maybe he'd been the victim of one of The Face's tricks all these years and was only now realizing it.

The Face was quiet and still in his mind.

"What are you?" Elliot asked aloud. The Face withdrew further. Elliot had tried to figure it out a number of times over the years, but with no luck. He suspected that The Face was not human. When it pressed close it seemed to have a muzzle, and black eyes with no whites. Elliot couldn't be sure what The Face was, and it didn't want him to know.

One thing was certain, The Face was very, very old. Elliot could sometimes feel the heavy weight of its years. What could live that long, though? His tired mind probed The Face again. It seemed to twist and turn away. Elliot pushed harder.

The Face lashed out, Elliot saw teeth and heard a scream within his mind.

"Elliot, are you okay?" Gerald was in the doorway. Elliot realized he was sitting bolt upright in bed, sweating as if he'd run a marathon. He looked down at himself, his hands were buried in the blankets of his bed.

"I'm..." Elliot was at a loss for words.

"You screamed." Gerald was white, his face as pale as the day they had drug Elliot out of the lake. "I've never heard you scream like that."

"I don't know." For once, not smiling or scheming, Elliot felt something. He was afraid.

Gerald stepped closer, slowly as if approaching a spooked horse. He crouched in front of his brother, his face still pale, but his brow determined.

"Whatever has happened to you. Whatever changed you. Let me help you, brother," Gerald paused. "You've always been different, but it wasn't always like this."

Elliot searched his brother's eyes and wished for the first time that he could explain his peculiar situation.

But he could not.

The Face pressed close to him then. It pushed and pushed until it was viewing Gerald through his eyes. Elliot tried to push back, beads of sweat popping out on his forehead from the effort. Gerald watched the struggle on his face with growing concern.

Elliot felt that he was losing the battle. Any moment, and he would blackout.

"Get out!" Elliot roared. Gerald fell back on his bottom from the sudden shout. He scrambled to his feet and ran from the room.

Elliot saw his brother leave and surrendered to the darkness.

Neveah

Neveah walked home, her head reeling. Ruth, her tutor, was actually a ...a what? Three-hundred-year old Native American woman? Older even? And she was apparently magic.

"Magic is real." Neveah whispered to herself. The absurdity of it overwhelmed her for a moment and she stood in the field and laughed. She laughed and laughed until tears came to her eyes.

Then she was crying.

"Elliot is possessed by some old Native American legend." She wiped tears from her eyes and tried to calm herself. She had crumpled like a wad of paper in the field. "I'm going to marry a monster."

She looked around and realized it was getting dark. She had stayed far too long and knew her mother would want to know where she had been. It didn't matter.

The numbness of the previous days crept back into her body.

"If I just never got up, would anyone even notice?" She thought about what would happen. How long before her family began looking for her? How long before they would even think to go outside. And then where would they look? In the stables, of course. But after that?

She shook her head. It benefitted no one, herself included, to lay shivering in a field half the night. They would find her eventually. And she would still have to marry...

"A monster." She said it again and again.

One step after another, she finally made it home. She sat in the doorway and rested for a moment. She could not believe how tired she was.

Suddenly the door behind her opened.

"There you are!" It was Jillian, her mother. "I've been looking everywhere for you. Where have you been?"

Neveah tilted her head up to look at her mother. She shrugged.

"Out."

Jillian pulled her to her feet. "Come inside. You need to eat something."

"Is that why I'm so tired?" Neveah meant it sarcastically.

"You've barely eaten in days. Yes, it's why you're so tired." Jillian had not noticed the sarcasm. She towed Neveah along, half dragging her down the hallway and sat her in a stool by the kitchen island. Jillian made a sandwich herself, waving away Harry, the chef.

"Eat this. Eat all of it."

Neveah made a face, but she took a bite anyway. She didn't care if she ate or not. It seemed to make her mother happy though. She took another bite, chewing mechanically.

"There you two are!" William said. He burst into the room. For the first time, Neveah was immune to his enormous presence. Neveah and Jillian both eyed him with suspicion.

"Why are you so happy?" Neveah was in a blunt mood and did not want to have to guess what he was up to.

William frowned. He still wasn't used to this new Neveah that felt nothing.

"I have good news." He pressed on, ignoring the icy stares of his wife and daughter. "There's going to be a party!"

"A party?" Jillian asked. "Who's party? Is now really the time for attending social events?"

"My dear, it will be Neveah's party!" Neveah stopped chewing the food in her mouth. It suddenly tasted of iron.

"What?" Jillian was shaking her head, as if to clear it.

"To announce her engagement, of course!"

Neveah spat the food from her mouth. She looked down and saw that blood was there.

"Neveah!" Jillian shouted. "You're bleeding!" Her hands went to her daughter's face, searching for the source of the blood. William went pale. He fumbled through a drawer looking for a towel or napkin.

Neveah ignored it all. All she could think about was marrying *him*.

She imagined for a moment the life set out before her. Neveah could see it unfold like a short film. The social engagements, the big house, the elaborate dresses. And behind all of that, the lonely nights, the empty days, the wondering what her husband was doing and worrying, always worrying. Even an optimistic view of that future with a monster like Elliot left her turning out exactly like her mother: cold, unhappy, alone. An un-optimistic view of life with someone like Elliot left her insides quivering. It assumed she would have a "life" with Elliot. He might just murder her on their wedding night.

Neveah felt a great breaking inside herself. It was as if her whole being shook and shattered apart.

"No."

It was a whisper, but William and Jillian both stilled all the same. Jillian's hand hovered near Neveah's face, napkin in hand.

"Excuse me?" William sounded as if he hadn't quite heard her.

"No," Neveah said it louder this time. She was dimly aware that the tea towel in her father's hand was shaking.

"Neveah..."

"No. I will not marry him." Neveah looked her father in the eye and dared him to argue with her. She had never stood up to him.

William did not say anything.

Neveah left her parents, blood from her bitten tongue still dripping from her mouth.

Chapter Eight

Creek Woman

In the days following the wolf's death, Joseph was transformed by his wrath. He swore vengeance on Rabbit, as I had done so many years before. I could not condemn his actions, because I had walked this same path. I knew that no reason would reach him. He must follow it to its bloody conclusion himself.

As a woman of my particular abilities, I went into the woods and did what I could to protect us, protect James, and the rest of the wolves. I had little I could do against Rabbit though.

I believe that Joseph knew this, too. Soon he packed for a long trip. He left to find the Osage tribe of his wife. He was looking for answers. I could not give him the answers he needed, and sent him with my blessing and a travel sack full of food and gifts for the elders. James and I stayed behind and hoped that he would return to us a restored man.

Joseph returned one day in early spring. He seemed changed again. He was resolved, somehow. I wondered what that would mean for us.

"Did you find the answers you were looking for?" I asked him, that first night.

"Yes," he said, looking into the fire. "But I did not like to hear them."

He spent the next few days with James, playing in the forest. I could hear their laughter even from where I sat in front of the house. I closed my eyes and hoped that this meant things were returned as they should be.

Then one night, after James was asleep, he took me aside.

"I want you to know that I love you." Joseph's eyes were serious as they looked into mine. "My heart will always belong to my wife, even though she is long gone. I think you understand that better than anyone. It doesn't mean that I don't love you still. You have been a better mother to James than I could have ever hoped for. You are strong and beautiful and I only hope that I have made you happy while you were here with us."

I had lived long enough that I knew what this meant. Joseph was saying goodbye. Then I realized why he had spent so much time with James. He believed he was leaving his son as well. I cried. I cried like I had not cried since Big Man-Eater's death. I cried more than when I left my tribe behind, more than when I left my homeland behind, more even than when I believed I would die alone in a cave.

"Please don't do whatever you are about to do, Joseph. James still needs you. I still need you!" I begged. "Whatever you believe you will gain, it is not worth losing your life with your family!" But I could see in his eyes that he had already made up his mind.

"Please, swear to me that you will take care of James," he asked, heart in his voice. "It is the only thing that gives me peace."

I swore to him.

The next day, Joseph went into the woods alone. I put James to sleep, made sure that he would not wake up until I returned for him and went to confront Joseph. I followed him. He was a good woodsman, but I had ways to conceal my presence. He trekked deep into the woods. The wolves followed closely behind. I trailed further behind so the wolves would not catch my scent.

I was too late. Joseph had performed a blood ritual. It must have been taught to him by the Osage elders. I had never seen such a thing before and did not understand what he meant to accomplish. When I caught up to him, his blood was spread everywhere. It was a mortal wound, I knew instantly.

He was barely conscious. I held him in my arms.

"Why, Joseph? Why do this?"

"For you. For my wolves. For James. For my wife. I think he killed her. I think Rabbit killed my wife. I've killed so many rabbits over the years. Other animals too." He coughed, blood sputtering out of his lungs and out of his mouth. I could feel the life force leaving his body. "But Rabbit has been trapped. I'm a trapper, so it seemed right. Rabbit can never leave here now. I did what I had to do. Please, please take care of James. Tell him that I loved him. Tell him that I always will."

It was not until much later that I learned that Joseph had trapped James too. The binding of his blood to the land meant that none of his descendants could leave any more than Rabbit could. They were all trapped. And as long as his line lived, Rabbit would seek vengeance for this act. And as long as his line lived, I would protect them.

Neveah

William was undeterred. He carried on making plans for the engagement party. Jillian and Neveah both refused to help him plan it and for the first time in his life he was forced to plan a delicate social engagement alone. Neveah went through each day with the usual routine, largely ignoring him.

"This princess isn't marrying anyone," Neveah whispered as she passed her father in the hallway. Her father's footsteps paused, but she continued on.

Ruth was waiting in the front parlor today for their tutoring. It was the first time they had seen each other since Ruth had revealed her identity to Neveah.

"So do we just keep tutoring like usual, now that I know you're a cat?" Neveah asked. "Well, not exactly a cat. But that sometimes you're a cat?"

"That I am sometimes a cat has no bearing on your education, little one," Ruth answered, setting out the usual books and papers from her bag. Neveah settled in the chair next to her with a sigh.

"He still wants me to marry Elliot," Neveah said, looking over her shoulder to the empty doorway. Ruth would know who she meant.

"Dear girl, your father doesn't want you to marry Elliot. He just doesn't know what else to do," Ruth said, pausing in her efforts.

"Surely he has options?" Neveah asked. "It feels as if he's given up."

Ruth was quiet for a moment, thoughtful. "I believe your father to be a resourceful man. He may have already tried to avoid this. Maybe he is even going along with it to buy time. But you must remember: Elliot is not like other boys."

Neveah had not considered this. Somewhere in her mind, she still didn't expect her father to keep so many secrets.

The woman in the photograph.

Conner's death.

Dealings with Elliot.

The list of mysteries were piling up and she had no answers to any of them.

"I don't think I would make a very good detective," Neveah said, trying to repress a pout. Ruth smirked at her without looking up.

"I rather think not." Ruth set out a final notebook. "Fortunately you have many other good qualities."

Neveah tried to not make a face at Ruth and failed. Ruth laughed regardless.

"Now, what can you tell me about the Peloponnesian Wars?"

Elliot

Elliot had changed. He knew it because when he looked in the mirror, he did not recognize himself. He was growing thinner all the time. He thought back and realized he couldn't remember the last time he had eaten anything.

The Face smiled in a corner of his mind.

Elliot went to the kitchen to find food. Gerald was there, washing his hands. Elliot was overcome with the sudden urge to plunge his brother's head under the water.

This urge shocked him. He had never felt the compulsion to harm Gerald. Gerald was different.

The water spattered in the sink, and Elliot remembered Gerald's intense fear of the water. Holding him underwater would terrify Gerald. Elliot stepped back into the hallway and left.

He hid in the bathroom, hoping Gerald had not seen or heard him. Throwing open the cabinets, he rummaged around.

There was a pair of nail clippers. He pushed it as deep into his nail bed as he could and snapped. Looking down, bright red blood welled at the corner of his nail.

Elliot took a deep breath and calmed himself.

Never Gerald. Never. The Face smiled again.

Elliot opened the window and climbed out. He had other things to focus on right now.

Slipping quietly through the forest, Elliot thought about what William had told him. Neveah was flat refusing to cooperate with their plans. William - Elliot laughed at the thought- was planning a wedding by himself.

Maybe it's time Neveah learned something about me. Elliot smiled at the thought. He'd really given a lot of thought to an engagement present for his future bride. But what to give her?

The answer was so simple. He arrived at a decision and set about putting it in motion.

❧ ❧ ❧

It was dark now. Elliot clung to the balcony outside of Neveah's room, listening.

He could hear her breathing as she slept. Desire welled up in him like a hot spring. Waves of it washed over him, making his skin flush and his hands shake.

At his waist hung a burlap sack. Inside was a common black snake. It wasn't poisonous, but it looked enough like a water moccasin to startle most people.

Elliot could just make out the soft sounds of sleeping. He suppressed the feelings of desire and they were immediately replaced with hate. He judged it was time and crept into her room.

Elliot stood beside her bed and gazed down. Neveah's hair splayed around her head on the pillow. Her hands were relaxed where they lay on the bed. Her beautiful face, peaceful. She looked small and perfect.

And vulnerable.

Elliot longed to fit his body to hers. He longed to put his hands to her delicate cheekbones.

And press. Press until he could feel them break beneath his hands.

Elliot's breathing quickened. Quietly, gently he lifted the snake from the bag and released it beneath the soft blankets of her bed.

She did not stir.

Elliot slipped back to the balcony, again listening.

The Face had been quietly watching. Now it grew excited and pressed closer.

The Face and Elliot both listened closely.

Neveah screamed.

Elliot was filled with a sudden release of tension, satisfaction flooding his body. The heady sensation caused him to gasp aloud.

Quickly he dropped from the balcony, barely registering the impact of the ground against his feet. He fled to the woods, his body still shaking from the experience.

Neveah

"It was a nightmare," Neveah said, holding the walkie-talkie close. She had taken to contacting Ash from inside her large closet. There was a niche underneath her dresses that suited her. It felt private and safe.

Safe. She certainly did not feel safe in her own bed anymore.

"A snake in your bed?" Ash repeated back to her. "I hate to say this, but it could have only been one person."

"Elliot. I know," Neveah answered. Just his name gave her the shivers.

"Actually, he did that to me once," Ash said. "I think it was a corn snake in my case though."

"What?" Neveah exclaimed. "Why would he do that?"

"Do you think he knows that we talk?" Ash asked. "I've suspected it before now. But if he knows that, he would know that I would know he was the one who put the snake in your bed."

Oh God. Neveah felt sick. "It was a message."

"I think so too."

Neveah did not want to think about what it meant. Elliot was marking his territory.

"Ash what do I do?" Neveah had asked him this many times before. She didn't really expect an answer.

"I don't know. Sleep with a knife?" Ash asked. He might have been attempting a joke, Neveah wasn't sure. She actually did sleep with a knife. It was tiny, but the only one she had.

"Can we talk about something else?" Neveah had that feeling of danger and fear creeping in on her. She didn't want to feel that while she was in her hiding place talking to Ash.

"I'm working on a dollhouse again." Ash sounded proud. Neveah's chest filled with a responding emotion.

"Really? That's great!" Neveah said, her voice vibrating with excitement.

Outside of the closet, there was a rustling sound.

"I have to go! I'm sorry! Bye!" Neveah whispered fiercely into the walkie. She turned it off, hating to not hear him say goodbye back.

The door swung open. Jillian poked her head inside.

"What are you doing in here?"

Neveah shrugged and crawled out from under the dresses. Jillian pulled her daughter in a sudden embrace. Jillian had been more affectionate in turns lately. Neveah was still not used to it.

"Your father wants to see us." Jillian's voice was heavy with disapproval. They shared a look and a sigh. Neveah followed her mother downstairs.

William was standing with a pile of color swatches on the kitchen island in front of him.

"I'm trying to pick out colors for the engagement party. I thought you two might want to weigh in here. What do you think?" William shoved the swatches forward.

Neveah stared down at them as if William had just passed her a dead mouse.

"You can't be serious, William," Jillian said, her hands going to her hips.

"Dear," William answered between gritted teeth. "I am trying to get Neveah involved in her own party."

"A party no one wants for a wedding no one wants!" Jillian snapped back.

The two began to fight in earnest. Neveah had never been front row for a real fight between them. She watched with disinterest.

Suddenly she felt so terribly tired. She turned and left. Jillian and William did not notice.

Ash

Ash opened his eyes and saw the ceiling. It was like most other ceilings, white and nondescript. However, he was suddenly gripped with the fear that it was about to cave in on him.

This happened a lot. Especially now that he was no longer taking those painkillers. The fear of it kept him awake at night. He hadn't admitted it to anyone. Not Neveah, not Ruth.

There was a noise outside, and Ash pulled his gaze away from the ceiling. There was a light knock on the door, and then Elliot was inside the room with him.

"Ashes, Ashes. We all fall down," Elliot said. He leaned against the closed door and smiled at Ash, hands in his pockets.

"You look awfully smug," Ash said, pretending disinterest. He sat up in his bed and reached for his crutches.

"No need to get up, dear brother. I just came to tell you about a little party I'm going to," Elliot said. His voice was as smooth as oil. "An engagement party."

Ash decided to take a gamble.

"I know," Ash said, his eyes meeting Elliot's.

"You do? How could you possibly know?" Elliot asked, his eyes not wavering.

"I know you know, Elliot. I know you listen sometimes. You think I don't know, but I do." Ash rose to his feet, unsteadily. Elliot stood as well.

The two boys had both risen to their full height, their chests swelling like peacocks.

"Oh Ashes. I know a lot of things. I never suspected you of knowing much though," Elliot said, smiling at Ash.

"Then you should know how I feel about your engagement," Ash said. "You should know I'd do anything for Neveah."

Elliot chuckled. "What exactly do you think you can do in your current state?" He quickly lunged forward and kicked one of Ash's crutches out from under him.

Ash caught his balance, but felt pain shoot up his leg. When he looked up, Elliot was already leaving. He listened to him laughing as he left.

Ash threw his remaining crutch like a javelin. It knocked the door open.

Elliot was right. What could he possibly do to help Neveah like this? He couldn't even do his own laundry!

Ash stooped to pick up one crutch, then hobbled forward to grab the second.

"Whoa, what happened here?" Ash looked up to see Gilly looking back at him.

"Gilly, what are you doing here?" Ash tried to sound normal but couldn't quite manage it.

"I was in the neighborhood?" Gilly answered. "I thought I'd check in on you."

Ash plopped down on his bed. "Well come in. The place is a wreck though."

"Yeah, I can see," Gilliy laughed. "How's the homework going?"

"See for yourself," Ash gestured to a notebook and stack of papers on his desk. Gilly leaned over and looked at it. He frowned.

"Did you have someone do this for you?"

"No," Ash answered, frowning back.

"The handwriting is so neat, I thought with your left hand being in a cast, it'd be a mess."

"What? You're crazy. That's how I always write."

"Dude, this is not your handwriting."

"What do you mean? Of course it is," Ash answered. To prove it, he reached over with his right hand and wrote something down. "See, my handwriting."

Gilly was silent for a moment.

"What?"

"Ash, you're left-handed."

Ash blinked. He looked at his right hand, holding the pencil. Could that be right?

"No way. You're joking," Ash said. He knew Gilly wasn't joking.

"We've been in the same class since the fifth grade. You're definitely left-handed."

"Oh...." Ash said, remembering what the doctor had told him. "I think I know what this is."

"You really don't remember being left-handed?" Gilly scratched his head, looking down at Ash.

"The doctor said this kind of thing might happen. I had a brain injury or something. It could change...anything. My memories, my personality, my...." Ash's voice trailed off.

"That is super weird, dude. What else has changed?" Gilly asked.

Ash was wondering that same thing.

Neveah

Neveah could hear the house and yard filling up with guests. She looked herself over again in the mirror and took a deep breath.

"Rapunzel goes to a very awkward party. Then hopefully ruins it," Neveah said to herself.

Neveah squared her shoulders, stepped out of her room and walked downstairs. Her elaborate engagement dress trailed lightly behind her. She felt the weight of it like chains. Her heart pounded in her ears and she wondered if anyone else could hear it.

She stepped outside. Guests were milling around the inground pool. William had brought in large braziers and filled them with burning wood to keep the guests warm. They wandered from brazier to brazier sipping wine.

Elliot was there. He wore a white suit, the fire turning his auburn hair dark. Neveah was struck by his beauty. She had never noticed before. His damaged soul had ruined a perfectly handsome person. Who would he have been if Rabbit had not possessed him? They would never know.

Elliot's eyes met hers with a predatory gleam. She felt a responding shiver down her spine and looked away.

Neveah recognized Gerald, Ash's other step-brother, hanging around awkwardly by a table filled with upscale hors d'oeuvres. She stepped closer, leaning over to pick up a mini quiche.

"Ash wasn't invited?" Neveah said, not looking at him. Gerald, likewise did not look at her. They seemed to have an unspoken understanding.

"I'm not sure *we* were invited, actually. My Mom was pretty salty about it," Gerald paused. "Elliot insisted we come. He's gloating, you know."

Neveah sighed. "I doubt this party is going to go the way he planned."

She stepped away. The area around the pool was full of people. Neveah judged that everyone was present. Neveah saw her father smiling at the people next to him. Elliot was at his elbow, shaking hands and laughing. Jillian was gone, hiding in her rose garden. The crowd seemed to part in front of her as if she were a plague carrier.

Neveah wished Ash were with her.

Now or never.

She reached the wine table. Bottles of the stuff crowded a table, all her father's vineyard label. Quickly, Neveah picked up two bottles of red, one in each hand. The people around her noticed. She saw some turn and whisper.

Neveah stepped to the poolside and raised her arms.

More people were looking now.

She slammed the bottles down with all her might against the concrete.

Crash!

Everyone was looking now.

Wine was running away in rivulets between pieces of broken glass. In her beautiful white dress, she knelt down and scooped as much wine into her hands as she could. She smeared the dark red wine against her dress, staining it the color of blood.

The base of one bottle was intact, a well of wine still inside. She picked it up and poured it over her head. The sticky liquid ran down her face and hair.

There was an audible gasp.

Elliot smiled at her from across the party.

Do you understand my message? Neveah thought.

"I don't want to get married. I'm not property to be passed between hands. I would rather die," Neveah said, pitching her voice so the crowd of onlookers could hear.

William's face grew dark and he moved through the crowd like a thundercloud.

Neveah rose to her feet. Willing herself to stand her ground, she did not move. Neveah met her father's eyes, tilting her head back to do so.

William slapped her hard across the face.

The sound echoed in silence. The guests were shocked. Delicate hands went to throats and clutched wine glasses tightly.

Pain exploded across the left side of Neveah's face and tears filled her eyes. She was determined not to cry and set her jaw.

"You have shamed me," William said, his voice thick with anger.

Neveah's eyes scanned the crowd of onlookers. Elliot winked at her and took another sip of wine. He was not threatened.

"What do you call what you've done to me then?" Neveah asked, her voice a heated whisper. She spun on her heel and left.

As she rushed to the house, she passed Gerald. There was sympathy in his eyes.

Neveah rushed upstairs and closed the door to her room. She locked it. She went into her closet and shut and locked that door as well. Climbing underneath her dresses, she grabbed fistfuls of the material and screamed.

Hot angry tears burned trails down her face. She longed to just leave, leave and never come back. As brave as she had been with her public stunt, she was not yet brave enough to leave.

She cried even more.

Ash

Ash was pleased with his work. It had been more than a little tricky to build a new dollhouse with one arm in a cast, then later a sling. The concussion had not helped. Along the way he had to rely on muscle memory to help him. And he had altogether forgotten how he'd made those little mailboxes.

Dr. Henderson had warned him this might happen. There was no way to predict how his personality and memory would be affected by the accident. Still, Ash was shocked every time a new side effect made itself known. Since seeing Gilly, he had tried to use his left hand more often. It was awkward. He did not know if it was because of the concussion or the sling.

The most shocking side effect was his driving. He had climbed into his old truck, stuck the key in the ignition and then...nothing. He had no idea how to put the thing in gear.

But he was determined to reclaim this part of his life. Weeks of perseverance and more trial and error than he'd like to admit had won the day. He had finished a dollhouse.

This one was special, too. This one was for Neveah.

He just had to figure out how to deliver it to her. His body was still too weak to carry it. He could no longer drive it. And it seemed rude to ask Neveah to carry home such a heavy gift alone.

He hadn't figured out how Neveah was going to get it home either. She would have a lot of explaining to do if either of her parents saw her lugging it through the front door.

Sigh.

Yes, the job was only half done until he figured out how to deliver it. But at least he had built it.

"Your young lady has had a rather difficult evening," Creature said, entering the room as silent as a shadow. Ash was no longer startled by her sudden entrances and exits.

"She has?"

Creature looked meaningfully at the walkie-talkie on the floor. Ash stooped to pick it up. He paused.

"What do I say?"

"If I know her like I think I do, you won't need to say much at all. She will probably talk enough for both of you," Creature said, making one of those exceptionally human expressions.

Ash looked at the walkie again. "You're probably right." Creature said nothing. Ash looked and she was already gone.

"Rapunzel?" Ash said into the walkie. "Are you there?"

There was a long pause. *Maybe she doesn't have it with her right now?*

The walkie buzzed, Ash could hear it crackling from the other end, but there was no voice.

"Are you okay?"

"No. I'm not okay," Neveah answered, her voice cracking. Ash reacted strongly, his body filling with emotions at the sound of her voice. He stuffed down those feelings to focus.

"What happened?"

"Daddy threw me an engagement party. It was awful," Neveah answered. "Your family was there. Gerald can tell you what happened. I...I did something."

Ash waited for a moment. What should he say? What would help?

"Daddy is so angry with me. I don't know what will happen. I don't know what he will do." Neveah sounded small, not like the big personality he was so accustomed to.

"Run away." Ash said it without thinking. He forged on, "You're not stuck like I am. Grab some things that you can sell, get out of there. Run. You can take my truck if you want. I have some money I can give you, too," Ash paused. "Don't marry Elliot."

There was silence. Ash was filled with an awful dread. Had he just said something unforgivably stupid? His chest was painfully tight, thinking of her leaving. But he felt even worse when he imagined her married to his step-brother.

The silence had drug on for a while. He imagined her throwing the walkie-talkie. He imagined her shocked or mad at him. He was still imagining when it sounded again.

"Ash! Help!"

Neveah

"Don't marry Elliot," Ash said. Neveah stared at the walkie-talkie. Could she do it? Could she just leave and never come back? Did she dare?

Then Neveah thought about Elliot smiling, his eyes gazing at her like he already owned her.

She grabbed her jewelry box and flipped the lid open. She owned a few pieces of jewelry her father had given her as birthday presents. Neveah stuffed them into a backpack. She grabbed her laptop, her camera, anything that might be worth something.

She tripped on her dress, the items sprawling in front of her.

"I have to change," Neveah said. She stood and rushed into her closet. Grabbing a plain shirt and jeans, she slipped out of the dress and threw on the clothes. She picked up tennis shoes, and carried them to the bed.

On hands and knees she grabbed the items she had dropped. It was here, shoving her laptop and camera into her backpack that her father found her.

The door flew open and slammed against the wall. William filled the doorframe, his eyes furious, hands clenched.

"What have you done!" William shouted at her.

Neveah was filled with a new kind of fear. She was sure he would hurt her. She rushed back to the closet, anything to get away from him. Reaching out, she grabbed the walkie-talkie.

"Ash! Help!" Neveah shouted into the walkie. William grabbed her ankle and drug her out of the closet. She dropped the walkie when he jerked her backwards, her elbows dragging on the carpet.

William pinned Neveah against a wall. He shook her, hard. Her head hit the wall behind her. Pain and fear flooded her system. She kicked out with her feet, but William was too strong.

"Do you know what you've done? You stupid, stupid girl! Don't you understand?" William was shouting.

Then Jillian was there, hauling on his arm.

"Let her go! She doesn't know!" Jillian was shouting. She grabbed William by his hair. "Let her go or I will call the police!"

William jumped away from them both. He shook his head as if to regain his composure.

"She doesn't know? She saw the body the same as you. She's met Elliot. She should know." William looked at Neveah. "Don't you see? You've killed us all."

William left as quickly as he had come.

Sobbing, Neveah slid down the wall where he had left her.

Chapter Nine

Ruth

The years went by quicker than I could have imagined. I guarded Joseph's line, first as a woman, then later as a cat. It became easier and easier to observe them, instead of living amongst them. I had watched so many die, passing on to that next plane that I might never know. My heart could only bear so much loss.

And always, I was hunting Rabbit. He was there, trapped, lurching through the forest in whatever form he could manage. I found and lost him more times than I could remember.

It was as if we were two ends of a compass, always chasing each other, but never meeting. I had begun to lose hope that the curse would ever end.

Nathan had been a good-hearted man, but lacking. I doubted any son of his would be able to help me catch Rabbit, much less kill him. And I had not been able to find Rabbit in several years. What was his new hiding place?

I was surprised by Asher's ability to persevere. Even in the face of suffering and loss, he carried on.

I began to hope.

Elliot

Elliot woke to someone shaking his body. He opened his eyes and saw his mother staring back.

"Elliot! Wake up!" She said, her voice shrill. Elliot pulled away from her and rubbed his face.

"Where am I?" Elliot asked.

"Do you not know?" Abigail asked. "How did you get here?"

Elliot looked around. He was lying in their backyard. The sky was dark, the lights of the house the only light around. The last thing he remembered was meeting with William. He couldn't remember what was said, what he'd done. Nothing.

"I don't know what you did to William, but he's terrified now," Abigail said. There was no question in her voice. He looked back at her. She was sitting back on her heels, her shoulders slumped. "As soon as I found the lighter, I knew."

Elliot said nothing.

"You started the fire that killed Nathan. You've been working with William all this time behind my back, haven't you? And I suppose you know about my relationship with him as well? There's no use hiding it now. There's no telling what horrors you've committed while I thought you were just catching squirrels in the woods. Am I right?" Abigail's voice was calm. She didn't need an answer.

"You're right, Mother." Elliot answered her anyway.

"Whatever you do, whatever plan you have cooked up, don't come back," Abigail said. She didn't sound angry, just so very tired.

"What?" Elliot asked.

"Don't come back. I can't stop you. I can't control you. All I can do now is try to protect Gerald from you. We're leaving and I'm not telling you where we're going. Don't look for us." Abigail said. She turned and walked back into the house, turning the porchlight off as she went. Elliot realized she had not said she loved him, had not bargained with him, had not even said goodbye. The Face pressed in close then, grinning at Elliot.

For the first time, Elliot realized that he had let The Face ruin his life.

And The Face was laughing at him.

Angered, Elliot turned towards the last loose end keeping him from Neveah. Elliot kicked open the door to Ash's shed.

It was empty. Where could he be?

In the middle of the floor was a large dollhouse. Elliot, of course, had known about his step-brother's little side business. He had not known Ash was back at work again. Stepping closer, he saw the name. Carefully written on a tiny card, it read *To Neveah, From Ash.*

Elliot's eyes went white. He could not allow Ash to get any closer to Neveah. His hands shaking with anger, he pulled a lighter out of his pocket. His hands fumbled and it dropped to the floor. He bent to pick it up, and quickly set the dollhouse on fire.

With any luck the whole place will burn down! Elliot could just hear the faint pop and crackle of the fire taking hold. It did not give him any relief, though.

He turned and headed to the one place Ash would want to be right now.

➹ ➹ ➹

Elliot was right, of course.

He crouched behind one of Jillian's rose bushes and saw Ash quietly crossing the yard. He looked left and right, and seeing no one, hobbled forward on his crutches.

Ash seemed to dither for a moment, looking at the dark windows.

"He doesn't know which window is hers, does he?" Elliot said softly. Ash stooped to pick up a rock, pulled his arm back unsteadily to throw, and...

Elliot tackled him before the rock could leave his hand.

Ash grunted on impact, toppling like a house of cards beneath Elliot's weight. His crutches flew out. Ash couldn't break his fall.

Elliot straightened, putting a knee on Ash's chest. He raised his fist to hit his step-brother only to realize he was too late.

Ash was already knocked out cold. His head had hit the concrete of their patio.

Elliot smiled, "This might be easier than I thought."

He took out a length of rope and began tying Ash securely. He'd have to wait to play his final trick on Ash. He wouldn't take any chances though. When the wedding was over, he would have Ash exactly where he wanted him.

Neveah

Neveah pressed the button on her walkie one more time.

"Ash, are you there?" She had been trying to reach him all day and had given up the code names. No answer.

She would have to find another way.

Neveah felt more like Rapunzel than ever. William had locked the house down. No one had been allowed in or out. He had used chains and a padlock on the balcony door in her room. The bottom floor of the house was shuttered and locked as if expecting a hurricane.

Maybe he was expecting a hurricane.

Neveah finally realized how afraid her father was.

After the party, William had disappeared for a few hours. Whatever had happened then had shaken him deeply. At first she thought the threat of a wedding might be gone.

It was not.

"I wanted to give you a beautiful wedding, at least. That option has been taken away from me," William had said, his face pale.

"What do you mean?" Jillian had asked.

"Elliot wants to marry her tonight." William stood and looked out a window. Neveah could just see that his hands shook.

"William, this is insane! He's just a teenager, what can he do to us?" Jillian shouted, flinging an arm wide.

"What can he do to us?" William spun on his heel to glare at her. "What can't he do? He's killed our security guard. He's snuck into our home more times than I know. He has evidence he's holding against me. He...he..." William's hand went to his forehead.

"Jillian, he could take everything away from us. Everything we've worked for," he paused. "He could kill us. I can't protect us from this."

"Then leave. We can pack up and leave. Right now." Jillian's voice was unwavering. William blanched.

"I've contacted everyone I know. I've called in all the favors. No one will help us. We are on our own," William paused. "Besides, we have nowhere to go."

Neveah was filled with longing. If only they could just leave and get away from Elliot. A small part of her mind whispered, *but Ash...*

"You *can* leave. We could change our names, if we had to."

But William couldn't leave. He didn't say it, but his face made it clear. Whatever his reason, he wasn't going to leave.

William left the room. Jillian had gone pale.

"I've never seen him like this," Jillian said, looking at her daughter.

➹ ➹ ➹

It was twelve hours later and Neveah was getting dressed for her wedding. Jillian was there, making final adjustments to a dress that wasn't meant to be worn for months yet. Neveah no longer attempted to hide the walkie-talkie from her mother.

"Who is he?" Jillian finally asked, a sewing needle between her teeth.

"He's Ash. He's my... friend." Neveah blushed. Jillian raised an eyebrow.

"Can he help us?"

"I don't know," Neveah answered. "He's Elliot's step-brother."

Jillian's hands paused in their work. "Ash...Price?"

Neveah frowned. "How did you know that?"

Jillian did not answer. She continued sewing.

Neveah sat looking at herself in her mirror. She looked pale and thin to her own eyes. It couldn't possibly be real, this waking nightmare.

"Pack a bag," Jillian said. "Just in case." Neveah gaped at her.

"Is that where we are, Mother? You want to help me run away?"

"Better that than watch you marry that monster."

"If I run, he might kill you." Neveah did not specify if she meant Elliot or her father. She honestly didn't know herself.

"Let them try," Jillian answered, then said no more.

Ash

Ash woke to his head pounding. He was immediately reminded of the moment he had woken up under the rockslide, and felt a momentary panic.

He closed his eyes again and tried to focus on his breathing. He could smell the lake and frowned.

Ash opened his eyes. It was dark, wherever he was. What happened? Where was he?

Then he remembered. Neveah's frantic voice crying out for help. His slow walk to her house through the woods on crutches. A hard impact from his right sending him falling, then darkness.

Elliot. He knew instantly it could only have been his step-brother. Neveah said that the security guard had never been replaced. Who else would be lurking around the property in the dark?

His panic returned. Ash's heart felt as if it would burst from his chest. His mending limbs ached. His head throbbed. Ash tried to put his arm out, but found that it was secured behind him. He pushed his legs out and found that they, too, were secured tightly. He could barely move at all.

Ash remembered Neveah's words. The body of the security guard had been bound and gutted like a pig.

That was when Ash knew he was going to die.

Neveah

Jillian already had a bag packed. Neveah felt that she was beyond shocking anymore and said nothing when Jillian set her own bag next to Neveah's. The two women had scoured her bedroom for valuables and packed them away in silence.

"This is crazy, Mom," Neveah said.

"Sometimes life is crazy," Jillian said simply. She handed Neveah a small knife. "Tuck this into your dress. I sewed a pocket into it."

Neveah did so wordlessly. None of this mattered if they couldn't get out of the house.

Jillian took out a flash drive from her purse. She looked at it long and hard, then handed it to Neveah.

"If you can get away, take this to the police."

"What is this?" Neveah tucked it into her dress with the knife.

"It's everything. I've been collecting evidence against your father for some time. There's enough in there to convict him and Elliot both. The police can give you some protection if necessary." Jillian's voice was steady as she met her daughter's eyes.

Neveah was still shockable after all.

"What? ...Why?" Neveah spluttered. "I thought you supported him."

Jillian flexed her fingers and sat at the edge of Neveah's bed. "I did in the beginning."

Neveah perched next to her. "But then something happened."

"Neveah you had a brother. I was married once before." Jillian looked away. "My first husband...died," Jillian paused. "When he died, I had nothing. No money, no family, no way to support myself and a child. Your father, he took me in."

"Where is my brother?"

"William had one condition. He would see that my son was taken care of, but he didn't want him in the house. William wanted us to have our own family, for me to forget my past." Jillian fidgeted, something Neveah had never seen her do. "I had no choice. Or rather, I couldn't see any other choice. I accepted his conditions. Your brother went to live with a foster family, but William made sure he was taken care of. He was supposed to have a good life. But a little boy doesn't forget his mother." She paused again. "I didn't forget him either."

"When he got a little older, William hired him. He took a special interest in him because he was my son. In the beginning I supported that. I wanted my son to have a good life and I thought William was helping. Too late I realized that William was corrupting him. He became bitter, angry and blamed us for his troubles."

"What happened to him, Mom?" Neveah's voice was a whisper. She already knew what Jillian would say next.

"Soon, William made him believe that his half-sister was the reason he could never be with his mother. You've met him, Neveah. His name was Conner."

Neveah felt as if she had been slapped. *Here you are, little sister.* That's what he had said. The words came back to hear clearly.

"Did he...? Did he really want to kill me?" Neveah choked on the words.

"I don't know. I don't think so. I think he thought that if he took you, he could make me come with him as well," Jillian's eyes were glassy and distant. "I think he just wanted his family back."

Neveah stood and went to the window. She saw the chains across her balcony doorway, the heavy padlock dangling there. Neveah suddenly couldn't breathe, she was suffocating.

"I have to get out of here!" Neveah cried, her hands clawing at her dress. "I can't do this." Frantically she turned and looked around for anything. Surely there was a way out.

"Neveah." Jillian's voice was firm. Neveah did not hear her. "You have to calm down. We can figure this out. We just have to be patient."

"Patient!" Neveah yelled. "I'm about to be married off in a few hours and you want me to be patient?"

The door to her room opened then. Jillian and Neveah spun on their heels, expecting William.

Ruth stood in the doorway.

"Neveah, we have to get you out of here," Ruth said, blowing into the room like a winter wind.

"That's what I've been trying to do!" Neveah said, gesturing to the locked door.

"Ash is missing," Ruth said the words as she walked to the balcony doors.

"What?" Neveah asked, feeling shocked again. Her blood drained from her face.

"I've sent Gerald to look for him, but we must hurry. I believe Elliot has him." Ruth looked from Jillian to Neveah. "Stand back."

They moved away from her and watched as Ruth began to transform. Neveah watched her mother out of the corner of her eye. Jillian did not seem surprised at all.

Just as before, it was hard to say exactly when the change happened. One moment Ruth was standing there, the next something much larger was there.

A mountain lion.

Only this mountain lion filled the room, her shoulders touching the ceiling, her tail knocking the wall as it switched through the air.

William rushed into the room, shouting. He stopped dead at the sight before him.

"What..." William began.

Ruth turned and roared. The sound threw William backward. With a kick of one massive hind leg, an opening appeared where there had once been a window. Ruth swung her massive head towards Neveah and Jillian.

"Go!"

The two rushed forward and jumped.

Neveah's ankles screamed with the impact of jumping from such a height. Her mother rolled and rose to her feet expertly. Where did she learn to do that?

"A-plus escape, princess," Neveah muttered.

"What?" Jillian asked.

"Nothing." Neveah tore the bottom part of her dress, so that she could move more freely, and rushed forward. "We have to get out of here. Elliot will be looking for me soon."

Elliot

Elliot stalked through the woods towards William's house. His head hurt. The Face had been pressing close and trying to take over Elliot's body all day. He had fought it back but was growing tired.

He wanted to remember what came next though.

Elliot imagined Neveah in a wedding dress waiting for him. After this, she would be his and no one could stop him.

His mother wanted to kick him out? Fine. He didn't need her.

But Gerald. Elliot's mind shuttered the thought away. He could not accept that he would never see his brother again.

William was subdued. Ash was trapped. Neveah was waiting. His plans were all coming together nicely. He just had to keep hold of his body long enough to see it finished.

He burst through the forest, and immediately knew something was wrong. There was a gaping hole in the side of William's house. A hole, coming from Neveah's room.

Elliot sprinted forward, kicking the front door open. He took the stairs two at a time. At the top, he found William lying on his back in front of Neveah's open bedroom door.

As he moved closer, a woman primly stepped over William's form and met his eyes. She was tall and dark, her green eyes flashing.

"You had better run, Rabbit. I've got you now," she said.

It was the last thing Elliot remembered before turning to run against his will. The Face had taken over.

Neveah

Jillian drove her SUV down the road at a reckless pace.

"We have to get to Ash's house. Maybe Elliot will be there," Neveah said.

"We need to get away from Elliot. Not closer."

"Then maybe Gerald will be there. He will know better than I will where Ash could be." Neveah's feet tapped against the floorboard. She pulled at the heavy dress.

"I think we should just leave, Neveah."

"Mother! Ash will die!"

Jillian was quiet for a moment. "Honey, he may already be dead. You don't know what you're dealing with here."

"I think I do, actually." Neveah regretted her words. The last thing she needed was to have an argument with her mother.

"Why were you not freaked out when Ruth turned into a big cat?" Neveah asked, remembering. Jillian's eyes darted towards her daughter.

"I don't 'freak out,' Neveah."

"You sure did when Elliot hung a body over your bed." Neveah glared at her mother, daring her to deny it.

"I suppose I didn't 'freak out' because I knew Ruth could do that," Jillian said, the tires of the SUV kicking up gravel as she turned into Ash's driveway.

"What?" Neveah shouted. Jillian was already climbing out of the vehicle though.

Neveah was quick to follow. "Mother!"

Gerald threw open the front door. "Neveah!"

Jillian stopped hard. A woman was standing behind Gerald and the two of them looked at each other warily.

Neveah realized she recognized the woman. From the photograph with her father.

"Elliot has Ash," Gerald said, interrupting her thoughts. "I've been looking all day."

"Where could he have taken him?" Neveah asked.

"He loves the woods. But that's where I've been looking. I haven't found anything." Gerald was pale, a pulse visible in his temple.

"Is there somewhere else he likes to go?" Neveah asked. Gerald shared a look with his mother. If possible, Gerald grew even paler.

"The lake," his mother answered for him. "He loves going to the lake."

"Get in the car then," Jillian said. Neveah and Gerald stepped forward. Jillian turned to leave then paused. "You too Abigail."

Elliot

Elliot had finally lost control. The Face had pushed him out of his own body. Elliot was still inside, watching, but he could no longer make his body move.

It was painful.

The Face was slowly forcing a drastic change on Elliot's body. His face hurt beyond words. It felt as if his bones were reshaping into something alien. His hands were curling inward, and he could see that The Face was having some difficulty dragging the large bag to the lake.

Ash was inside, bound up so tightly that he could barely wiggle. The Face had thrown him into a large burlap sack that Elliot had never seen before. Elliot suspected that Ash had lost consciousness somewhere along the way. Even as The Face dragged him over the rocks, he did not move.

Elliot felt surprise. From his new place in his own mind, he could see more of The Face. The Face now became The Rabbit. After all of these years, he would have never guessed that a rabbit of any kind was his cohabitor.

Elliot also felt a strange relief. All of his scheming was at an end. No longer would he have any say or control in the actions of this peculiar body of his. If Rabbit decided to burn down the town, he could no longer be blamed. If Rabbit decided to run away, to hurt, to maim, Elliot was free of the consequences.

If Rabbit decided to kill his stepbrother, well, he wasn't responsible for that anymore either.

The long pier of the lake was before him. The water here was deeper than at the other shorter docks. Elliot had thrown enough into it, listening to the deep gulps of the water as it closed over the items, to know that it was deep. He'd even swum in it a few times, just to be sure.

Most people would not drown from diving here. However, Ash was bound tightly, secured in a sack, and likely unconscious. He would die.

But what is the joke? Elliot asked. Rabbit loved a good trick, above all else. How did throwing someone in a lake in a sack make for a good trick? It just seemed like simple murder to him. But all the same, Rabbit was brimming over with excitement.

In a flash, Elliot saw the past. Rabbit, all four limbs stuck in a dark, sticky substance. A woman wrapping him in burlap and throwing him into a river.

Rabbit had fought hard enough that he almost lost all of his life force. His powerful spirit had sustained him long enough to break free and make the shore. It had been a surprising drain on him, and had taken a long time to recover. Rabbit still felt the fire of anger for what was done to him.

Elliot felt something new in that moment.

Sadness.

Ash was going to die. Elliot was surprised by this new emotion. He felt the same sense of loss that he had once felt when he lost his father's watch. Something irreplaceable was being taken from him again, and he barely had the language to express it.

Rabbit had reached the edge of the dock. Ears (for Elliot now had new ears, which heard much more) twitched and turned. The sound of footsteps were quickly approaching. Several sets of footsteps.

Ash's body was heavy, it was difficult to drag it any further. Rabbit heaved hard on the bag.

Ash stirred, throwing out his limbs as much as he could. He cried out, a sound of pain and panic.

Elliot saw, with shock and horror, his little brother running forward. Gerald leapt, hands outstretched for him.

Rabbit kicked Ash into the water.

Rabbit reached his hands out to meet Gerald. Their bodies crashed into each other, Gerald's force pushing them both over the edge.

Elliot felt the water hit his back.

Elliot saw Gerald's face grow panicked as the water closed over them both.

Rabbit moved to strangle Gerald. Elliot screamed. With all of his will, he fought against Rabbit.

Not Gerald! He cried out. He tried to pull the hands away, the hands that were no longer his own.

Rabbit did not let go.

Chapter Ten

Ruth

Ruth stepped over William's prone form, once again a woman. She saw Elliot charging up the stairs. Then, there it was, that instant flash of recognition.

"You had better run, Rabbit. I've got you now." Ruth said the words calmly. Elliot's face changed, and he quickly turned and fled. Ruth heard the front door slam open. She calmly descended the staircase and left the house.

Now that she knew where Rabbit resided, it would be a simple matter to find him again. It was always the catching of Rabbit that was difficult. He always managed to slip her traps. It was impossible to trick a trickster, as she had learned through the years.

Of all the people and creatures she had known, why did it have to be him that lasted to the end? Ruth closed her eyes and felt the sun on her face. She missed Big Man-Eater. She missed Joseph, and James, and all the others she had lived with and loved.

Ruth opened her eyes, turning into a cat again. She began to run through the woods. There was somewhere she needed to be.

Neveah

Neveah jumped out of the SUV before her mother had stopped it. Gerald followed behind quickly. His longer legs meant that he soon outran her. They were both pounding the ground to get to the fishing pier. They had seen Ash's truck and they both knew.

As she ran, Neveah became dimly aware of drag marks on the trail. The trees opened up. Gerald was already halfway down the pier.

Elliot was horribly misshapen. His head sprouted comically huge ears. His face had contorted into that of a large white rabbit. Elliot-Rabbit had a big sack that he was dragging down the pier.

The sack began to move, to cry out.

Ash!

Rabbit kicked it into the water.

Gerald jumped headlong into his brother, and they both fell into the water.

Neveah did not pause, but kept running. At the end of the pier, she dove without hesitation. She pulled her body tight to cut the water. Coach Yeats would have been proud of her pointed toes.

The cold was shocking. It stung like needles. As soon as it closed over her, she kicked hard to propel herself downward, her muscles protesting. The muddy water was dark and she instantly lost sight of the struggling sack.

A moment of panic. What if she couldn't find him?

The water was icy cold, but she pushed downward again as hard as she could. Her hands stretched out and she felt the mud of the bottom of the lake. Frantically she searched around. Her lungs screaming for air, she strained to keep searching.

At the last moment, her fingers grazed the rough material of the bag. She grabbed it and pulled as hard as she could. Her feet dug into the mud.

Instead of swimming up, she tried to pull Ash up the incline to the shore. Her lungs burned, but she was afraid to let go and surface. What if she never found him again?

On the verge of passing out, her hair broke the surface of the water. Instantly, two sets of hands were around her. She finally let go when she felt them take hold of the bag holding Ash.

Coughing, spluttering, Neveah collapsed on the shore.

Jillian and Abigail had waded into the water in their dresses and coats and were together hauling Ash out of the water. They bent their heads to the task of cutting him out. Neveah crawled forward on her hands and knees, still struggling to catch her breath. She shivered uncontrollably from the cold water.

Ash wasn't breathing.

"He needs CPR," Jillian said. She tilted his head back and began pumping his chest, hard. Abigail and Neveah watched on in horror.

"Please wake up! Please wake up!" Neveah was saying. Without realizing it, she had begun crying, and wiped away the tears that began to cloud her vision.

A loud splashing sound drew their attention away.

Elliot, or rather Rabbit, was rising from the water and climbing onto the pier. Elliot was gone now. His head was that of a large rabbit, his forearms had shortened and ended in curling paws. He grinned at them, his smile stretching too far across his face.

Jillian continued to heave on Ash's chest. Ash still wasn't breathing.

Rabbit's face twisted, his claws reaching up to cover it.

For a moment, he was Elliot again. His boyish face was stripped of his usual glib smile. All that was left was naked fear.

"You must leave! Run!" Elliot shouted.

Then he was gone and Rabbit was back.

"He's right. You must flee." Ruth was suddenly on the beach beside them. She reached down, her hands gently glowing. She touched Ash's chest.

Immediately, his eyes flew open and he began coughing up water.

Abigail, Neveah realized, had disappeared.

Jillian and Neveah tugged Ash to his feet and began rushing back to the SUV.

"Ruth!" Neveah called.

"Go, little one. I will be fine." She turned to face Rabbit.

Rabbit fled into the woods. Ruth calmly followed.

Ash

Ash thought he was dead.

It was a huge relief.

But he felt a deep sadness when he thought of Neveah. He'd never even kissed her. It occurred to him then, floating on the air like a ghost, that he might have even loved her.

Suddenly there was intense pain. Ash was back in his body. Everything hurt. His chest felt on the verge of exploding.

His eyes flew open. Ruth, Neveah and a woman he'd never seen before were all beside him.

None of them were looking at him.

It was just as well. As soon as his eyes were open, his mouth was open too. He began vomiting lake water. His throat and lungs burned. He coughed, tears streaming from his eyes with the strain.

Hands were pulling him to his feet. Water was still streaming from his nose and mouth. He stumbled forward, sucking fresh air in as quickly as he could.

Ash's head was pounding. His limbs ached. His wet clothes chaffed. He was dimly aware of ground passing by and the hushed labored breathing of the people around him.

Then Ash was lying on the backseat of someone's vehicle. When the vehicle lurched into motion, he thought he would vomit. There was nothing left in his body to throw up.

"Neveah we need to decide what to do next. We can't leave the county, can we?"

"Well no... wait, you know about that?" Neveah's voice jumped up an octave, making Ash's head throb.

His head was starting to clear enough to realize he was dry heaving in Neveah's mother's car.

So much for good first impressions.

"Can we go to a hospital?" Ash asked, his voice weak. He'd managed to sit up, but only just.

Jillian met his eyes in the rearview mirror.

"You're Nathan's boy, aren't you?" Jillian's voice was heavy with meaning.

Ash just nodded.

Jillian grabbed the emergency brake and turned the wheel. The SUV swung around and was racing in the opposite direction in a moment.

Ash vomited. Apparently he was not completely empty.

"Who are you?!" Neveah exclaimed.

Jillian glanced at her daughter, then focused on the road ahead.

"My first husband was best friends with Nathan. I was good friends with his wife. The four of us worked together for years to end the curse."

Ash gaped at the woman sitting in front of him.

"It obviously didn't work." Jillian's eyes met his in the mirror again. "I'm sorry. After your mother died, and my husband died... Nathan and I lost touch."

"I can't believe you knew about this!" Neveah's hands were gesturing wildly. "All of this, all along!"

"Neveah, now is not the time," Jillian's voice was steady.

"Not the time! Not the time? Apparently it hasn't been the right time for 16 years." Neveah was hysterical. "Do you know everything? Did you know I was sneaking out to see Ash? Did you know I was investigating Daddy?"

"I knew about your investigation. You're not a very good detective, are you dear?"

Neveah made a loud noise of frustration.

"But I didn't know you were sneaking out to see Nathan's son."

"Well that's something, I guess."

Ruth

"Go, little one. I will be fine," Ruth answered Neveah.

She did not wait to watch Neveah and Jillian drag Ash's body through the forest back to their vehicle. She had pushed enough life into Ash's broken body to know he would survive. Instead she turned her attention to the lake.

Poor, frightened Gerald.

Ruth stepped to the water's edge and transformed herself into a fish. Sliding into the water, she grew to a comfortable size. Big enough to not be bothered by predators. It did not take her long to find Gerald's body. Turning into a beaver, she caught his clothes in her teeth and pulled him to the shore.

Gerald's body still held some warmth despite the frigid cold of the lake. His expression had a peace to it that it had not carried in life. Ruth, a woman again, touched his boyish face.

"In life, you were so afraid of the water. You showed true courage in the end, child," Ruth said to him. She sensed that Abigail was still there, hiding in the woods.

Ruth stepped away from the boy and entered the forest. She left Abigail to grieve for her son in her own way.

A few yards away from the lake and from Abigail, Ruth changed again. This time she chose a bird, a bird much bigger than had been seen in a long time.

A thunderbird.

She flexed her huge wings and slowly took to the air. Ruth could see her own shadow cast on the tree tops. Below, she could hear the smaller animals fleeing from her. Her sharp eyes could see them scurrying away.

It did not take long for Ruth to find Rabbit's trail. He had not been in his own body for a long time, and Ruth was a skilled tracker. Joseph had seen to that. Rabbit had fled back to country he knew, the places he haunted when the forest was still untouched and wild. Ruth smiled. Rabbit was going to try to hide, but she knew every hiding place here.

Landing some distance away, Ruth chose to appear at first as a woman. She could hear Rabbit scrabbling around in a burrow and knew he was there. The sounds stopped and she waited. He had seen her.

"There's no point in hiding. I know you are there," Ruth said. Rabbit's long ears appeared first, then his head. His nose twitched in the air, smelling her.

"How did you find me so quickly?" Rabbit asked.

"You've gotten clumsy and old," Ruth said. She settled on the ground in front of him, cross-legged.

"Have I?" Rabbit asked, smiling. It was the same smile she remembered from so many years prior, when he was conning Alligator into meeting the devil. Ruth did not answer him, merely waited.

"A game, old one?" Rabbit asked. Ruth laughed, an unkind one.

"Old one? Not as old as you!" Ruth said.

"You're the oldest woman I've ever met!" Rabbit said, pulling at an ear with his foreleg.

"Am I?" asked Ruth. "Do you know many like me then?"

"You are the only one like you, I suppose," Rabbit answered. Silence passed between them. They were not friends, but they had known each other a long time. "Why have you lived so long? Do you know?"

Ruth shifted her weight. "I do not."

Rabbit smiled at her, as if smiling at a shared joke.

"You don't?"

Ruth frowned.

Rabbit laughed, one heel thumping the ground in delight.

Ruth rolled her eyes.

"You sour old hare! You don't know either! No one does. No one that's left anyway."

Rabbit laughed even more, flipping onto his back. His feet kicked at the air.

"Are you saying that you know the answer?" Ruth asked. Outwardly, she tried to show no emotion, but inwardly she quailed. She had never known the answer, but of course she wanted to know. Why had she been chosen to live this unnaturally long life, cursed to watch everyone she loved die?

Rabbit quieted and wiped the tears of laughter from his eyes.

"Why yes, I do know why," he said. Ruth was quiet. Of course she wanted to know, but Rabbit was her enemy. Rabbit had made her long life so miserable, had trapped her here along with himself, in a manner. What would she give to know the answer?

"I propose a game, then," Ruth said. Rabbit's ears perked up immediately. He ever loved a game.

"A game?" Rabbit asked. "What game?"

"A race."

"A race? With me? There's no way your human legs can compare with mine! I'm the fastest rabbit that's ever lived!" Rabbit said, puffing up his chest.

"Then you agree?" Ruth asked. "If you win, I will leave this place, and you, forever." Ruth's heart ached to even say the words.

"And if you win?" Rabbit asked.

"Then you have to tell me why I have lived so long," Ruth answered. Rabbit barely thought the matter over. Instead, he jumped up and gave the ground a strong thump with his foot.

"A game it is then!" Rabbit laughed.

The two of them agreed to race back to the lake. The first one to jump into the cold water would win the race. Rabbit's eyes gleamed the whole time. Ruth crouched down in a runner's position, and counted.

"One, two, three! Go!" Ruth said, and shot off on her human legs as fast as she could.

Rabbit, of course, was right. She had no hope of winning this way. His form shot ahead of hers in a moment, laughing all the way. Ruth smiled. It seemed that Rabbit did not know everything.

Rabbit

Rabbit bounded ahead, thinking about how easy this would be. He could already smell the water. He kicked his feet, he was so excited. It was a good trick, and one he hadn't even set up. Had she really believed she could run faster than him?

Rabbit's feet hit the ground beside the water. How far ahead was he now? He imagined her form laboring through a field a mile or so behind him and laughed again. He stepped forward, all four feet touching the water.

"I won! I won!" Rabbit jumped and splashed up and down the

rocky beach. He looked up and saw the promontory he'd jumped from so long ago, just before he'd trapped that boy, Elliot. Thinking of that day, Rabbit pushed a little deeper into the water.

He had gotten more than he had bargained for with Elliot. The boy had a damaged mind, and it had muddled Rabbit's sensibilities along the way. That one was always setting fires and killing things. He didn't care for killing things. No, he just loved a good trick. A game.

Rabbit paddled around the lake, reveling in his victory. The cold water lulled him until he was half asleep. He thought about some of the tricks he'd played over his long life. He thought of life and death differently than others. Dying just meant changing from one living form to another. One of his favorite tricks was to grant immortality to animals. Somewhere in his homeland, a large mosquito was probably still buzzing around the swamps. He had once even granted it to a girl...

Suddenly a large form surged up from the water's depths. First there was nothing visible except jaws, teeth surging out of the water like a shark. Then a snout, fur and claws were recognizable amidst the roiling lake. An animal the size of a school bus was closing in on him quickly.

Big Man-Eater! But no! He was dead!

Rabbit turned and tried to swim away, desperately shifting his form to give himself any advantage. But it was too late. Big Man-Eater's jaws were already around his neck. He kicked hard with his feet, but couldn't break free. He felt the heat of Big Man-Eater's breath on his body and knew this was the end. He felt his magic bleeding away.

Rabbit was dying. Him and that old mosquito, he supposed. Real fear gripped him.

How had Big Man-Eater survived?

The man-eater laughed. It was the laugh of a female. Rabbit stilled in her mouth.

"That's right, Rabbit. You've been tricked once and for all." It was Ruth. She had tricked him!

Rabbit's last thought was that he should have picked a different girl to trick with eternal youth all those years ago.

Ash

Ash woke up to find Neveah's large eyes peering down at him, her brow creased with worry.

"You're awake!" Neveah squealed. Ash winced.

"Too loud!"

"I'm sorry!" Neveah answered in an exaggerated whisper. Her hands clenched at her cheeks; she didn't seem to realize how loud her whisper was.

Ash slowly sat up. Looking around, he recognized the place.

"The hospital. Again." Ash's mood soured. If Beverly and Dr. Henderson found out he was there...

"You're awake! Good!" Beverly's cheerful voice said. "I've already notified Dr. Henderson of your arrival. He should be here any minute to look you over."

Neveah squeezed Ash's hand. He looked around again. Ash was sitting on a patient bed in an ER stall. Neveah's mother was visible in the hallway, talking on her cell phone.

"Where is Abby?" Ash asked. "And Ruth? I thought they would be here with us."

"Do you remember what happened at the lake?" Neveah chewed her bottom lip.

Ash thought back. He could remember being in a burlap sack, his panic. He remembered the chill of the water and shivered.

He remembered waking up.

"Did your mom give me mouth-to-mouth?" Ash asked, the memory coming back, sharp and absurd in retrospect. Of all the people...

"*That's* what you remember?" Neveah's eyebrows rose in a comical sort of way. Ash laughed out loud. Despite herself, Neveah laughed too.

"That's not the only thing I remember..." Ash answered, doubling over. He had been tired and hurting and afraid for so long. It felt good to laugh.

"Good. I don't want you thinking about my mom's mouth on yours!"

"And who's mouth should I be thinking about?"

Neveah went still, blushing deep red.

Ash had felt this moment before. But this time, he knew exactly what to do.

He slipped off of the bed, steadying himself. He put his hands on Neveah's cheeks, feeling the softness of her hair against his fingertips.

"There's only one person I can think of," Ash said. Her eyes were large and round, but she wasn't pulling away. He leaned forward slowly. He wanted her to have time to turn away or tell him no, if she wanted.

Their lips brushed. Ash felt a thrill rise through him that trumped all of the aches and pains. Neveah made a little noise, and he kissed her soundly. Her hands gripped his shoulders, pulling him closer.

"Ahem."

Ash let go immediately. Neveah's mother was glaring at him like she might throw him back in the lake.

"I think we had better leave Ash to recover. He's had enough excitement for one night."

Neveah scurried out of the room, stopping to wink at him before she left. Ash sat back on the bed, smiling to himself.

Beverly stuck her head in the room and asked, "Are you ready to see the doctor?"

"I'm ready for anything, Beverly."

Ash

Ash thought they would never be done with him at the hospital. Because of his recent concussion, they ran some extra tests on him to make sure the oxygen deprivation had not given him complications. Eventually, he was let go.

It was not until Ash had left that he realized he had missed his own birthday.

"I'm eighteen now," Ash said to no one.

The shed he called home had burned to the ground. He suspected Elliot had done it, but could prove nothing. Fortunately the main house was unaffected. With no other alternative, he moved in. There was no one to protest. He had looked everywhere, but he could not find Abigail or Gerald.

The story of his near-death in the lake had caught the attention of some journalists. The story had been spun quite a bit, but he was nonetheless a local celebrity. It was on the news all across the state, and maybe even further. Ash had been home alone for two days when the police showed up at his door, making a fuss.

"Can I help you?" Ash asked, opening the door. The two policemen standing outside looked at each other.

"We are going to need you to come down to the station with us. We have some questions for you," one said, a large man with heavy knuckles.

"Is this about my accident?" Ash asked.

"Among other things," answered the other policeman, a smaller man who looked like a marathon runner. Ash grabbed his wallet and keys and locked the door. He rode in the police car, feeling nervous the whole way to the station.

Inside, he was seated in a small room that held only a metal table and four chairs. He was told he wasn't in trouble, then left alone. Ash saw his reflection in the one-way glass and shivered. He wished he had brought a jacket with him. The cold made his legs hurt.

The door opened and a squat man in his fifties bustled into the room carrying a thick folder under his arm. A police officer, this time a lady, followed him.

"Hello, Asher. I'm Mr. Taylor. I'm your lawyer." The man held his hand out for Ash to shake. He looked at it like it was an untapped nuke, then decided to shake his hand anyway. He didn't want to be rude.

"Do I need a lawyer?" Ash asked, looking at the police officer. She smiled.

"You're not in trouble. He's not that kind of lawyer anyway."

"I don't understand," Ash said, looking between the two as they sat down across from him.

"Mr. Price, I'm here because I'm the executor of your father's will," the lawyer said. "You have a rather impressive trust fund left to you by your father. Abigail Fisher was issued checks monthly for your care since his passing. Now that you are eighteen, you will receive those checks."

"What?" Ash asked, sure he had misheard.

"You're eighteen, aren't you?"

"Yes, sir."

"Then we need to discuss how to handle your money."

Ash blinked.

"And I'm here because we suspect that Abigail has been using this money for other purposes, forcing you into child labor unlawfully, and lying to this lawyer about your care for years." The police officer said. "Also, we needed to talk to you because Ms. Fisher and her sons Elliot and Gerald have gone missing. No one has seen them since before the accident."

Ash blinked again.

"Do you understand what we are saying to you?" The lawyer asked, looking into Ash's eyes.

Ash just laughed. And laughed and laughed.

Neveah

"I can't believe you haven't already tried this," Neveah said, kicking a pebble along the roadside. Ash shrugged.

"I wanted you with me when I tried it," Ash answered. They held hands casually. Ash still hadn't relearned how to drive, so they had decided to walk to the end of the county. It was three miles from Neveah's house. They were close now.

"What did the police decide about Abigail?" Neveah asked. They had returned three more times to questions Ash about Abigail Fisher and her missing sons. He didn't have any answers for them. No one did. The few of them involved knew Gerald was dead. They suspected Elliot was as well. But what could they tell the police? Elliot

309

had turned into a giant rabbit and killed his own brother. They would be in a looney bin with a story like that.

Jillian had convinced them that the best plan was to pretend ignorance. Elliot had thrown Ash into the lake and disappeared. They hadn't seen where he had gone, they were too busy trying to save Ash. They pretended to have not seen Gerald or Abigail since the engagement party.

"I think they have decided I'm not a good suspect, at least. I mean, I didn't know Abby had been taking money from me. And apparently she had loads of enemies," Ash shrugged. "I'm just glad they aren't dragging me down to the station anymore."

"I think Mom and I are just getting started with that stuff." Neveah's mother had flipped on her father. She had handed over a mountain of evidence against him to the police. He was charged with a litany of crimes, running from tax fraud to murder.

Ash squeezed her hand. "It has to be hard, having to answer all those questions about your dad."

"I thought it would be. And...it is," Neveah sighed. "Now that I know more about Conner, it's easier though. He was a damaged person, ya know? He'd had a lot of bad things happen to him that kind of messed him up. And my father exploited that for his own purposes. He used that to manipulate my mother. Who does something like that?"

They could see the sign up ahead. The county line was just a few yards away.

"Are you nervous?" Neveah asked.

"Extremely."

Ash walked the distance, pausing to look back at her.

"Here goes nothing, I hope." Ash stepped forward.

Nothing happened.

Neveah and Ash stared at each other, gaping. Ash stepped forward again.

Nothing happened again. Neveah squealed and ran forward. Ash picked her up and swung her around.

The curse was broken!

🗲 🗲 🗲

Ash and Neveah had looked for Ruth. They finally had decided that, if she was still alive, she didn't want to be found. Then Ash had a dream.

A pack of red wolves came to him. They were making excited yipping noises, circling in his front yard. He followed them down the street, and then back into the woods. Just inside the canopy of trees, a man waited. He was dressed in furs, and when he looked up, Ash saw his own eyes reflected back.

"Come with me. She's still out there," the man said. He turned and led Ash through the forest. Deep, deeper than he'd ever ventured there was a cave. Ash wondered if this was still part of the National Forest, or on someone's property. The man stopped.

"She's in there, waiting. You need to take her home."

Ash woke up.

❧ ❧ ❧

"So you had a dream," Neveah said, breathing hard as they trekked further into the forest. "And a pack of wolves told you where Ruth was?"

"No. The wolves led me to a man, and he told me where she was."

"Hmm...and if we hike all the way out here and there's no cave?"

"Then I stop eating pizza late at night."

Neveah grew quiet. Ash turned and looked.

There was a cave.

They entered the cave quietly, not sure what to expect. They found Ruth. She was herself again, not a mountain lion or a small black cat. Her long dark hair was spread out beneath her like a blanket.

"She looks so peaceful." Neveah said. Ash nodded. The two of them knelt beside her, unsure what to do.

"I don't really want to notify the authorities about her. There would be an investigation and who knows what they'd turn up," Ash said.

"What should we do then?" Neveah asked. They looked at each other and then back at Ruth.

"I think we should take her home," Ash answered.

Epilogue

Neveah

It took some convincing on her part, but finally Jillian relented.

"I swear you better not make me regret this," Jillian said, her tone hard. Neveah smiled at her mother.

"You won't. I promise." Neveah had practically danced out of the room to call Ash. The phone rang- she had a phone!- and after two rings he picked up.

"She said yes!" Neveah said, not waiting for a 'hello.'

"Really?" Ash answered, knowing immediately what she meant.

The three of them set out the next day. Jillian drove. Ash still hadn't relearned how to drive. His truck wouldn't have made the long trip anyway. They loaded Ruth's body carefully into the very back. They had wrapped her as respectfully as they could head-to-toe in muslin cloth. She was clutching that old woven pendant in her hands.

"You could always buy a new car, you know," Neveah said, setting her bag in the backseat.

"I like my truck," Ash said, buckling his seatbelt. Neveah laughed as she settled into the passenger seat. Jillian rolled her eyes as she started the SUV and they pulled slowly away from her house.

Neveah turned and looked in the back. They had covered Ruth's body with some blankets. How could they explain it if someone saw her back there?

"Do you think she found peace in the end?" Neveah asked.

"I hope so. She waited long enough for it," Ash said.

It took them two days to reach the southern part of Georgia that Ruth had described. It might have been a shorter trip, except neither of them had ever been this far away from home. They convinced Jillian to take her time.

Neveah kept her promise to her mother to be good. Aside from holding hands and a few stolen kisses, Ash kept his distance. Every night Ash went to his hotel room, Jillian and Neveah to theirs. Ash emerged every morning from his room looking happier than the last.

Finally they reached the deep forest of southern Georgia. The vehicle Ash had rented looked out of place, creeping down the dirt track they had found. It was a state park now, protected and secluded. An animal wildlife refuge. Ash and Neveah thought it was likely the best place to lay her to rest. She had been like a wild animal herself in some ways.

"This place reminds me of Ruth," Jillian agreed.

They did not know how the Creeks buried their dead when they still lived in their homelands, so they decided to bury her the only way they knew, a rectangular grave cut with a shovel. Ash spent hours digging the thing out, never complaining. Neveah sat on the hood of the car, keeping watch for park rangers and hikers who might pass by.

Jillian hiked further down the road, hoping to spot anyone coming their way. When Ash was done, he wiped the sweat from his brow and took Neveah's hands.

"Are we doing the right thing?" Ash asked.

"I think so. She deserved to come home. We don't know exactly where that was, but she spent a lot of time talking about the Indian Removal to me. This is the place from the pictures she showed me. This is the place she talked about. This is where a portion of the Creeks lived. I think we must be close," Neveah said, brushing Ash's hair back from his forehead. He rested his head on her knee for a moment.

"Okay. Nothing left to do but put her to rest," Ash said, finally.

He carried her body to the gravesite in his arms. It took all three of them to lower her into the grave on boards. Neveah sprinkled spring wildflowers over her body.

"Should we say something?" Neveah asked. Jillian and Ash nodded. He looked around at the tall trees, and then down at Ruth.

"Thank you. You did a lot for my family. I don't think we could ever repay you. I didn't know Joseph, but I think he would have honored you for what you did. I hope you find peace now," Ash said. Neveah looked down at Ruth, her tutor, her eyes filling up with tears.

There was a sudden wind that rushed in. Neveah's hair rose up. They could hear voices on the wind, laughing. Neveah looked around. Faded images of people appeared. All of them with the same dark curling hair and blue eyes as Ash's. Then Ruth was there, laughing with them, embracing them. Some of them were serious, holding a hand over a heart or bowing to her. Some of them laughed with her. One man, dressed in furs, put his hand to her cheek tenderly.

They all turned, and suddenly Ruth's ghost was running. She ran to a big man who picked her up and spun her around.

It was Big Man-Eater, her husband.

Ash moved to stand next to Neveah, and took her hand in his.

The images began to fade, disappear. Before they did, Ruth turned to them and opened her mouth.

"He's still alive." Then she was gone.

Ash turned to Neveah, his eyes wide. "Who's alive?"

But Neveah didn't know either. Ash had crossed the county line, surely that meant that Rabbit was dead? Who else could she mean?

After they finished burying Ruth, they walked back to the car in silence. Neveah looked back one last time, and noticed a set of unusually large paw prints on the ground nearby.

"I have a feeling it's not over yet."

Far away, on a lake shore...

"Wake up!"

Elliot opened his eyes. His mother was crouched over him, shaking his shoulders.

"I'm awake," he muttered, trying to sit up. Abigail looked around and sat back, giving him some room.

"We have to leave, and quickly," Abigail said. She sounded nervous. "What do you remember?"

Elliot shook his head. He was filthy with lake water. Rubbing his eyes with the backs of his hands, he thought about what had happened. The memories came rushing back.

Gerald is dead.

Elliot groaned.

"Gerald..."

"Yes, he's gone." Abigail looked pale.

"And I..." Elliot paused, looking at his mother. "I'm alone."

Abigail frowned at him. "I'm right here."

But Elliot knew she would not understand. For the first time in a long time, he was alone with his thoughts. The Face, Rabbit, was gone.

"I'm ready to go, Mother."

Keep reading for a preview of the second book in the Native Legends series, The Thrown-Away Son!

Available Now!

Prologue

Abigail

Abigail shook her son's shoulder. He was so pale, but she could see the soft rise and fall of his chest. He was alive.

"Wake up!" she said again.

Elliot's eyes opened, flat and black but aware. He looked up at her, then his eyes slowly gazed around, taking in his surroundings.

"I'm awake," he said, then began easing up to a sitting position. Abigail leaned back on her heels where she crouched next to him. She glanced over her shoulder. They were only a few yards down the beach from where everything had happened.

From Gerald.

It was only a matter of time until people came looking for them. They would need to start moving soon. Her eyes rested on the form of her dead son, then back to the living son at her side. He was all she had left.

"We have to leave, and quickly," she said. "What do you remember?"

Elliot shook his head, sending droplets of lake water around him. His gaze turned inwards, taking inventory of himself, his memories maybe.

"Gerald..."

"Yes, he's gone."

"And I..." Elliot's eyes met hers, seeing her for the first time. "I'm alone."

Abigail frowned.

"I'm right here."

Elliot's eyes were looking in her direction, but he wasn't seeing her anymore. A familiar experience.

"I'm ready to go, Mother," he said, rising easily. He began stalking down the beach ahead of her, his feet leaving no marks on the rocky beach.

Abigail felt a shiver run through her. He was all she had left, but she couldn't shake her apprehension.

"We'll have to take your brother."

Elliot stopped in his tracks and looked back at her.

"And do what with him, Mother?" His voice was sharp and accusing.

Abigail swallowed hard.

"They will come looking for us. And what do you think they will do when they find your brother's body on the shore?"

"Are you concerned about what the police will think of you?" Elliot turned away, his head swinging so sharply that more lake water went flying out of his hair.

"No," she answered, then. "Yes. I think they will tie us to his murder. And then we'll go to prison. Is that what you want, Elliot?"